Meat Won't Pay
My Light Bill

Kurt Eisenlohr

Future Tense Books

MEAT WON'T PAY MY LIGHT BILL
a novel
© 2000 Future Tense Books & Kurt Eisenlohr

Cover design by John Richen
Book layout by Kevin Sampsell
Author photo by Jennifer Procter
The artwork herein is also by the author.

ISBN 1-892061-08-2

Future Tense Books
PO Box 42416
Portland OR 97242

E-mail: futuret@teleport.com
http://www.teleport.com/~futuret

For Columbus, Kook, Bug, and Sidney

*Special thanks to Ritah Parrish, Kevin Sampsell, and
Mykle Hansen*

It is the hand of God and the lack of fire escapes
Carl Sandburg

Sane, sane, they're all insane
The fireman's blind, the conductor's lame
A Cincinnati jacket and a sad luck dame
Hanging out the window with a bottle full of rain
Clap hands. Clap hands.
Tom Waits

FIRST MEDITATIONS

A nurse. White light. A large silver tray.

The nurse is digging the shit out of me with a spoon, piling it high atop the silver tray. The spoon is silver too—and I am born with it in my ass; a backward child born of backward but well-meaning parents. I am told I was a breech-birth, pulled from the womb ass-first with the indelicate aid of forceps—silver, no doubt. In an earlier world, I might not have been born at all. My mother and I may well have died right there in the saddle.

I was three years old and hadn't had a bowel movement for more than a week. I refused to. I would sit in the corner and hold the shit inside. After a while, all that shit hardened in me. I couldn't have shit even if I'd wanted to. I would sit in the corner and howl. My parents didn't know what the hell. I had been howling since birth. I didn't want to shit. There wasn't much to know.

I was howling when the nurse dug it out of me. They had given me a dozen enemas that day but the shit held its ground. It wasn't going anywhere. I feel sorry for the nurse now. She was grossly underpaid, no doubt, and had to spend her days spooning strongholds of shit from the stubborn, recalcitrant assholes of strangers. She was gentle about it, however, as gentle as was possible, given the grim nature of her work. She squeezed my hand every now and then. To reassure me, to be sweet.

"It'll be over soon, honey," she said. "You're a brave little man. Most boys would be crying by now."

I let out another howl.

I thought she was the devil. I thought she was God.

ARE YOU READY FOR THE COUNTRY?

I took it because I didn't know how to do anything, yet needed to eat just like the people who did know how to do things, and this one seemed to require neither talent, skill, nor knowledge of any sort. It was a job.

I heard about it from a guy at the bar.

"They'll take anybody," he told me. "They'd hire a hunchback at this point."

That was another reason I took the job. Always go with the sinking ship. No chance of longterm commitment.

"I'm going to go down there," I said. "I'm going to go down there today."

And I did.

But first, I had a few more drinks.

The boss didn't feel it was necessary to look at my application, which was a shame, being that it was a fairly entertaining piece of fiction. He was a balding, weary-looking man, standard issue, late 40s or 50s, grey hair, grey face, large of chest and belly, stout but run down as an old discarded clock, the fatigue showing in both his eyes and in his mind. Yet there was a certain kindness there, a gentleness of soul which was immediately apparent. Maybe this had worked against him, maybe life had clubbed him half to death and he had come here to hide.

Then again, maybe I was reading him wrong and he was just another horse's ass who believed that the hiring and firing of people was not only of great, universal importance, but also his God-given right.

"I need a job," I told him.

I handed him my application. We were standing in aisle 3, two men who had once been boys, among the meat and dairy products.

"What's your name?" he asked. He had my application in his hand, my name printed out in large block letters across the top.

"Lupus Totten," I told him, hating the sound of it. I always felt like a fool whenever I had to say my name aloud. I felt like a fool even without having to say my name aloud.

"Lupus? Like the disease?"

"Yeah, like the disease. You can call me Lou."

"Any relation to Chuck Totten up on the lake there?"

"No, no relation."

"Well, that's all right. When can you start?"

I was three thousand dollars in debt to a surgeon in Grand Rapids. I had no money. If I wanted a pack of cigarettes I had to dig through the trash for returnable cans. If I wanted a drink, I had to beg them at the bar. My weight had fallen to one hundred twenty-five pounds, fully clothed. I glanced toward the deli counter. Behind the meats and the cheeses and the chocolate mousse stood three young women, all of them grossly overweight. One appeared to be a halfwit, no evidence of any light behind her eyes, just two dim holes going back into her head, a string of sliced ham dangling from her lips. She saw me staring at her and slowly sucked the meat into her mouth, down her throat and into darkness.

"Next week," I said.

The boss's name was Jack Philly. He didn't own the place, just ran it, and he took no discernable pride in that. It didn't seem to matter much to him. You got the feeling that if the place went up in flames and the fire trucks were called it wouldn't have been of great concern to him whether those trucks ever came or not, that either way would have been just fine. So what might have been a small dark corner of working-class hell turned out to be a small but welcome patch of heaven. Which is to say, the job was incredibly dull, but things could have been worse. Jack Philly gave me the fifteen-minute training session.

"See this tube of meat?" he asked. We were in the meat cooler. It was fucking cold in there. We weren't wearing coats. "This is chuck. See this tube of meat? This is ground round. It's darker, see? Has less fat. It costs twice as much and isn't worth a shit on the grill."

I nodded. I hadn't slept in days. My mouth hung agape. I was on my way to becoming a useful member of society.

Jack held up a knife. "Now all you gotta do," he said, "is cut the tube and get the meat out." He cut the tube, peeled back the plastic. He walked it over to the grinder. It looked as if he were walking a big red dick of a date to the prom.

I nodded again. I looked around for a clock but there wasn't any clock in there.

"Now," he said, "you take the meat and you push it down into the hole. Don't use your hands. Don't even fucking think about using your hands. Always use the stick."

"You working for the Pope?"

"What?"

"Nothing. Just a joke."

"I don't get it."

"That's okay," I said, "neither do I."

He pulled a club-like orange stick from the wall. He waved it around as he spoke, an inch or so from my nose. I stepped back. His breath was coming at me in frosty little cloudbursts, an admixture of sewer fog and dead fish. But you only noticed this smell when he opened his mouth to speak or breathe.

"A guy lost his arm right up to the goddamned elbow last summer," he said. "You can't sell that stuff. But it's up to you."

"I'll use the stick," I said.

Jack turned the machine on and pushed the meat down into the hole with the stick. The machine made a grotesque wet sucking sound. Blood spurted into the air, and the meat came out the other end, a million red worms. It fell onto a tray. He gathered it up in his arms.

"Now, you take this and put it back into the grinder, you run it through again. Only this time, when the meat comes out you cup it in your hand, gentle, the way you'd cup a woman's breast. Like this ..." He tossed the meat back into the machine, turned it on. The meat began to ooze out. He cupped it in his palm, forming a B-cup. He placed it on a small styrofoam tray—very quickly—and did this again and again until all 20 pounds of meat had been cupped and trayed.

"Now all you gotta do is wrap and weigh them," he said. "Nothing to it."

I gave it a whirl. He was right. There was nothing to it.

"I'll let you do the rest of these," Jack said. "I'll be in my office. Give me a holler when you're finished."

I worked the grinder, poking the meat down into the hole with the big orange stick, poking, poking, pushing, pushing, pushing, cupping those breasts. Ten pounds, 20 pounds, 30 pounds, 40 pounds, 50 pounds ... It was oddly sexual and the closest I'd come to having it in quite some time. But it was damned cold in there.

When I stepped from the cooler I was blue and had a rock hard-on sticking out in front of me. The warm air hit my face and my glasses fogged. I walked into a wall. The new guy.

The Deli Maidens stood there smiling, eyes on the new protrusion. I was a caucasian Isaac Hayes. I was Shaft. The combined weight of the women before me was probably in the neighborhood of 600 pounds. Too much for even Shaft to get his libido around.

My mast fell. The Deli Maidens frowned.

First day on the job, and already I was becoming popular. And unpopular.

It was a Zen thing.

It was a small-town grocery store, and the employees, all seven of us, were allowed many breaks. There just wasn't much action.

After the first week, I knew how to work it. You performed your various duties, and when you were finished you sat around at the picnic table out back, smoking cigarettes and gazing off into space. You made slight, insipid conversation, read the newspapers, drank coffee, ate donuts, cracked jokes. If a customer needed some special service or had a complaint of any sort, you became indignant and crushed out your smoke, appalled at such a gross violation of etiquette. You took care of whatever the problem was, then made your way back to the picnic table: "That fucker just tainted a perfectly civilized afternoon. What is *wrong* with these people?"

You were paid a pittance and you gave as much in return.

I was sitting in my kitchen one night. I'd just cracked a pint of whiskey. I had my paints and brushes spread before me, a large canvas propped against the wall. I was just back from the bar and half in the bag. I was a genius, I was a giant among men, I was immortal, I was going to paint my masterpiece and make all the history books when—

I saw the hand snake around the corner, thin, white, bloodless.

The hand turned out the lights.

"HEY! WHAT THE HELL!"

It wasn't my kitchen.

The grocery store was a good place to nap away the days but it wasn't paying off. I took home $130 per week. There was the bar to consider, food, rent, cigarettes. A man just couldn't make it on that, the mathematics didn't figure.

I kept getting threat letters from a collection agency in Lansing. My surgeon had gone mad. He wanted his three thousand and change.

"What is wrong with these people?" I kept thinking.

I was forced to rent a room from my mother. *In* my mother's house. My mother's cups, my mother's saucers, my mother's coffee pot, my mother's plates, my mother's forks, knives, spoons ...

"Two weeks," she said. "I'm giving you two weeks. Then you're out of here!" Well, one could only hope.

The house was over a hundred years old, and

getting older by the hour. I had a room upstairs. It stank
up there. There were dead rats in the walls, live rats in
the walls. There were squirrels and winged things, bats,
birds, and unnameable things. It was also insanely hot
up there; you could hardly breathe. There was a small
window but the window was painted shut, to open it
would have meant breaking the glass and the glass was
a goddamned antique and not to be broken. At night
the mosquitoes would descend upon me, moths would
crash against the lampshade, fall to the floor, work their
way up the wall, do it all over again. I would writhe in
agony half the night, abandon any hope of sleep three
hours before having to be at work, leap out of bed, grope
through the dark for a light and fall down the stairs
trying to find the fucker.

The woman was trying to murder me.

She had rented me the room in a last-ditch effort
to finish me off.

***

Things were slow at the store. Jack Philly and I were
out back at the picnic table eating a second lunch, company food on company time, not that the company was
aware of it. We were bluecollar Davids, pissing on the
Italian shoes of Goliath while he slept or had his attention focused elsewhere. It was the American way. You
just took and took and took, in retaliation for having
been taken all your life. Jack had had a triple bypass six
months earlier but there he was, chocolate milk and
apple pie three times a day, shoveling it in, getting his
payback, getting his fair share.

I pushed my steak aside and lit a cigarette.
Donnie Lynn, the produce girl, was telling us about her
new tattoo.

"I had it done last night," she said. "It's still bleeding. Don't tell my mom."

Her mother's name was Linda Lee. Linda Lee worked at the grocery store too. She was a "floater," she was Jack's right-hand man. Milk, meat, produce, deli, cash register: Linda Lee did it all. She was a workhorse, she was a powerhouse, she was my second favorite person on the planet. She weighed close to 300 pounds and was funnier than most of the comedians I had seen on TV. I kept telling her she should chuck the grocery bullshit and get on a sitcom.

"See, it's a ROSE!" Donnie Lynn said. She was up against the dumpster in a police-search stance. She had her jeans down around her ankles, her big white pimpled ass in the air.

"Oh, Jesus Christ!" Jack said, chocolate milk shooting out his nose. He began to choke and gag.

"Hey, the man has an addled heart," I told her. "You're gonna kill him. Look—"

Jack had gone from pale to purple. He kept hacking away. Donnie Lynn's rose was blue, with a black stem and two twisted yellow leaves. It was still raw, more like a wound than a work of body art. Blood and sweat were running down into the crack of her ass. Jack was gripping his chest, coughing, gasping, laughing, choking to death.

"Don't tell my mom," Donnie Lynn said.

She kept shaking that awful rose.

Donnie Lynn should have been in show business, too.

***

I was in need of money. I was in need of a lot of things, but I'd decided that money should be my first priority. The rest, I'd deal with later. Right now, I needed cash.

I was in the Sause Box, telling one of the bartenders all about it.

"I need more money," I told her. "I can't make it, I can't even afford to sit here."

"Want another?" she asked.

"Well, yes. But I can't afford it."

She poured me one. Bourbon, splash of water. I gave her two singles, took a sip. It was a good drink, like I knew it would be. I was in my favorite bar. They always tipped the bottle high. They were very kind that way.

I walked over to the jukebox, dropped fifty cents down the slot. Billie Holiday sat up through hip-hop and the grave. She began to do her thing again:

One dark and stormy night
Big John was feeling blue
Things just didn't seem right
So he didn't know just what to do

I had always liked Billie Holiday. She could perform miracles given even the world's worst lyrics. I enjoyed hearing her in the bar. The bar was the perfect place for her, she belonged there, and when you listened to her, so did you. Also, by playing Billie Holiday I was able to drive many of those who did not belong in the bar *out* of the bar.

I started back to my stool, back to my good bartender, back to my good drink. Thomas Wolfe was a liar, you could always go home again.

I was stopped short by a small, leather-clad Mexican, white t-shirt, home-rolled cigarette, macho swagger, the whole tired shtick.

"Gimme a cigarette," he said.

I pointed out the obvious.

"Yeah, but I want one of *yours*."

It was the same all over the world. There was no peace, there never would be any peace. We were already fucked, plucked and buried.

"Listen," I said. "I've got a drink waiting for me over there. I'd like to get back to it."

"I should kick your ass for that," he said.

"For what?"

"Your moustache."

"I don't have a moustache."

"I know. I should kick your ass."

"Oh, shit ... Listen: let me get back to my drink. Maybe the whiskey will put some hair under my nose."

The asshole seemed to get a kick out of that. He laughed, turned back to his buddies at the pooltable, hitched a thumb my way.

"Alright," he said. "But I've got my eye on you, chump. I think you're a fag who plays fucking fag music. I've got my eye on you. Don't forget that."

"I won't forget that," I said. Then I forgot about it. I'd attracted this sort of trouble my entire life. I'd gotten used to it over the years. The guy lingered there, giving me the territorial eye. I walked around him, made it back to my drink. Why I'd ever left it was beyond me.

"That guy giving you any trouble?" the bartender asked. "If he is, let me know. We don't need that shit in here."

"No, it's alright."

The women bartenders, no matter what their size, could almost always get a man out of the bar. They'd lay the scolding mother routine on them. They'd guilt them into submission:

Now, if you boys can't play fair, you're not going to play at all!

If you want a drink, you say PLEASE!

One more word out of you, and you're going home!

It provoked a Pavlovian response that went all the way back to the womb. The men would either back down or head for the door. They'd apologize, bow their heads like little boys, stare at their shoes. It was an amusing thing to see, and it was a terrible thing to see. If a male bartender had gone that route he would have had his balls wrapped around his neck, an equally terrible thing to see. More conditioning. Once you came of age you were required by ancient law to stomp the old man's ass into the ground. Someone had carved it in stone somewhere.

"Hey," the bartender said, "are you really serious about needing money?" The bartender's name was Angel. That was her last name. No one seemed to know what her first name was.

"Angel," I said, "I'm a wanted man. The powers that be have caught on to my bullshit, they want me to settle up. I'm fucked. The world is round, there is no music in space."

"Come again?"

"I said you pour a good drink."

"Well, if you're serious, we're going to be needing some help here as soon as the Summer picks up. Once the tourists get into town we're going to be swamped day and night. It'll be hell."

"I'm used to that."

"You need another one," Angel said. She filled my glass, straight up this time. Poured herself one. "On the house, champ."

"Thank you, my Angel."

"No sweat."

I held up my glass. "Here's to hell," I said.

"Here's to hell, Lupus."

We knocked them back. The guys at the pooltable had turned on one another. The Mexican who had his eye on me was beating one of his friends over the head with a poolstick. The guy had apparently fucked up a shot and caused them to lose the game they were betting on against the other two friends. The winners stood there laughing. When the guy getting the stick caught one of them with a jab they stopped laughing and joined in, kicking the poor bastard to the floor and giving him the boot. Bob Seger's "Old Time Rock and Roll" boomed from the jukebox, keeping time with the boots and the blood and the beer.

Angel poured me another shot, grabbed a baseball bat from behind the bar and stomped on over there:

"ALRIGHT YOU ASSHOLES! ONE MORE MOVE AND YOU'LL NEVER HEAR MUSIC IN HERE AGAIN! I'LL SMASH THIS JUKEBOX INTO A MILLION FUCKING PIECES!"

All at once, the beating stopped.

Those good old boys really loved their Bob Seger.

***

The line was busy. I hung up. I began to pace.

I smoked a cigarette, tried it again.

1-312-267-6050.

It was my girlfriend's number. After three years I'd finally memorized the thing. I'd been calling every night for a month and a half, driving my phone bill skyward, past the clouds and the financial point of no return. She'd dumped me in May. It was June now. I was trying hard to patch things up.

There was some static on the line, some crackling and popping sounds. Then the phone began to ring. It rang and rang. I wondered where she could have gone so quickly. I let it ring some more. I let it ring on and on.

After a while, I gave up. It was 3 a.m.

I tried to read a book but it was no good, my mind kept wandering away from the words. My body wanted to move, keep moving. Soon, I wasn't able to see the words at all. All I could see was her face. I put the book down, paced the floor for a while, tried not to think. I picked up the book again, sat down, opened it—then decided to go for a walk. I took three sleeping pills and put on my shoes. I figured I'd walk around town until it was time to go to work.

Stillwater was small. They didn't even call it a town, they called it a village and left it at that. All the village of Stillwater had going for it was Lake Michigan. It sat right there along the shore, and during the Summer the village was beautiful. There was the lake, the beach, the trees, the sand dunes, the sun. It was during the Summer that the tourists came and the locals bitched and moaned and made all their money. They had to make it fast, and then make it last, because once the leaves fell and the tourists left it was famine all over again. So far, the tourists had not arrived. It had been a cold Spring, and now, halfway into June, it was still cold. The sun was rarely out, it rained much of the time. Without the tourists there to piss their money away, business was slow and jobs were few. Everyone was worried about their pocketbooks, their rent, their car payments. I enjoyed the absence of the crowd, the peace and the quiet of that. But I was in need of money like everyone else, and when you're chasing the God Almighty dollar there is no possibility of peace. Peace is the property of the rich and the blissfully insane. If I could have gone blissfully insane I would have. But my insanity was of a more common, miserable kind. All lumps, no light.

I wound up on Hitchcock Street, the main drag, or what passed for it. Hitchcock was about a half mile in length. All the shops were there, the Post Office was there, the bars and the restaurants were there, the drugstore, the grocery store. I walked along up the center line, listening to the echo my boots made as they struck the pavement. I felt like a ghost, like a lost character on a long forgotten movie set. Maybe I was. I'd been away from this town for years. Now I was back, and most of the people I'd grown up with were gone. They'd either gotten out and moved on, or they'd stayed and drunk themselves to death, or simply senseless. Either way, I recognized almost no one. And worse, almost no one recognized me. Funny thing was, I was related to half the people in town.

I came to another streetlamp, then I saw him. He was in the light, holding a broom. He had a hump in his back and a small, triangular-shaped hat on his head. And he stood there, hunched like that, sweeping the dirt off the street. I'd seen him before, I was seeing him all the time, it seemed. I'd see him at night, I'd see him in the morning, I'd see him during the day—always at this corner or that, hunched over his broom, sweeping the street clean, sweeping it even after he'd swept it, sweeping away at nothing. He looked to be about 70, and his hump was bigger than his head. I was always tempted to talk to him, but the man appeared to have much larger things on his mind. Besides, to talk to him would have been to risk understanding him, and I didn't want to understand him. I was afraid that something might click, something deep inside of me, and I would lose my grip, let go, once and forever, and pick up a broom of my own. I was about ripe for that.

I walked right past the old guy. I might as well have been invisible. He just kept on sweeping. And I just kept on walking. It happened that way every night.

I thought I'd catch the sunrise. I walked to the beach, out onto the pier. It was a good pier, solid stone; it would last for centuries. I was early, the sky was still dark. I looked at the lake, listened to the waves. It was a big dumb body of water and it didn't know my name. I couldn't understand what people saw in it. It was cold and wet and there were a few million industrially diseased fish down there eating and shitting up a storm. The sound of the waves made me have to urinate. I hauled it out and pissed at the fish, then waited in front of the grocery store for the sun to come up.

Linda Lee unlocked the door. She had on a clean, colorful dress and her hair was done up nice. For a three-hundred-pound mother of four, she looked pretty good.

"You look like shit," she said.

I walked to the timeclock, found my card, punched it.

"I'll be in the milk cooler," I told her.

"Alright."

I went around back to the milk cooler. It was stacked to the ceiling with overstock, milk, cheese, eggs, things that would perish long before we put them on the shelves. I sat down on a box of Johnsonville Smoked Sausage. I lit a match. Someone, Donnie Lynn most likely, had drawn an enormous cock and balls on the wall. I let the match burn down until it reached my fingers. I let it burn my fingers, then it went out. I looked around. It was dark and cold. I wasn't quite sure what the hell I was doing in there.

I stepped out into the equally dismal light of day.

An old mongrel dog was staring at me. He was standing by the dumpster, a huge, pitiful-looking beast with a sagging back. He began to growl. His eyes narrowed to small yellow slits. I walked back into the grocery store and took a New York Strip off the shelf.

"This steak has gone bad," I told Linda Lee.

"Alright," she said. "Whatever."

I went back into the alley. I tossed it to the dog. He tore right into it. It was a perfectly good New York Strip. The sun was not shining. I could hear birds singing in the trees. I had a headache and a bad back, I'd had both my entire life it seemed. I sat at the picnic table next to the dumpster and the fruitflies and felt my head and my back ache and watched the dog eat the steak. After he finished he saddled up beside me and laid his head against my leg. He passed gas and gazed up at me with the unmistakable look of love in his eyes. I'd made a friend for life. After that, the beast came by every morning. I couldn't get rid of the goddamned thing. I named him Kafka and before long he was following me all over town. Everywhere I went, he was there, too. I'd leave work and he'd follow me to the bar, I'd leave the bar and he'd follow me home. When I woke up, he'd be waiting outside, ready to follow me back to work. Every morning I tossed him a perfectly good steak. That dog was eating better than I was. It occurred to me that I ought to take *two* steaks from the store every morning. One for Kafka the Mongrel Dog, and one for my mother. She'd been badgering me for rent.

My two weeks had come and gone. Long ago.

***

The TV was turned up loud, very loud. One of my mother's relatives had given her a stereo hook-up and a stereo to hook it up to. The dismal commotion of Hollywood could now be heard all over the house. It climbed the stairs and clawed my door, voices boomed and glass shattered, the rats in the walls awoke, gun shots rang out, chips of paint shook loose from the ceiling. The woman was obviously deaf. Technology would be my cross.

I was drunk and trying to paint another masterpiece. I had her lips down, her breasts, her dark, miraculous eyes, her raven-black hair, the creamy curve of her hips and thighs. She was done primarily in yellow, a crazed, blazing Van Gogh yellow: A sex-maddened goddess writhing in the light of a thousand orgasmic suns. Yellow.

Downstairs, however, a different scene was unfolding. I tried to ignore it, but the information crashed through nonetheless.

Andy Garcia was hot on the trail of a psychotic serial killer. He was a cop and he had fallen in love with a blind woman who had witnessed something—with her ears—and was now being stalked by the serial killer. The blind woman was a curvaceous knockout (one could sense this, even from upstairs), she had great legs, a remarkable ass and a keen intellect. Andy Garcia wasn't bothered by her blindness. The young, unsullied nubile body and keen intellect more than made up for the dark glasses and cane. It added to the mystery, made her sexier, that much more vulnerable and alluring. The guy couldn't keep his hands off the bitch. He was about to lose his cop job over the scandalous smell of it all. He didn't care, though. All he cared about anymore was climbing into the sack with the blind woman and catching the crazed serial killer who had her number. He had a personal stake in it, he was obsessed. He drank heavily and cold-cocked anyone who got in his way, including his fellow officers. The noise was deafening. Gunfire was exchanged, a female shrieked, reasonable men lost their reason and hurled obscene racial epithets, fine china broke, the world was coming to an end.

I tried to concentrate. Concentration was key, even under the best of circumstances. I started in on the vulva, then went to work on the vagina, imagining the tip of the brush to be my tongue, concentrating on that. Before long, I'd painted a fairly tasty-looking vagina— and in the process, pulled wood. I took my cock out and began to stroke it while admiring my work. A large part of art is simple appreciation.

Downstairs, Hollywood was still spilling blood and shaking the walls of the world—mine, in particular. Some sort of explosion took place down there, causing a piece of plaster to fall from my ceiling—directly onto my masterpiece, the one that was to make me immortal throughout the ages, the single painting that would lock me firmly into history and secure my place among the greatest artists of all time. Another high-fidelity shockwave hit the room and rattled my spine. I got up, threw open the door and went crashing down the stairs:

"WHAT THE HELL IS GOING ON DOWN HERE?!"

"THIS COP IS TRYING TO CATCH A SERIAL KILLER, HE'S IN LOVE WITH THIS BLIND GIRL AND THE BLIND GIRL IS ABOUT TO BE SLAUGHTERED BY THE SERIAL KILLER AND THE COP IS DRUNK AND HE'S SHOOTING EVERYBODY AND THE SERIAL KILLER IS A COP TOO ONLY NO ONE KNOWS IT YET EXCEPT THE BLIND GIRL AND THE COP WHO'S IN LOVE WITH THE BLIND GIRL HAS BEEN ACCUSED OF MURDER, ALL THE OTHER COPS THINK HE'S THE SERIAL KILLER BUT HE'S INNOCENT AND THEY HAVE HIM CORNERED AND HE'S DRUNK AND HE'S SHOOTING EVERYBODY AND THE BLIND GIRL CAN'T SEE ANYTHING AND—"

"ARE YOU SURE SHE'S NOT DEAF?"

"NO, SHE'S BLIND! THE BLIND CAN HEAR BETTER THAN BATS, YOU FOOL! SHE CAN HEAR A PIN DROP FROM ACROSS THE HALL AND HER SENSE OF SMELL IS HIGHLY ADVANCED—THAT'S HOW SHE KNOWS WHO THE SERIAL KILLER IS!"

"DO YOU REALIZE THAT YOU ARE SHARING SPACE WITH THE WORLD'S GREATEST UNDISCOVERED LIVING ARTIST?"

"SIT DOWN AND WATCH THE MOVIE!"

"WOMAN, I AM GOING TO BE IMMORTAL. LIKE BEETHOVEN'S NINTH, LIKE COCA-COLA, LIKE THE PYRAMIDS!"

"AW, SHUT UP YA MORON!"

"DO YOU THINK PICASSO HAD TO WORK UNDER THESE CONDITIONS?"

"PICASSO DIDN'T LIVE WITH HIS MOTHER!"

***

Jack Philly and I were on our hands and knees, two men who might have once held promise, putting together a Food Club creamed corn display. We were stacking the cans of corn into an enormous pyramid, one atop the next, working toward the ceiling. The whole thing was Jack's idea. He had one of the girls make up a sign, some stroke of genius phrase-making he'd come up with while lying in bed the night before:

CREAMED CORN
AT 4 FOR A DOLLAR
IT'S ONE OF THE WORLD'S 7 WONDERS
BUT OUR SALE WON'T LAST FOREVER

The sign was written in a large, florid female hand. Each letter was a different color, all of them blinding, all of them leaping out at you in tandem. The sign was now propped against a toilet paper display, awaiting the completion of the pyramid.

We were still laboring at the base. It was frustrating work. You'd finish a layer, then move inward a can and build upon that. If you weren't careful you could disrupt something and the entire structure would topple. We'd been at it for nearly an hour. I had a hangover. Jack had glasses, but he never wore them. Our pyramid kept toppling. The Egyptians had gone through generation after generation of Hebrew slaves before getting theirs up. Jack Philly and I were in danger of working through our lunch break.

"This was a brilliant idea, Jack."

"Don't start in on me, Totten. You're still the new guy here, don't forget that."

"It's almost noon. This is ridiculous. We'll never

finish before lunch."

"We'll work straight through dinner if we have to."

"Jack, it's hopeless. Be realistic. Let's give it up and get one of the girls to build us a sandwich."

"Do you always give up on things so quickly?"

"Yes. It's easier that way." I dropped the can I was holding. I stretched out on the floor, closed my eyes. Jack put his foot in my ass. It was a big foot. I got up.

"Keep stacking," Jack said. "This isn't Cancun. We're being *paid*."

"But this is insanity! Even if we do finish the goddamned thing, the first person who walks through here will knock it over. They'll be crushed to death and we'll be sued. LOCAL INNOCENT KILLED BY IRRE-SPONSIBLE CREAMED CORN DISPLAY. Think about it."

"We can't stop *now*. The deli girls would think we'd failed!"

"Jack, you're 55 years old. I'm 30. We work in a grocery store and we are building a pyramid out of creamed corn. There are many who would say that we've already failed. Why should you care what the girls think? They're all forty pounds overweight, they live in small trailers in the woods and their husbands and children have driven them insane."

"The girls look up to me."

"Why do you hire so many fat women? It is some sort of fetish you have?"

"No, just the opposite."

"I don't get it."

"Keep stacking. I have to take a shit."

Jack wandered off to have a shit. His shit-breaks were legendary. I added a few more cans to the pyra-mid. Then I stretched out on the floor again and went to sleep.

I was the King of the Village. It was a village of women and the women were all mine. I was lying on a bed of gold and several obscenely young Nubian slave girls were fondling me with palm leaves. The Nubian slave girls were topless, they wore short grass mini-skirts and had multi-colored jewels bobbing in their navels—a gift from their benevolent King. They were virgins, all. And they were in competition with one another. They fought nightly to determine which of them would have the honor of wrapping their lips around the King's royal cock. The King was to eventually puncture each of the young Nubian hymens—in his own good time. But I didn't feel up to it just yet. My girlfriend was the Queen, and the Queen was insatiable. When the Queen got through with me there was nothing left. All I could do in the way of kingly duties was to lie around in the sun, eat expensive cuts of meat and wait for my strength to return. The Queen would be back at any moment. We had a Cadillac parked out front. Soon we would drive to Sears and piss away a fortune on things we did not need ...

I heard a voice in the fog. Something kicked me. I had a hard-on.

I opened my eyes. I didn't see any virgins.

"Wake up!" Jack said. "Jesus Christ, I'm gone five minutes and you take a vacation."

"Look, Jack, let's just forget about this pyramid nonsense. The Egyptians had slaves. We don't have shit."

"What the fuck do the Egyptians have to do with anything?"

"Let my people go, Jack."

"We're going to finish this thing. Get off your ass—NOW!"

"Alright! Alright!"

Linda Lee walked by. Then Donnie Lynn. Then Cheryl, Sue and Betty. The Deli-Maidens, in formation.

"Hello, boys! Having fun yet?"

"Look—Lupus has a *boner*!"

"But you can hardly *see it*!"

"He must be a EUNUCH!"

There was much laughter and gaiety. You would have thought they ran the place. They probably did. I watched all that cellulite jiggle by, back to the deli counter from whence it came.

"You never told me why you hire so many fat women, Jack."

Jack didn't look so good. He took a hanky from his pocket and wiped his forehead. His doctor had him on Xanax. He popped one. What he needed was a five-year nap. But life had slapped him upside the head too many times and he couldn't think clearly anymore.

"Two summers ago," Jack said, "I hired a girl named Jamie Dean. She was eighteen, a redhead. Real slim, but shapely—I mean, there was something to grab ahold of there besides bone. It was probably the red hair, though. I've always had a thing for redheads. My whole life, I'd wanted to lay into a redhead—just once—but I'd never even come close. They always terrified me— one glance and I'd begin to sweat. I'd see that red hair, get an erection and run away. I'd been a coward all my life. So when Jamie Dean walked in, I hired her on the spot."

"Guts."

"Yeah. But I never thought anything would actually happen. I just figured she'd brighten up the place a bit."

"Like flowers."

"Do you wanna hear this or not?"

"Yes, yes. Go on."

"Shit, I don't know where to start. She had that red hair ..."

"Yeah, I caught that."

"Well, she had a body on her, too. And breasts-- Jesus, it was like they were struggling to get out of her blouse, like they *needed* to get out. And her *ass*, oh, my God, her ass was shaped like a *heart*, like a Valentine— but upside down, you know?"

"Nice."

"Yeah. And she'd stare at me with all that, she'd watch me watching her."

"So she was interested."

"I couldn't be sure. Shit, I was old enough to be her father."

"Maybe that turned her on."

"Maybe. Hell, it must have. We became friendly right off. We'd make smalltalk, you know. Tell off-color jokes, flirt ..."

"Jack, every working stiff in America does that. It kills time and helps you to forget that you're wasting your life. You were *bored*. Let me tell you something, if it weren't for women at the workplace, I'd go fucking mad. I won't even *take* a job unless the women outnumber the men three to one. If the scale's tipped the other way, fuck it, I'll go on welfare, I'll starve. Who wants to work with a bunch of guys? I *hate* sports. What the hell would I have to talk to them about? Hey, you need another can there. You're gonna make this thing collapse again."

Jack grabbed another can and shoved it into place. Slowly, but surely, we were raising our ridiculous display. Blame it on the folly of ancient man.

"But with Jamie Dean it was different," Jack went on. "There was something there, it was like a current you could feel."

"Running between the two of you. Electric."

"Yes, exactly."

"So what happened?"

"Well, we were in the meat cooler one day. I was showing her how to work the grinder—out of nowhere she cups my balls and starts kissing me, deep, on the mouth, lots of tongue. I thought I was going to have a coronary. Christ, I was married! She could have been my daughter! The whole thing was twisted."

"Taboo."

"We did it standing up. Lupus, even her *cunt* hair was red. But it was so light you could barely see it. She weighed ninety-five pounds."

"Ninety-five pounds? That's too fucking skinny."

"Ninety-five pounds. It was like child-rape!"

"Keep your voice down, Jack. Someone might get the wrong idea." It was strange, the things a person would confide to you while putting up a pyramid. It seemed that men could only truly talk to one another while diverted. Maybe that explained the general obsession with sports. Keep your eye on the ball, and when the other guy isn't looking, spill your guts.

"Oh, get off it," Jack said. "No one's listening. Besides, she was eighteen. I checked her application."

"Why are you whispering?"

"I'm not whispering," he said, in a whisper.

"Alright, I hear you. So what happened next? You made it with a boney, eighteen-year-old redhead with big tits and a heart-shaped ass and now you hire only heifers. I don't get it. That's discrimination, by the way."

"Nonsense."

"The thin and the beautiful deserve a chance here, too. You could be taken to court. Some little waif's gonna get you, Jack."

"Some little waif *already* got me."

"Okay. So what was this horrible thing that happened?"

"I fell in love! Day and night, all I could think about was Jamie Dean. Jamie Dean, Jamie Dean, Jamie Dean! I lost my goddamned mind."

"Yeah, it works that way sometimes."

"I started coming home late every night. My wife would have dinner on the table and I'd be fucking Jamie Dean in the backseat of the car. My wife's car!"

"I thought you had a bad back."

"How do you think I *got* the fucking thing?"

A customer came wandering up the aisle, old and bent, forever lost. She had a head of lettuce in her hands, her shoes didn't match. Jack got off his knees. It was his job.

"Can I help you, ma'am?"

"I'm looking for SALT," the woman said. "I can't find any SALT."

"The salt is in aisle two. Let me get it for you."

"Over in Hart they put the salt right where you can see it. Here, you hide everything."

"We have plenty of salt here, ma'am."

"You never have what I WANT here, you never have ANYTHING!" The woman was turning in circles now, hostile, impatient, angry. Whenever I began to worry that my life might be cut short by a horrible accident, drug abuse, violence or disease, all I had to do was observe the old men and women who staggered through the store every day to realize that death was not the enemy, not always the thing to fear.

"I want SALT!" the woman shouted.

"Follow me," said Jack. "We'll fix you right up."

"I want SALT! Why is there no SALT? I want to talk to the MANAGER!"

"I'll get you your salt, ma'am."

"I don't want SALT! I WANT TO TALK TO THE MANAGER!"

"I am the manager, ma'am. We have salt, let me show you."

"WHERE IS THE SALT? I CAN'T SEE ANY SALT! WHY ARE YOU HIDING IT FROM ME? I AM GOING TO SCREAM NOW!"

She began to scream. Jack ran for the salt.

The woman was clearly insane. Half the people in town were insane, but the elderly were the most insane of all—they'd been at it longer. Tuesdays were the worst. Tuesday was Senior Citizen's Day. They got a five-percent discount. They'd begin lining up at the door an hour before we opened, lying in wait to seize the castle and poke and prod the produce, searching throughout the morning for the perfect melon, the perfect cucumber, the perfect peach. It was on Tuesdays that you began to see the beauty in euthanasia. The problem with most people, however, was that their minds and their souls became sick long before their bodies did. The majority of them didn't *appear* to be in any pain. You couldn't kill them and call it a kindness.

Jack came trotting back to the pyramid, short of breath, beaten. He'd probably squander the remainder of his life dealing with this same sort of less-than-nothing bullshit. Maybe that didn't bother him. Maybe he didn't think about it. Maybe that was for the best. You think about a thing like that too much and you wind up being the guy on the six o'clock news wearing the flakjacket and holding hostages.

"Did you get rid of her?" I asked.

"Yes. I ended up *giving* her the salt. I'd swear these people are nuts."

"They are."

"Ever see her husband?"

"I don't know."

"The old guy who comes in? Wears that green suit, stinks, always muttering to himself?"

"Oh, him, yeah. He was in here the other day. He peeled an ear of corn, took a bite, then put it back."

"Yeah, that's him. They're rich as hell, those two. They own a whole stretch of lakefront property. The old man used to run with Al Capone. He carries a picture of the guy in his wallet."

"We're living in a godless era, Jack. You were telling me about Jamie Dean." I picked up a can, put it into place. Jack did likewise. We weren't getting a hell of a lot accomplished. If there had been a taskmaster lording over us we would have been given the lash by now.

"Right. I fell in love with her," Jack said. "I really did. You can love your wife, and at the same time, be in love with this other person, too. It's the damnedest thing ... I felt terrible about it. But I couldn't stop. After awhile, I got to feeling so guilty I couldn't live with it anymore. I told my wife. I thought she might understand. I thought that maybe I could love them both."

Here was a man truly touched by the angels. Or something more ominous than angels.

"Jack, you're an innocent."

"She threw me out. Just like that. She divorced me. I lost everything."

"I'm sorry, Jack. That's a tough one."

"Jamie Dean and me, we kept seeing each other. We really carried on there for awhile. We had ourselves some fun, we really did. I think she loved me, Lupus. But it got so she wouldn't do any work. She'd sit around in the back room talking on the telephone all day. Everyone knew what was going on by then and they were mad as hell. They thought I was playing favorites, that

I was just paying Jamie Dean to sleep with me. I'd go back there to tell her to get to work, but then I'd see her sitting there with her skirt hiked up and no panties on ... you know, playing with herself. I swear to God, she'd *wink* at me with that thing. I'd end up giving her the afternoon off. I'd end up giving her a raise! It was insane. I was in love with her, I was totally helpless. And I still loved my wife!"

There wasn't anything to say. I worked at the pyramid and let Jack tell it.

"Then I lost Jamie Dean, too. She got a job at the K Mart over in Muskegon. I helped her move. She had a new boyfriend, some young guy. I never met him, though ... I carried in the couch. I had my heart attack right after that, right there in her new apartment. I haven't seen her since. I'm still in love with her."

"What about your wife?"

"We're living together again. She let me come back after I had the heart attack. I built us a house last Summer. She has her own bedroom now. She likes that."

"You don't sleep together?"

"Well, we never did, really. My wife's religious. She doesn't believe in sex except to have children. And we had a son early on, and that's all she wanted, just the one."

"How old is your son?"

"Twenty-four. He's in prison. He went in on his eighteenth birthday. He won't be getting out."

"Christ, what's he in for?"

"Rape, attempted murder."

It was terrible. I didn't know what to say.

"I used to be a cop," Jack said.

"Jesus ..."

"Yeah. I used to hate people like him. I still do."

It was Greek Tragedy. It was the whole fucking

town, in a nutshell.

"Shit, Jack, you oughta write a book."

"What the hell for?"

"Yeah, I guess you're right. During my twenties I went a little nuts and read all the classics. "

"This conversation is depressing."

"So are the classics."

"Let's talk about something else."

"Sure."

We didn't talk about anything after that. We worked away at our pyramid in silence.

By three o'clock we were nearly finished. I was hanging from a crossbeam, putting the last glorious can on top. I got it in place, climbed down.

We stepped back and took a look at what we'd done.

The thing was enormous. Awe-inspiring. Ridiculous.

It looked dangerous as hell.

"It's too goddamned big," Jack said. "Look at it! It'll kill us all!"

"No, it's fine," I said. "It's perfect. Let's go across the street and get a drink."

"We have to take it down."

"Are you crazy? I'm not getting near that thing."

"We'll use sticks," Jack said. "Go see if you can find some really big sticks."

"Sticks?"

"Yeah. Big long sticks."

"Oh, fuck ... Alright. Wait here. I know just the place." I made for the door.

"Don't be gone long," Jack yelled at my back. "And make sure they're big."

I walked to the bar. Angel was pouring. They

were tall and strong and good.

I dropped fifty cents into the jukebox.

Billie Holiday sang.

***

It was 2 a.m. The moon was casting shadows across the kitchen floor. It wasn't romantic like in the movies. It wasn't anything.

I went upstairs to my room. I'd thrown an old mattress on the floor the day I'd moved into the place, while still suffering the delusion that sleep was a necessary ingredient to good health. There was a shitty little scarred-up dresser in the room, and above it hung an antique mirror with a crack running down the center. On the mirror I'd taped a picture of my girlfriend, the lovely Tia Correlia. In the picture Tia Correlia was three years old, all innocence and big brown eyes. She was wearing a ragged little nightdress. She had dark curly hair and was jamming an Easter egg into her mouth. Looking at that picture had always made me feel good. Now it broke my heart. I sat down on my mattress and pressed my hand to my chest. I stared at the little Tia Correlia. The little Tia Correlia stared back. A woman now. Full-grown, caught in the currents of life. We used to dog-fuck on the kitchen floor, the rent overdue and the sun coming up ...

I went outside to the shed and found a can of spray paint. Van Gogh yellow. I looked at the moon. I shook the spray can, listened to the ball rattle. Then I walked to the beach, up the shore, and out onto the pier. At the end of the pier there was a tower with a flashing green light at the top. There was a ladder running up the side and a sign, at the base of it, which said DO NOT CLIMB. I stood there, shaking the spray can, listening to the rattle. There was something comforting in that. I watched the light at the top of the tower blink on and off, green to black, black to green, and back again. I listened to the waves, the rattle of the can.

Then I began to climb the tower, one rung after another. Up up up. Into the light. Into the dark. And back again ...

Thirty minutes later, I was finished.

I had written her name down the side of the tower.

In Van Gogh yellow.

One hundred times:

TIA CORRELIA
TIA CORRELIA
TIA CORRELIA
TIA CORRELIA
TIA CORRELIA
TIA CORRELIA
TIA CORRELIA
TIA CORRELIA ...

The light blinked on and off. Green to black, black to green. Earth was 93 million miles from the sun. The moon was roughly 238,875 miles further removed and wasn't worth its weight in dogshit, no matter what Hollywood or the romantic poets said. The waves crashed against the pier. The paint ran. The sun remained hidden. The moon was insane. The light blinked on and off.

I sat at the foot of the tower, waiting ...

***

I was pacing back and forth in front of the Sause Box

the following morning, watching the sun come up, waiting for the OPEN sign to pop on and the doors to open. I had to get that bartending job. I had to get out of my mother's house, away from the rats and the mosquitoes and the ear-piercing glamour of Hollywood. More importantly, I had to win back the heart of Tia Correlia. I had to get to Chicago and persuade her to marry me. I felt that my survival depended upon it. Tia Correlia was my foundation, she was a goddess to me. Hell, she was my God. I had no religion. Without Her I was lost. It was obvious.

To accomplish this I needed money, cash flow, an income. I'd never been very good at making money. I seemed to lack motivation. I preferred to lie around in a pre-hypnotic, cipher-like state, and leisurely paint my way toward immortality and other poetic destinations—the gutter, for instance. This was one of the reasons Tia Correlia had given me the boot in Chicago. Painters rarely made any money, even when their paintings sold, and mine didn't sell all that often. When they did sell, it was usually to the mentally and financially unstable—fellow painters, in other words. It was a seemingly hopeless situation and it often got the best of me. Rather than surrender to the headaches and hemorrhoids of the work world, I would simply fall into a depressed state for three or four days, lying on the livingroom floor, staring at the ceiling or counting flowers in the wallpaper. Then I would rise and attack the canvas, working myself into a frenzy, painting day and night without pause. Then I would collapse, sleep, awake to the doomed and dreary prospects of a day job, and fall into a depressive fit once again—floor, ceiling, flowers, the shell-shocked thousand-yard stare. Life with Lupus was less than lovely. Thus my fall from grace with Tia Correlia, thus the boot from home and hearth. God knows the woman had good reason. But I hoped to change all that. I was going to burn my brushes and build bridges. I was going to work myself to the quick at what the world deemed serious, and rewarded as such. Which, in my case, meant grinding hamburger in a town 400 miles north. And now, if luck would allow it, pouring drinks for small-town drunks, as well.

I was sitting on the front steps when Angel came to open the place. She was wearing a baseball hat and bluejeans, well-rested, freshly scrubbed, sporty. She had short brown hair and a solid, slightly heavy, athletic build. She could have easily taken me in a fight. But then, Shirley Temple could have taken me, too. Fortunately, I had always gotten along well with women. Weighing a hundred and twenty-five pounds, I had no choice.

Angel pulled a set of keys from her pocket. She saw me sitting there and a disgusted look swept over her face.

"Shit, it's not even ten o'clock yet. Give it a rest."

"No, I'm here about the job you mentioned. I can't wait anymore. I need the money."

"The tourists aren't here yet. I can't hire anybody until the tourists show up. I told you that."

"Well, where *are* those pricks? I'm dying over here and the fucks are still picking out luggage."

Angel grinned. I must have looked desperate.

"They'll be here," she said. "Don't worry."

"I hope so ... I'm about ready to knock over a bank."

"Listen, when they get here, the job is yours. Alright?"

"Thanks, Angel."

"Don't thank me. By August you'll wish you'd never heard of this place."

I went back to my room and wrote a letter to Tia Correlia. I had written to Tia Correlia twice a day for the past month and a half. So far, she had not written back. I was worried. I was stricken to the point of spiritual hysteria. But I had great faith in Tia Correlia. I wasn't going to give her up without a fight. Or an epistolary novel. Whichever came first.

I walked to the post office and mailed off my letter to Tia Correlia and waited for the tourists to arrive ...

***

Lance Barley was lying in a heap at the corner of Second and Clymer. He was face down in the center of the road. His left arm was pinned beneath his belly and his right arm would have been pointed toward the rumored coordinates of the Christian Heaven had he been standing. He had one of his shoes clutched in that hand. Barley was six-foot-seven and one-half inches tall. He was a friend of mine. I kicked him.

"Barley," I said. "Wake up."

Barley didn't say anything. He rolled over. I kicked him again. He sat up.

"Suzette dumped me," he said.

Suzette was an old girlfriend of his, a pill freak with great legs, who'd put him through the wringer.

"Shit, Barley, that was a year ago."

"I know. *Exactly* a year ago."

"Oh ..."

"I thought you were living in Chicago."

"I was. But I needed a job. No one had the intelligence to hire me, so I came here."

"It's good to see you again."

"Likewise."

"What time is it?"

"I don't know."

Barley searched the sky for the moon. Found it. "Fuck, it's after 4. I have to be at work in a few hours."

"Me too."

"Shit ... You want a drink?"

"Sure."

Barley put his shoe on. Black high-top, size 12. He crossed the street and disappeared into a tall tangle of weeds. We'd become friends five years earlier, during a summer when I was out of work and out of hope and out of my mind, and had run back to Stillwater to hide. I was on tranquilizers at the time. Xanax, Restoril, Thorazine. Barley was on beer and LSD, self-prescribed. I carried around a black cigarette case in those days, it was leather and it had a little change pouch on the front and I kept my pills in there. The pills were all I had to keep me sane, the pills were the god and I never went anywhere without them. If I had to walk to the store or take out the trash or get the mail, the pills came with me—always a week's worth, on the off chance that I might get lost and not be able to make it back to the stash. So that cigarette case was always loaded with pills, and *I* was always loaded, stumbling, falling, losing things. I'd often lose the cigarette case and Barley would always find it, somehow, and explain to me what it meant in very cosmic terms. I was always grateful when he found that thing. It meant I wouldn't get sick that day. Barley and I soon became inseparable. We discovered that we had similar tastes in authors and books and historic disasters—Pompeii, in particular—and we swapped books and talked about authors and historic disasters and argued about these things while we drank and smoked and popped pills, ran cars off the road, gestured wildly, dropped hot ash, set couches and tablecloths aflame, got kicked out of bars and restaurants and the homes of friends. Barley was fresh out of the Army then and at a loss as to what to do with his life; he was just pissing it away in a state of semi-shellshock and waiting for a door and a better day to open. I was fresh out of the madhouse and doing similarly. For all our verbosity concerning books, literary giants and the end of the world, Barley and I never talked much about our personal lives. We didn't have to, we understood one another intuitively. It was a good thing we did; we were often too fucked up to make any verbal sense whatsoever. We had each made a bit of personal progression since then. But you needed a trained eye to see it.

Barley came stumbling out of the weeds with a bottle of rum. Bacardi 151, Rotgut of the Gods. He took a seat on the yellow line, cracked the seal. We sat there in the street and passed the bottle back and forth and caught up on what the other had been doing. Neither of us had been doing much so we didn't talk about that for very long.

"How's Tia?" Barley asked.

I took the bottle, tipped it. "She put the freeze on me six weeks ago. She's taking stock of our relationship. I think I've blown it. I may have to kill myself."

"You'll survive. I did."

"No, with me and Tia it's different. You and Suzette were completely out of synch. Tia and I fit like clockwork, we were born for one another. There's no other woman for me. Tia is the only one I've ever loved."

"Tia is the only one you've ever *fucked*."

"That too. But I mean it, there's no other woman for me."

"I don't know what to say to you. You romanticize everything."

"I'm telling you, Tia and I were born for one another. Nothing else makes sense."

"If you two are so perfect together, why is she dumping you?"

"Because I'm fucked in the head! I'm not blaming her. Christ, I drive *myself* crazy most of the time."

"She's a great woman, you know. I've always liked her."

"I know. I got lucky."

"I always thought you and Tia would end up married. I thought you two would last."

"I don't wanna talk about it anymore." I laid back and looked at the sky. The moon was up there, bright and crazy. My stomach was on fire and I felt half mad. Maybe a truck would come along and take me out, splatter my skull and snuff the grief.

"Have some more rum," Barley said. "It takes the edge off."

I had some more rum.

When I awoke I saw the sky. I saw a plane in the sky with a white tail trailing out behind. I heard birds singing, but I couldn't see them. Then I heard a horn. It was a loud horn. I sat up.

"GET THE FUCK OUT OF THE ROAD, ASSHOLE!"

I hadn't lost my shoes, my arms and legs were still attached. Everything seemed to be working except my mind, which felt like putty. Business as usual. I walked to the grocery store and punched the clock.

"You look like shit," Linda Lee pronounced.

I walked to the bathroom to vomit. Linda Lee followed me. I stuck my head in the toilet and let it go.

"Betty's sick today," said Linda Lee. "Jack wants you to run the register."

I coughed up what was left of my stomach lining, flushed and watched the blood and bright yellow bile swirl down.

At a quarter to 5, Barley walked through the door. He bought a T-Bone steak and a can of baked beans. I rang it up, bagged it.

"Where the hell did you go last night?" I asked. "You left me lying in the fucking street!"

"You don't remember?"

"No, I don't."

"You were going on about Tia. You were crying. You said you were going to kill yourself. Then you challenged me to a fight. You said nothing could touch you. You asked me to put a cigarette out on your forehead."

I was stunned. *Tears*? This was a first. I was breaking new ground, going where I had never gone before. Advanced alcoholism: The Final Frontier.

"I didn't do it," Barley said.

I owed him one.

I stole two steaks and took it easy that night. I gave one steak to my mother and tossed the other to Kafka the Mongrel Dog. Kafka was becoming a good friend of mine.

I went upstairs to my room. I was feeling that terrible variety of remorse all problem drinkers feel following a bender. Like I alone was guilty for the sins of Man, going all the way back to the murder of Christ.

I sat down and wrote a twenty-five-page letter to Tia Correlia. I sealed the envelope and put six or seven stamps on it.

Then I turned off the light, felt my heart breaking there in the dark, and prayed that the tourists would arrive and I would see Tia Correlia again.

CHILDHOOD
AND OTHER CRAMPED QUARTERS

We lived in a trailer, in a park, with other people who lived in trailers. I can still remember it, the orange curtains tacked to the windows, the avocado rug, the paneling on the walls. I have an old photograph, and in the photograph the trailer doesn't appear much larger than the car parked alongside of it. The car has no wheels.

I remember sitting in the trailer a lot. Me and my mother, and maybe my brother as well, who would have been just a baby then, if indeed he was anything at all. My father worked nights in a gas station. I was never quite sure what he did during the day. Maybe he had another job. Maybe he was President of some exotic third-world country no one had ever thought to name.

We were always watching television. There were no other children in the trailer park, there seemed to be a ban against them. It was just me and my baby brother, if he was even a baby yet. Maybe it *was* just me in the trailer park. Me and my mother. And the kids I saw on *Sesame Street*.

Surrounding the park itself were four *busy* streets, cars racing every which way at once. People going to work, coming from work, looking for work. These streets were nearly impossible to cross on foot, they were streets of perpetual motion, streets of the daily dull and mundane war. None of them were named *Sesame Street*. I would turn from the television to the window, then back to the television again. Occasionally, I would go outside.

"Stay close to the trailer," my mother was always warning me. "If you don't you'll be run over and killed and your father can't afford any funerals." Then she would add, "And don't go hanging around the other trailers."

Everyone seemed to work at night, like my father. People—*working* people, in particular—needed their sleep, my mother said. Everyone except my father, I guess. The President of some faraway country, the one with no name.

The park was crowded, a trailer every ten feet or so, with ragged clumps of crabgrass between them. I was to play, as quietly as possible, on my parents' clump of grass. The sky was fair game, however; wide and without boundary, often blue and always open for exploration. I would lie on my back and watch for airplanes, for clouds that reminded me of things which were not clouds: fat ladies, gimps, geeks, aunts and uncles. I had been given a magnifying glass that year so I would be able to see "all of the small parts that make up the whole," and on sunny days I would sit alongside my parents' trailer and lord it over ant colonies, entire armies going up in gratuitous smoke, which was well within the rules of my universe, being that the ants were mute and bore their inferno with a quiet dignity. I never wandered from my crabgrass island. I did not want to be run over and killed by some harried American Dream Chaser late for work. I knew from the start that death was a no more viable means of escape than anything else, that to die was to screw the living out of their last lardered dollar. The solution lay elsewhere. But no one seemed to know what that solution might be or where to begin looking for it. There was always the television, of course, which, as I understood it, was more affordable than both life *and* death. We watched a lot of television ...

One day we watched a man walk on the moon.

The man wore a large, bubble-like helmet over his head. There was a window cut into the helmet, right where his face was, so the man could look out at things. We watched him walk around up there. He took giant floating steps, he planted a flag, jumped up and down. He waved hello to the rest of us back on Earth. I could see the Earth hanging there behind him in space. It didn't look like much. The Earth was small, much smaller than I had ever imagined it to be, and I wondered how it was possible that I could be living on it, that we, all of the people in the world, could fit. No wonder the trailer park was overcrowded. How could we all fit into the trailer park when even the planet itself was too small? Of course there was a ban against children. There just wasn't anywhere to put us.

The man on the moon kept waving at us, he waved and waved. And I waved back. I wanted to be that man. I wanted all that space to jump around in. The man said that he was taking "One small step for man, one giant leap for Mankind." Which meant that he was taking that step not only for himself but for all of us, my mother informed me. In other words, there was no reason for me to stray too far from the trailer.

We watched that man walk around up there all day. I thought that was a pretty great day. When I got big enough, I would go to the moon too. I would stand up there on the moon and wave back at all the people in the trailer park.

I had met a boy named Emmett Rosenfelt, who lived in a real house, in an actual neighborhood, with kids and dogs and carports, a few miles from our trailer and its tinfoil antenna. Emmett told me he had, among other enviable treasures, a trampoline in his backyard, and that I was welcome to come visit any time I felt like jumping around in the sky with him. He said we would pull underwear over our heads and become astronauts, something I had done plenty of times on my own, but only while sitting in a cardboard box, never actually airborne—unless you counted the time I jumped off the roof of our trailer and dislocated my hip.

I felt a need to jump around. I informed my mother one day that I was going to walk to Emmett Rosenfelt's house, which was in a real neighborhood and was as big as a castle and had a trampoline out back. I told her where this magical place was.

"Oh no you're not!" my mother said. "To get there you have to go up Division Street where all the whores and junkies live and you'll be murdered for sure!"

There was no arguing with her. To do so would have been futile. She was the Lawgiver, plain and simple.

Neil Armstrong wasn't on the moon that day, so I watched *Big Valley* instead.

That night a tornado touched down in the trailer park. My mother was crouched in front of the radio because she knew that if she turned on the television during a storm, lightning would fist through the screen and kill us dead and my father would wind up on Division Street with the whores and the drunkards and the junkies, ruined from the cost of our funerals.

The man in the radio was going on about storm and tornado warnings. No one was to go outdoors, we were to take immediate shelter in our basements and cellars. I sat at the window, watching the trailers blow over. The park looked completely deserted.

"Hey Mom ..."

"Be quiet! I can't hear what the man is saying!"

I saw a trashcan tumble by. A picnic table. A sock. I saw my father out there. He was wearing his work uniform, a pair of bright blue coveralls with the legend SUNOCO DOES IT BETTER emblazoned on the back, running toward our trailer in the wind and the rain, waving his arms through the air like a true lunatic. His mouth was moving but whatever he was shouting got sucked away with the wind. Maybe another boy, miles away, heard what my father was shouting that night. I watched a lawnchair tumble by with nobody in it. Maybe that lawnchair belonged to the father of the distant boy, a boy whose father sat around all the time in a lawnchair. Except for tonight. The Night of the Great Tornado.

"Hey Mom, Dad's outside ... I think he wants us to come out," I told her.

"Oh, Christ!" my mother screamed. Our trailer was beginning to rock, back and forth, to and fro, as if it couldn't make up its mind as to the proper direction in which to topple. If my brother was born he was a baby at the time, and surely my mother grabbed him on our way out.

We hid under something, I can't recall what it was now, but it provided us with a bit of shelter. We watched our trailer tumble away like a big tin can and waited for the worst. But the worst never came. Suddenly everything was calm again, the way it had been just before all swell hell broke loose.

We rose from the rubble. Having seen *The Wizard of Oz* that year, I found myself looking for the witch's red shoes, but I didn't see them anywhere. It was still quite a show, however, even without the dead witch. The park looked like a great box of toys some outsized, petulant child had thrown to the floor in a fit of inspiration or disgust. But we'd been spared, we had come through it without a scratch. It was a small miracle. Something to look back on and consider when belief began to wane.

My father and I poked around in the ruins for awhile, the personal belongings of our neighbors, the stuff of their very lives. Well, they hadn't had any more than we had had. It was all rubbish, junk, things that seemed important until you saw them scattered over the ground. My father picked up a plate and sailed it through the air like a cheap flying saucer. He put a plastic bowl on his head and twirled a string of fake pearls from his finger, batting his lashes and pursing his lips. Then he smiled at me and said, "Well, son, I guess we'll be moving, eh?" He pulled a silver flask from his pocket, tipped it, and whistled a tune any fool could dance to.

"WE'RE RUINED!" my mother screamed.

It was the grandest night of my life up to that point. Even better than the time Ziggy Teagarden pulled the fire alarm in school and we all had to file out onto the lawn right in the middle of a quiz concerning the Various Birds of Michigan, for which I had exactly none of the answers.

***

We had a cat that for one reason or another we never did get around to naming. We just called him "Cat." I would say, "Hey, Cat," and the cat always knew who I was talking to.

I'd found the cat in an alley one night after sneaking out of our apartment to explore the new neighborhood. Someone had tied rocks around its ankles and the cat was trying to walk with these rocks dragging along behind him on the cement. He would wheel around, as if chasing his tail, trying to get at the rocks. Then he'd give it up and try to walk again. I untied the rocks and carried him home with me.

I woke my mother up trying to sneak back into the apartment. That cat made a lot of noise.

"WHAT ARE YOU DOING OUTSIDE? IT'S AFTER MIDNIGHT! YOU COULD'VE BEEN KILLED!"

I told her I'd found a cat.

"YOU WHAT?"

"I found a cat. He's hurt."

My mother seemed only to hear what she wanted to hear. Everything else had to be repeated twice—thrice if the news entailed a torn shirt.

I showed her the cat. I told her about the rocks tied to its legs and the sad way it had been afraid at first but finally warmed up to me and licked my hand and purred. I told her I wanted to keep it. I told her that the cat would never make it on the street, that the world would kill it for sure. She could see for herself that the cat no longer had a tail, that in the past someone had chopped it off.

"Who in heavens would do such a thing?" my mother cried. She bent down to pet it but the cat shied away. It rubbed up against my leg then ran into the bathroom. I brought him back.

"He's scared," I explained.

My mother ran her hand along the cat's spine, the way cats like it. The cat arched its back. He looked like a Halloween cat, like a witch's cat. Only without the tail.

"He needs a bath," my mother said. "The poor little thing ..."

Then she cuffed me upside the head.

"WHAT WERE YOU DOING SNEAKING OUT OF THE HOUSE THIS TIME OF NIGHT?"

I got to keep the cat.

We were living in an apartment on Wealthy Street, which was in one of the poorer areas of Grand Rapids, despite its rosy name. There were billboards plastered up and down the street, big as barns, advertising all the latest luxury cars, especially Cadillacs, but most everyone in the neighborhood rode the bus. My father had landed a teaching job, something he had gone to college for, on the G.I. Bill, after leaving the Army several years before. He could afford a car now and an apartment on Wealthy Street. The car hardly ever ran. So my father rode the bus a lot.

Wealthy Street wasn't all that far from the trailer park we'd been living in. Division Street was about a mile and a half away, maybe less. If you drove west down Wealthy you crossed Division. There, just as my mother said, you'd see hookers and their johns, the hookers climbing into the kind of cars you saw on the billboards. You'd see hobos, derelicts, drunks, madmen. A place called GOD'S KITCHEN, where the homeless lined up for bowls of soup. Next to this was a place called GOD'S GARAGE, a rather handsome looking building, if you used GOD'S KITCHEN as counterpoint, in which I assumed the Almighty must have parked His car. Later I learned it was a recreational center for disadvantaged youth, a place for the children of the poor to lift weights, don gloves and beat one another senseless in the ring. You'd see drug addicts, dealers, the only gay bars in town. Once I even saw a man walking up the street in his pajamas. My father told me that the man was probably mentally ill. But I had seen my father wandering around in front of our apartment before, laughing to himself and shaking his fists at the stars, wearing nothing but his boxershorts.

Beyond Division Street were the highways, and then, further still, the suburbs. Everyone wanted to buy a house in the suburbs some day. The suburbs were a quiet, safe haven, nothing bad ever happened in the suburbs, it was one big picnic there and no one ever walked around in their pajamas. My father vowed that one fine day we would make it to the suburbs.

I was happy just to be out of the trailer park. Compared to the trailer park, Wealthy Street was a paradise. The trailer park had been a tomb. Here you heard music, sirens, voices. There were bars and Take-Out stores, there were people, people everywhere, standing around, hanging out of windows, sitting on porches, leaning in doorways, playing cards, playing basketball, people singing, people shouting, people arguing, people who didn't sleep all the time or appear to be dead the moment they stopped moving, or the moment they began to. All was chaos, color, life. I could be as loud and unruly as I wanted, I could step outside and scream, light matches, smash bottles in the street. There were abandoned buildings to explore, strange characters to spy on. It was like living in a movie, it was one big playground, full of brick and broken glass. My crabgrass island had expanded to an entire city block and beyond.

I lost all interest in television. It was no longer necessary. The show taking place in the street was much more exciting, and I ran wild with it. I was out and about most every day, smashing things, examining and exploring, with Cat along as my scout. We'd chase mice, hunt rats and pigeons. Cat would flush them from the trash and I would take wild potshots at them with beer bottles and rocks. I was a lousy shot, but Cat was a first-class scout, even without his tail. Cat had been around, he was streetwise and knew the ropes. He was so disfigured the other cats never gave him any trouble. They'd see him coming and cross to the other side of the street, scared shitless. So Cat was never mauled and he always got his rat. People were a different story, they were bigger, madder, more dangerous. I was the one who kept an eye out for those. If they came too close or got a little too strange, I'd give Cat the signal and we'd run like hell. We never had much trouble, though. We were too insignificant to bother with, I guess. Small game. But we were always on guard nonetheless. With human beings, caution was key.

Around dinnertime my mother would stick her head out the window and scream "LUPUS!" at the top of her lungs, and Cat and I would head on home for something to eat. After the Night of the Great Tornado my mother had become a bit less overprotective of me. Maybe she figured that the elements of life and death were beyond her control. You either made it or you didn't. We'd survived the tornado okay. Also, my father was in a slightly better financial position now, and a funeral wasn't as likely to be the ruin of him.

Math and History. Those were the subjects he taught. He taught at Grover High, one of the inner-city schools. Most of the students there were black. Even his boss, the Principal, was black. My father would occasionally lay down some racist remark, usually at the beginning or end of each week, always while drunk or hung-over, about "savages" and "welfare babies," but he was always inviting students over to the apartment to tutor them privately if they weren't catching on in class. The students seemed to like him, black or white. He was a goof, he made learning fun, even math. He'd fold the newspaper into a Dunce Cap, stick it on his head and say, "If *I* can learn algebra anybody can." He'd bound around the livingroom swinging a saber, put on a Cavalry uniform (he was a Civil War buff) if the subject was a particularly important battle and he felt that he wasn't quite getting the human drama across. Sometimes his boss would come to the apartment and he and my father would drink and carry on all night, laughing and tossing bullshit back and forth like old friends. Drink seemed to break down the barriers of race. In our apartment, as long as the booze was flowing, everyone seemed to get along. I don't know how it worked in other apartments.

Most of the adults I came into contact with drank. They all appeared to be carefree, happy people—at least while they were drinking. When they drank they always danced and sang loud chaotic songs, sometimes getting into near arguments over the lyrics, which no one could ever quite remember, always inventing their own as they went along, changing them to suit the mood and occasion, which could mean something entirely different to each person in the room, moods being unpredictable and apt to have almost nothing to do with circumstance or occasion. I always loved it when the adults got together to drink. It meant movement, action, event. All the dull rules of conduct went out the window and were replaced with dance, with raucous song.

My father was a good singer. He was the best, the biggest, the loudest singer around. My mother never drank at all. Probably because she was the one who had to clean up the mess in the morning. My mother had the television, and me. She had my little brother, who was definitely a baby now.

***

Kindergarten.

I didn't want to go.

I had a feeling it was a trick to get rid of me, that if I went to school I would never make it home again, never see my parents, never see Cat, my G.I. Joes or Wealthy Street again. But I had to go anyway, there was no getting around it. I pleaded with my father:

"You're a schoolteacher, why can't *you* teach me?"

"Because he has to teach everybody else," my mother said. "That's his job, he does it all day."

My father nodded in agreement. He had a beer in his hand and was half asleep at the kitchen table. When you had a job there wasn't much left of you at the end of the day. Getting a job was another thing I would try to avoid.

They drove me to school the following morning. The car was working that day. I said goodbye to my bedroom and all the broken-down buildings that I loved. I gave Cat a hug.

"After this you'll have to walk," my mother said. "It's only four miles. You're a big boy now."

My father told me not to worry. School could be

a lot of fun, he said. Then he looked at his watch:

"Oh, Christ! I'm late again. I hate this goddamned job."

I walked up to the school, opened the door built for giants. When I looked back I saw my mother wiping her eyes with a hanky. My father didn't look too happy either. I didn't know what the hell to think. I'd given up trying to figure it out. My mind was blank, a perfect zero. I scratched my new crewcut and walked on in. I caught my shirt in the door, tearing it up the back. I knew I'd catch hell for that when I got home. If I got home at all. An unfamiliar terror spread throughout my belly, pointed and icy, sharp, stabbing. I burst into tears, choked them back, and walked on up the hall.

We were seated, roll-call was taken.

Our teacher's name was Miss Underbell. Miss Underbell was old, older than my mother, even. She must have been sixty at the time, snow-white hair, bottle-thick glasses, baggy nylons, an army of rats possibly nesting between her legs. She seemed nice enough, however. Her voice was soft and sweet and she told us of all the fun we were going to have that year. We were going to learn how to read and write and fingerpaint, we were going to be given napmats, crayons, notebook paper. But I was terrified. I missed my parents and I hadn't even been away from them ten minutes yet. I missed my bedroom, my little brother, the chaos and freedom of Wealthy Street, the noise and the people and the light. I kept wondering when it would all be over and I could go home again. I'm sure a lot of the other kids were wondering that as well. Yet they seemed to be taking it better than me; they seemed relatively calm, whereas I was literally shaking in my seat. Miss Underbell was a *witch*, she had rats between her legs, her teeth didn't look real, her eyes were all wrong. The fish in my aquarium had eyes like that. Dolls had eyes like that.

There was another boy who appeared to be just as terrified as I was. He had his face buried in his hands, shaking his head back and forth in the universally acknowledged NO motion.

It was Emmett Rosenfelt! My underwearing astronaut friend!

Emmett's parents were rich as kings, at least in comparison to mine. I could understand why he would have rather been at home. His mother was a notorious alcoholic and his father owned a poolhall on Division Street; he was never home so Emmett pretty much had the run of the place. His mother lay in bed all day, drinking and listening to symphony music. She never bothered anybody and nobody bothered her. I liked her right off. You rarely ever saw her, and when you did it was always exciting. She'd wobble to the bathroom wearing nothing but her panties and bra, she'd wave at you and smile, then disappear into her bedroom again. And you would hear all of that powerful and majestic music coming from under her door, music like mountains rising from the earth, music violent as the history of man, bloody as the sword or as soft as the wings of a bird. The world might have been a much better place had more people lived the way Mrs. Rosenfelt lived. I imagined it must be real nice in there with that music. I wanted to be in there, too. I wanted that room, that door to open and close, that music. Emmett's mother was a true goddess, so beautiful and mysterious. And Emmett, he had all those great toys to play with, guns, trucks, soldiers, that big trampoline in his backyard. He could also go into the refrigerator any time he pleased. Emmett's refrigerator was always full of soda pop. He had it made.

Miss Underbell approached Emmett first.

"It's all right," she told him. "There's nothing to be afraid of, Emmett." She was kneeling beside his desk, nylons sagging at the ankles, stretched to burst everywhere else, stroking Emmett's greasy mass of hair. Her dress was riding up her thighs. She had fat thighs, old lady thighs. Emmett began to cry.

"Now, Emmett, look around. No one else is crying, are they? Why are you crying? We are here to learn and have fun."

Emmett's face was a bright red mess. His mouth was twisted wide and the tears kept coming, faster and faster. There was a long green string of snot hanging from his nose. He'd blubber and a big green bubble would form in each nostril, grow large, then pop, and then another set of bubbles would form. He looked awful. School looked awful. Miss Underbell looked horrific. I was homesick. I had to go to the bathroom.

"No one else is crying, Emmett. What's wrong? Aren't you a big boy?"

Big Boy. I was beginning to grow suspicious of that phrase. There was more to it than met the ear.

I broke. The terror came rushing out, there was no holding it back any longer. I'd failed some sort of test, some strange rite of passage—the first and probably most important.

I laid my head on my desk and began to wail. I was a coward. I would never make it to manhood, never learn to read or write, never learn how to fingerpaint, work in a gas station, ride the bus with the lunatics of Wealthy Street. I had to shit and thought I might do it right there in my pants. I was subnormal, a flop. I'd end up dying alone in a madhouse, I'd end up insane, a zero, wandering up and down Division Street in my pajamas. I wailed. Emmett wailed. I wailed louder, longer.

"Oh, this is ridiculous!" Miss Underbell said. She arrived at my desk in a huff, the dark hull of her body filling the sky—the Hindenburg, destined to explode.

"What in God's name is the problem?" she demanded.

I couldn't tell her. My legs were crossed, I had my hands jammed in my crotch, my face felt hot, my stomach hurt. Emmett had stopped crying. He was staring at me with terror in his eyes. Everyone was. They knew I had to shit, that I was about to shit myself right there in my seat for all the world to see. They were afraid that the same thing might happen to them one day. The whole room crossed its legs and waited for the outcome. I wanted to be unborn, to crawl back into the womb and call it a day. Not that I knew what a womb was. I hadn't even learned how to fingerpaint yet, and perhaps never would.

"The restroom is at the back of the classroom," Miss Underbell informed me. The tone of her voice made her disgust quite clear.

She pointed to the back of the classroom. There was a door back there. On the door was a sign with the word GO written on it in large green letters. I knew that word. Miss Underbell kept pointing at it. Her finger looked like a long brittle stick. The rest of her was fat but her hands were very thin. She had the thinnest hands I'd ever seen, the hands of a skeleton, bones jutting out, wrinkled, her dry skin covered with nauseating liverspots. There were no rings on her fingers. She only used them to point with.

I stood up and began walking toward the GO sign. The shit was halfway out of my ass. I could feel it hanging there, weighing down the seat of my pants. There was a girl sitting at the back of the class, right next to the bathroom, a pretty little Mexican girl. There were some other girls back there too, but none of them were as pretty as the Mexican girl. They were all clustered around her, small moons orbiting a major planet: goofy white girls. I was a rancid piece of meteor debris falling by and fouling the universe. The Mexican girl had much better legs than Miss Underbell had, and they poked out of her bright and festive yellow dress, not quite touching the floor, dangling there, pretty as anything, with little lace shoes at the end. Later on, I developed a near-fatal crush on her—Melia was her name—but I never told her, so Melia never knew. I figured I had already blown whatever chance I may have had with her by shitting my pants that first day. Melia didn't look like the type of girl who would shit herself or associate with anyone who did.

I opened the bathroom door, stepped through, closed it. There wasn't any symphony music playing, but I felt better in there. I thought maybe I could just stay in the bathroom until it was time to go home.

I was wiping my ass when the door swung open.

It was Miss Underbell. She seemed even more ominous now that I was sitting on the toilet. I'd taken my pants off. My underwear was lying in the sink with the water running over it. "All You Need Is Love" was Number 1 on the charts. I had a wad of toilet paper in my hand.

"You didn't change the sign!" Miss Underbell said. "When we go to the bathroom we *always* change the sign from GO to STOP. STOP when we are *going* and GO when we are *finished*. We do this so others will know when the bathroom is free and when it is not free. If we don't change the sign someone is likely to walk in on us when we are doing our nasty. Now that would be rather unpleasant, wouldn't it, Lupus? Unpleasant for all of us, yes."

I could see the lovely Melia. She was peering around the corner, grinning in at me from behind the wall of flesh and authority that was Miss Underbell. She would never be my sweetheart, not now, not ever. Melia, my first great unrequited love. She stuck out her tongue, made a horrible face, then disappeared. Another face appeared. Then another, and another—a whole parade of monstrous, grinning little faces. I was on display, I was being held up as a living example of subnormalcy.

I wanted to disappear. I put my head in my lap. I put my hands over my head. I had shit in my hair ... Years later, I took the ferry across Lake Michigan to the Milwaukee Zoo and watched *Bobo the World's Largest Orangutan* do the exact same thing.

My second day of school was much like the first. Only I didn't shit myself this time. I cried again, but I managed to control my bowels, if not my emotions.

Emmett did a little better too, but not much. Melia looked as lovely as ever. Her dress was a brilliant blue-green this time, as brilliant and as beautiful as the sea, with lots of lace around the edges, a very short dress that floated on the breeze of her every graceful movement—so you would catch a glimpse of her panties every now and again, which were pink and, of course, spotless. None of us knew what sex was yet, but everyone seemed very interested in Melia's panties. Looking at Melia's panties almost made me forget how horrible school was. But not quite. I got to thinking about the previous day, which had been a true nightmare. Maybe today would be a nightmare too.

I put my head down on my desk and tried not to

think about it. I thought about Melia's panties instead, the mystery there. I thought about the pyramids I had seen in picture books. I thought about golden calves. The Sphinx. King Tut. *The Impossibles. Mr. Magoo.* I could hear Emmett sniveling in the distance. People whispering.

I opened my eyes.

Miss Underbell was hovering over me, a great grey tower of false teeth and knowledge.

"Come with me," Miss Underbell said.

She led me out of the classroom, into the hallway. There was a coat closet out there, right next to the door.

"I want you to stand in the coat closet," Miss Underbell said. She'd opened the door and was pointing in at the coats and the brooms with her long bony do-it finger. She didn't explain, she just kept pointing that finger toward the darkness. I knew I wasn't going to hear any joyous music in there. Mozart was dead. It was Wagner now, it was Schoenberg, Helter Skelter and mad hippies crawling out of the desert to smear the Hollywood Hills with blood and gore.

I stepped inside. Miss Underbell closed the door. I heard a key turn in the lock. I heard the clack of her heels as she walked away. After that, I didn't hear anything. I was alone in there with the coats and the brooms.

After an eternity, it was time to go home.

The same thing happened the following day. And the day after that. And then the next.

Miss Underbell had informed me that she would have no "Mama's Boys" in her class. I was being toughened up, stripped of the Mama.

Was this the way it worked in all schools? I wondered. In my father's school? What would High School be like? If you were fool enough to enroll in college they sent you to Belson, no doubt.

I dropped out right then and there.

I wouldn't be going on to Belson.

One day during that first week Miss Underbell climbed into the coat closet with me.

I never told my parents about having to stand in the coat closet every day. And I didn't tell them what Miss Underbell had done to me either. I didn't know how. The most I ever told my parents was that I hated school. Every morning my mother would have to drag me into that building kicking and screaming. I wouldn't even walk, she had to carry me through the door and drop me down. She'd apologize to Miss Underbell for all the trouble.

"He's still afraid," my mother would explain. "I'm sorry, I don't know what's wrong with him."

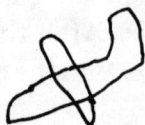

ENOLA

After that first week of school Miss Underbell left me alone. I was back in the classroom again, a mixed blessing, perhaps. The coat closet had had its advantages. After the terror of that first day, I'd almost grown to like it in there. It was better than being in the classroom with a load of shit in your pants, better than being on the toilet with your pants *off* and the whole carnivorous world staring in at you and laughing. I'd pile a few coats on the floor, make myself comfortable, and go to sleep. I'd dream I was a bird, sailing high over the city, over treetops and cesspools, over schoolyards and mad kindergarten teachers, dropping my dung onto the heads of all. But then Miss Underbell had climbed inside, and there went the neighborhood.

So I was back with the others again. Changing the sign from GO to Stop and Stop to GO. Emmett was getting the closet treatment now.

He didn't submit to it as silently as I had. He made a hell of a racket in there. Miss Underbell had gone so far round the bend that she simply pretended to ignore it, as if it wasn't happening. You could hear Emmett screaming all over the goddamned school. Some of the kids had begun to cry, and there she sat, showing us how to construct paper hats.

Emmett wasn't in there fifteen minutes before the Principal and half a dozen other faculty members filled the room.

"WHAT IS GOING ON HERE?" the Principal roared.

We got to go home early that day.

All he did was scream, I thought. Why didn't *I* do that?

Emmett hadn't even had his pants pulled down.

Emmett must be a real Mama's Boy, I thought.

It was never mentioned again.

We got a new teacher and everyone forgot about Miss Underbell, who had been carted off to receive free psychiatric help, no doubt. After a while, I forgot about her too. Completely. That first week of school seemed like a bad dream. And then it disappeared. I didn't even dream about it anymore.

I went to school, which wasn't so awful now that Miss Underbell was no longer there. I stuck close to Cat and we went on weekend rat safaris together. I looked through my father's history books. I thought about outer space. Jumped around on the moon with Emmett Rosenfelt.

One small step for Mankind, one giant leap for Lupus.

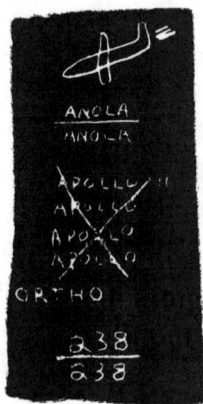

DON'T LET IT BRING YOU DOWN

All at once, the tourists arrived.

They came like a swarm of locusts, like roaches running from the light of all the major cities, Detroit, Chicago, New York, some from as far as L.A. Summer in the city was intolerable. Those who could afford to got out. They headed for small, picturesque towns such as Stillwater, and made those towns intolerable for the people who lived there. The tourists were a cash cow, however. They were needed. The survival of the town depended upon them. Economically, at least.

So, for the locals, it was a love-hate relationship. Suck the tit, sure. Then bite the fucker.

With the arrival of the tourists came the call from Angel. The Sause Box was swamped, awash in a sea of sun-visors and fluorescent t-shirts, holiday drunks and howling children.

The very idea of being at the beck and call of these idiots was anathema to me. Certainly it was better to starve? To go mad and hug the walls, or to swallow the pill of darkness and simply *take*, to rob, pillage, rape?

But no, one did not win back the hand of the fair,

raven-haired maiden in this way. One was forced to choose, rather, a ridiculous yet necessary form of bondage—bankteller, waiter, dishwasher, priest, cabbie, frycook, tax accountant, janitor, CEO—and try not to think too much while hurtling inanely toward the grave.

Well, I was a grinder of hamburger.

Turned bartender.

***

I walked into the grocery store and demanded that Jack Philly accommodate my new schedule.

"Jack, I can't work nights anymore. No early mornings, either."

"What?" He put down the box of Ding-Dongs he was holding.

"I got a job at the Sause Box. But I still want my forty hours here. I can't have any part-time shit. I'm thinking eleven to five."

"Impossible," Jack said. "Besides, that doesn't add up."

"We spread it out," I told him. "I work a six-day week. That'll give me forty-two hours. You can pocket the overtime. Assuming you have no conscience."

"Listen, I've got six other employees to keep happy. Most of them have been here for years. Shit, these women would hit the ceiling, they'd pitch a fit. It wouldn't be fair."

"Jack, I'm the best."

"Linda Lee's the best."

"Well, then I'm second best. We leave Linda Lee where she is and fuck with the schedules of those further down the food chain."

"You're third best, Lupus. *I'm* King around here. Hell, you're not even third best, come to think of it."

"I'm worth my weight in gold. I'm a pillar, I'm

holding the place up!"

"You're dreaming, punk. You don't weigh that much."

"Come on, Jack. Stick with me here. Show a little compassion."

"You've been here eight weeks and you're already fucking with my sanity."

"Oh, come on, Jack. Face it, you love me. I'm the son you always wanted, the one who never went to prison."

Jack winced at that one. I felt like an asshole. I hadn't meant to say it, but there it was, a small murder committed. Cruelty came so naturally to human beings, so thoughtlessly easy. We were defective. Christ was the model, the one to emulate. But that fucker hadn't been to town for over two thousand years.

Jack let my comment roll off him like a joke. The way I'd meant it, perhaps. He popped a Xanax and pointed to my long, greasy hair.

"You're more like the daughter I never had. The one who always said yes to the gang bang—punk."

I thought that was rather good. Jack Philly: tough guy. Men were amusing. We could only express affection for each other through insults and degradation. Blame it on history, blame it on the nature of the cradle.

"Yeah, well ... whatta ya say, Jack? I need the job at the bar. And I need this job too. I need the cash. I'm trying to win back the hand of a maiden here. I'm doing all this for love. You know damn well I'd rather lie around drinking beer all day."

"You're pussy-whipped."

"Of course."

"That can be dangerous."

"Yeah, I'm aware of that."

"So when are we going to meet this princess,

anyway?"

"Good question ..."

The possibility of never seeing her again took all the wind out of me, all the bluster and bullshit. I suddenly felt like falling to the floor and sobbing, no more armor, no more false bravery. But I was sober, and unless he's falling down drunk, a tough guy doesn't sob.

Something got in my eyes and Jack looked away.

"Oh, for christsake," he said. "I'll see what I can do."

"Thanks, Jack. I appreciate it, really."

"I can't believe I'm agreeing to this."

"You're in the top eight, Jack. You're practically one of the best."

"Yeah, whatever." He walked toward the meat cooler, then turned back. "That Barley friend of yours puked in the bathroom sink this morning. I've been saving it for you."

Jack was alright. He was a lot like the father I'd once had. The one who died on the job at age forty-seven and whose funeral we could not afford.

***

The following night I was at the Sause Box, tending bar.

It seemed strange to be on the serving side—backward, almost cruel. A world of bottles within reach, none of which I was allowed to drink from. Not according to law, at any rate. In Stillwater, the law wasn't all that hard to get around. But it being my first night on the job, I thought I'd best play it cool, by the book. I'd much rather have had my ass planted on a stool. But this was apparently my Season In Hell. They say every man has to have one.

All the regulars were there along the bar, lined up in their usual configurations—hardcore local drunks.

The rest of the place had been taken over by tourists. The regulars were quiet, staring listlessly into their drinks or at the woodgrain in the bar. The tourists were loud and obvious, screaming for beer from across the room, playing all the worst jukebox music, carrying on as if at a cock-fight. They personified every asshole I'd ever gone to high school with. Back then, I simply tried to avoid those people. Now I wanted them dead. They had gotten worse with age. And apparently so had I.

Just like the grocery store, the Sause Box had a predominantly female staff. Me and a short-order cook named Easy were the token males. Easy had a lazy eye and spent most of his time in the kitchen, so I was pretty much the only cock in the henhouse. I liked it that way. I was always a much better employee while working for and with women, happier, more at home. For one reason or another, women had a taming effect on me. I could never say no to a woman. With men it was different; I became contrary, lazy, uninvolved—I just didn't give a flying fuck. Women were ultimately stronger in my world, a more powerful force. I felt a closeness with women. I adored them. They were just as cracked and as flawed and off-base as men most of the time, but they were more at ease with it, more natural, less ruled and informed by emotional fear. Man was a liquid. Woman was a solid. Women were also much nicer to look at. Maybe, deep down, I just wanted to dick them all. Like every other pig on the planet.

I eyeballed the bar, checking drink levels. I poured a few fresh ones, slid them on down.

It was easy keeping the regulars happy. You just had to crack them a beer every ten minutes or so, keep the whiskey going around, the Rum and Coke. Simple poisons, easily dispensed. None of the regulars would have ever thought to order a fruit or a blender drink, a daiquiri, a pina colada, a fuzzy navel. In Michigan, a man could be beaten senseless for such a violation. The tourists seemed unaware of the ancient laws. One would have thought these laws to be universal, but this was apparently not the case. You almost felt sorry for the bastards. But not quite.

A soft, doughy, unruffled-looking college-age zero wearing sweatpants and a jogging shirt waddled up to the bar.

"I want a pina colada!" he said, drawing stares from every professional drunk at the bar.

I had no idea how to make one. It was 9 o'clock and we were beginning to get busy. The place was filling up. Angel was flying around like a lunatic, doing ten things at once yet doing them all well. A pro. I hollered over to her for assistance:

"Hey, this guy wants a *pina colada*! What the hell!"

"There's a bartender's book right next to the cash register!"

"What? What color is it?"

"It's red. Maybe somebody moved it. Look around!"

There was a tourist grabbing her arm and giving her some shit about his drink being too strong. Angel had her own horrorshow to deal with. I was on my own. Donna Summer was screeching from the jukebox, singing baby baby baby and faking an orgasm. People were dancing. I was tending bar at Studio 54.

The regulars had become visibly offended, glaring alternately at Mr. Pina Colada and whoever the fuck it was who'd punched up Donna Summer on the jukebox; even the taxidermic deer heads staring dead from the paneled walls seemed to be seething over it all. You could smell the seeds of violence in the air. The only thing preventing it, for the moment, was the possibility

of one of the female disco freaks falling out of her hal-
ter-top and the local boys' general amusement at the
spectacle of me trying to put together a pina colada. I'd
found the bartender's book and was flipping through
the index while a constantly changing parade of ingrates
shouted drink orders at me.

"IN A MINUTE!" I kept screaming.

"Hey, BARTENDER! I NEED A FUCKING
BEER!"

It was just the sort of thing that created the kind
of hate that kept the N.R.A. alive. With every new drink
request I imagined myself hauling out a 9mm and dis-
charging it in the general direction of the disturbance.
Outlaw justice.

I kept flipping through the book.

Then I found it:

PINA COLADA DELUXE
1 1/4 oz. rum
1 oz. cream de coconut
3 oz. pineapple juice
1 oz. soft vanilla ice cream
1 pineapple chunk
1 maraschino cherry

"I can't make this fucking thing," I said to no
one in particular.

Crushed ice? Pineapple? Ice cream? A fucking
cherry on top?

A chick drink! It wasn't even a drink. It was des-
sert. And, of course, no one knew where the blender
was.

I had to leave the bar altogether and go rummag-
ing around in the breakroom. By the time I found the
thing and got it back to the bar the locals were in an

uproar. Fresh drinks were required, pronto. You didn't keep an alcoholic waiting long, the pros could suck it down almost as quickly as it could be poured. Being a sympathetic soul, I provided fresh horses for all those in need, including a tall one for myself, before attempting a shot at the pina colada—which seemed to piss off the guy who had *ordered* the pina colada.

"WHAT KIND OF HORSESHIT IS THIS?" he shrieked. "I WAS HERE FIRST! I SHOULD HAVE BEEN SERVED BEFORE THOSE PEOPLE!"

"Those people have been here all their lives, they pay the mortgage on the place. They've earned priority status."

"I WANT MY PINA COLADA!" He'd puffed himself up and was bellowing over the disco. Whatever macho effect this may have had was negated by the nature of the drink he was demanding.

"I'll get right on it, Missy," I said, thinking it was what John Wayne might have said had he been tending bar that night. I wasn't John Wayne, though. I was more like the guy that John Wayne was always shooting holes in. I'd never liked John Wayne. Too patriotic, too All-American. When it came to Westerns, I always rooted for the Indians.

"WHAT DID YOU SAY?" Mr. Pina Colada yelled. He appeared to have gotten larger, somehow. For a moment, I thought he might actually jump the bar and do some blood-letting. Not good. In Hollywood, the Indians usually died. In real life, the Indians usually died. I wondered where the hell Angel was. I wondered about that gene that made most Indians crazy when they drank.

I made the pina colada. Found the coconut, the pineapple, the ice cream, everything else. Threw it in the blender, whipped it up, put the silly-ass cherry on top.

I shoved it across the bar without comment, avoiding the tedium of further confrontation. Playing John Wayne required too much fucking energy.

When no one was looking, I dumped what was left in the blender into a coffee cup and had myself a taste of that pina colada.

You know something? It wasn't half bad.

But you didn't hear it here.

That night became progressively busier and more chaotic. Tending bar had always looked so simple from the drinking side. But in reality it was a pain in the ass. You never stopped moving. It taxed your energy and awareness, you had to cultivate eyes in the back of your head, juggle ten or more thoughts simultaneously, remember this, remember that, what drink was going here, what drink was going there and then the other place. Your fuse was always burning, being lit and relit, your patience pushed to the breaking point. It put you dangerously close to madness, murder, suicide. I'd always been close to madness anyway, so the feelings I experienced on the job weren't at all alien to me. Not that I enjoyed them. Serving the public was a job that could drive even Mahatma Gandhi mad, turn the Son of God misanthropic, cause the monks to lose their center and take to drink and chants of violence. I hardly needed any extra push in that direction. But there it was.

Toward the end of the night, even the regulars appeared to have taken on all the aspects of standard assholes. Whiny, bitchy, impatient, demanding. Just another gaggle of slurring mediocrity, just as bad as the tourists.

It was a troubling thought, to be sure, and I wished I was back on that better side of the bar, blissfully unaware of most everything under the bulblight, good or bad.

A mob of football-looking morons caught my attention from the far corner of the bar and began screaming for beer. Rather than throw in the towel and take a walk, as anyone with even a modicum of self-respect might have done, I sold out and trotted the shit over to them, reliving the jeers and derision of my youth, as if in a time-warp—jarheaded jocks descending upon me in the hallways of hell, the whole pathetic lot of us caught forever between Civics and Behavioral Science 101.

I felt a little better when I got home and laid out the tips I'd made. It was astonishing. I'd been stuffing money into my pockets all night without thinking, having neither the time nor the energy to consider the cumulative effect it might be having upon my wallet. At the time, it looked like nothing more than pocket change, 50 cents here, a dollar there. Yet I was raking it in all night long. Pennies from heaven, pennies from hell.

The total came to $97.50. Nine hours of horseshit and abuse. A fairly good payoff. And there lay the rub.

Two thoughts came to mind.

The first being that I was profiting off the misery and weaknesses of others, people much like myself. I was dealing a drug. I was like the guy on nearly every streetcorner in America, pushing shit for the Mob or the Man. It was just that the shit I was dealing was legal.

My second thought was: It's all a trap. I'd get used to the disposable cash, I'd come to depend on it, I'd be hooked. The years would fly by in a neon haze, scarcely noticed. I'd wind up tending bar till the end of my days, an aging crank with a scowl and a shaker in his hand, nursing an ulcer and hating humanity.

The first thought caused me no real guilt. I'd been exploited by the tobacco and liquor companies all my life and I bore them no ill will. They had what I needed, and I was happy to pay, financially or physically. I was a grown boy, an adult. If I felt it necessary to self-destruct, that was my business. I tended to my backyard and they to theirs. The rest could fuck off and follow their own path, or jack-off in tandem with their neighbors, or whatever the hell it was they wanted to do.

But that second thought stuck in my craw. I was slave to enough as it was —I didn't need to make the list any longer. Becoming a slave to cash seemed to me to be a far larger, far more disastrous failing. A more obvious, less interesting failing. The kind of idiocy that the majority of Americans were constantly engaged in, becoming chained to and blinded by.

But, for the time being, I had to play the game. My only real comfort was the thought that, in the process, I *might* be working my way back to Tia Correlia. Love was a wonderful and enervating thing.

I found myself drinking and smoking more than usual.

Life's compromises were endless, it seemed. You occasionally wondered if they were worth it. Or if you were simply selling your soul for a sack of dogshit.

That's when the drinking and excessive smoking came into play, I guess.

My mother began beating on my door at 9 a.m. I'd gotten out of the bar at 3:30, fallen into bed at 5:00.

Again, the woman was trying to finish me off, push me over the edge, drive me toward the blade.

I tore off the sheets and whipped the door open: "WHAT IS IT? A FIRE? IT BETTER BE A FIRE

YOU WOKE ME FOR!"

"IT'S 9 A.M.!" my mother screamed. "GET OUT OF THAT BED AND TRY TO MAKE SOMETHING OF YOURSELF!"

"WOMAN, YOU ARE LOOKING AT A MAN WHO HAS JUST RETURNED FROM A TRIP THROUGH ALL NINE CIRCLES OF HELL!"

"GET OUT OF BED, YOU BUM! COME OUT OF THAT CAVE OF YOURS! YOU DIDN'T WORK THAT HARD LAST NIGHT! I TALKED TO CELESTE!"

Celeste was one of the owners of the Sause Box. She and a friend of hers named Sally co-owned the place. I liked Celeste and Sally. They were always swilling scotch and yukking it up, trying to run the place while seeing double. My kind of women. They'd most likely been too drunk the night before to acknowledge my quality labor. I got about as much recognition in the work world as I did in the art and literary world. Me and Van Gogh. Me and Hansum. Oh, the world would come to know my name one day. The world would be damned sorry it hadn't kissed my ass a little more ... Well, it was a nice delusion. And the more you failed, the more you came to believe it. Perfect.

I stood in the doorway, scratched myself, said nothing.

"YOU SHOULD HAVE SEEN THE WAY YOUR FATHER WORKED AT YOUR AGE!" my mother screamed.

I'd seen the way that guy had worked.

"YOUR FATHER HAD AMBITION!"

I pushed the door shut and climbed back into bed.

"HE COULD'VE BURIED YOU WITH ONE HAND TIED BEHIND HIS BACK!"

I buried him with *both* hands tied, I thought.
Then nodded out and into dreamland.

Two hours later I was at the grocery store, cutting steaks from a side of beef. From bed to the butcher's block. Then to the bar. My old man had held down *three* jobs toward the end of his life, and never less than two—the eternal impossibility of making ends meet. No wonder the guy drank and smoked himself to death. It was the only way he could get a day off.

Despite all the work, he never did manage a way to make those ends meet. At least not comfortably, not without having to forfeit both health and sanity, not without having to lay down his life. It wasn't until after he died and my mother received a pile of insurance money and a pension from the U.S. Army that the ends finally met. Spend your life digging blindly, and find your pot of gold at the bottom of the grave. The American way.

I hacked at that expensive side of dead meat, up to my elbows in blood and gore. I was feeling a little unsteady from lack of sleep, unfocused. One had to be careful while cutting steaks. Those knives were sharp enough to cut through bone.

From outside the meat-cooler one of the girls yelled a standard lowbrow witticism: "LUPUS, STOP PLAYING WITH YOUR MEAT! WE KNOW WHAT YOU'RE DOING IN THERE!"

I heard it all the fucking time. It was as stale as the day was dull. If I was in there, or Jack was in there, one of the girls was sure to shout it, usually at the top of her lungs. But I was half asleep that morning. My nerves were ravaged, my mind was frayed. When I heard it, I jumped.

And brought the blade down on the wrong piece

of meat.

For a moment, I didn't even feel anything, the cut was so clean. Then the pain asserted itself and began to spread, white hot and larger than life. I began to scream.

Donnie Lynn stuck her head into the cooler to see what the problem was. Her hair was gathered into a crazy ponytail that shot straight up from the top of her skull. One look at her and you knew that humanity was a flash in the pan, a dimestore novelty, faulty by design and doomed to fail. Our extinction was inevitable. The cockroach would soon be King again.

In the meantime, I was hurting like a motherfucker.

"What is it? What is it?" Donnie Lynn said.

"I'VE CHOPPED OFF MY FUCKING THUMB!" I screamed.

"Bullshit," she said. She flipped her hair and leaned in through the door, trying to show off her cleavage and give me a hard-on or something. She should have worn a bra more often. It might have helped. The cutting table was awash with blood and gore, piled high with gristle and slabs of raw meat. You really couldn't see my thumb in all of that. It would have been like trying to spot cigarette ash in the ovens of Dachau.

Donnie Lynn chomped away at her eternal stick of gum. She blew a bubble, popped it.

I walked up close and waved my mangled hand in her face, the blood spurting, flinging it around for dramatic effect.

"I'VE CHOPPED MY FUCKING THUMB OFF!"

Donnie Lynn went pale and ran screaming from the cooler.

A moment later, Jack Philly appeared.

"Oh, for christsake!" he said. He grabbed my hand and assessed the damage. He looked his usual exhausted self. You could tell he considered the loss of my thumb just another pain in the ass, one more thing designed to fuck up his morning. I'd probably interrupted his coffee-break.

I was howling like a banshee. Jack had put on his glasses to get a better look at the thing. He peered real close then pushed my hand away.

"That ain't shit, Totten. What are you whining about? You only whacked the top off!"

"I'M DISFIGURED! I'M A CRIPPLE NOW!"

"It's just the tip! It isn't anything. You'll be fine."

"THE TIP IS ENOUGH! I'M AN ARTIST! I'M SENSITIVE!

"WILL YOU SHUT THE FUCK UP? WE'VE GOT CUSTOMERS OUT THERE!"

"I'VE DECAPITATED MY THUMB!"

"KEEP IT DOWN! BE A MAN, FOR CHRISTSAKE!"

"I CAN'T! MY THUMB'S GONE! I'M A PRIMATE NOW!"

"Yeah, well, you'd better find it, monkey boy. They might be able to sew it back on." He pulled a hardboiled egg out of one of the pockets on his apron, peeled it, popped it into his mouth, stood there, munching away.

"WELL HELP ME LOOK FOR THE GODDAMNED THING!" I said, not sure where to begin. Everything on the table looked the same to me, one big pile of blood, muscle and meat. Once butchered, it was hard to tell the difference between animal and man.

Jack and I began digging through the gore, trying to locate the top of my thumb before spoilage set in. The more I dug the more I bled, and the more confused the search became.

"Jesus Christ," Jack said. "Go have one of the girls put a bandage around that thing! I can't have you bleeding on the meat—I've gotta sell this shit!"

I left the cooler and wandered around the store looking for someone to wrap my thumb, leaving a trail of blood and alarmed customers in my wake. A suggestion of mortality, even the tiniest one, could really clear the aisles. I liked that. Moses parts the imbecilic sea. *Stand back, fuckers! Death does not brake for pedestrians!*

Donnie Lynn wouldn't get near me. She didn't like the sight of blood. Neither did Cheryl, Sue or Betty, apparently. I walked out back to the break table. Linda Lee was good with a gun, she gutted deer on a regular basis, in and out of season. I figured she could deal with a severed appendage.

I waltzed out of there waving the thing around, again, for maximum dramatic effect. Bad theatre, I had a flair for it. Linda Lee was eating a slab of roast beef, doing the daily crossword puzzle and swatting away flies. She saw my thumb hanging there.

"Hey, what's another word for unemployed?" she asked.

"Happy."

"Four letters."

"Wife?"

"This ain't the fifties, little man. You've been hanging around Jack too long. What'd you do to your hand?" She pushed her beef aside, gave me the once-over.

"Looks like you got yourself pretty good. Stay here, I'll be right back."

I waited there, watching the blood pour from my hand. *Death in the Afternoon.* It wasn't so bad. I could hardly feel it anymore. It throbbed more than it hurt.

Me and Hemingway, we were tough s.o.b.'s—old school. We could take it. Maybe I'd blow my brains out someday. Not any time soon, though. I wasn't famous yet.

Linda Lee came back with a roll of gauze and a raspberry longjohn in her hand. Those longjohns were good. We got a fresh batch in every morning. It was best to eat them before they cooled.

"Let's see what we can do here," Linda Lee said.

I gave her my hand and she went to work on it, patching me up while putting away that warm raspberry longjohn.

A few minutes later, Jack came out the backdoor. He had the top of my thumb with him. He'd put it in a Zip-Lock Sandwich Bag, along with some ice to keep it from spoiling before the doctors could sew it back on. He dropped it down on the picnic table.

Linda Lee picked it up, gave it a look.

"That ain't shit," Jack said.

Linda Lee called Donnie Lynn and the rest of the girls out of the store. "You've gotta see this!" she laughed.

"GROSS!" Donnie Lynn screamed. "LET ME SEE IT!"

They bellied up to the table and began passing the bag around, tossing it back and forth, laughing and screaming.

Around and around, it went. They were going apeshit. Kafka the Mongrel Dog ran up, joined the circle and began going apeshit too, growling and jumping at it, snapping, snarling, insane.

"KAFKA, GET THE FUCK OVER HERE!" I shouted. I didn't want him eating that thing. He turned and looked at me, then came charging over, howling as if in heat. He went straight for my hand, pulling at my bandage, licking and drooling, maddened with bloodlust. If I had been dead, that bastard would have eaten me. I yanked my hand back and pushed him away. Instinct was a powerful thing.

The girls were still tossing my thumb around, playing hot-potato with it while it died. Betty shoved it down the front of Donnie Lynn's blouse and Donnie Lynn shrieked and threw it to the ground. Kafka was over there in a flash, panting, growling, pawing at it.

I couldn't take it anymore.

"HEY!" I screamed.

Everyone froze. I'd never raised my voice at work before. They didn't know what to make of it. Even Kafka began to whimper. They all stood there, silent, staring at me.

"CAN I HAVE MY FUCKING THUMB BACK NOW?"

***

Well, it got me out of work that afternoon. And being that it happened on the job, the company was oblige to pay for all repairs. There was a bit of surgery required, but it was all on the cuff, that bill would never find its way to my mailbox. I hadn't thought of that. Hell, maybe I'd sue, go the whiny modern American route, stick it to everybody and their brother, even the score, walk away rich. The Proletariat puts the Man to the mat, David slays Goliath, the poor and the downtrodden cheer. I could reinvent myself with the settlement money, get a makeover, buy a new car, drive to Chicago and announce to Tia Correlia that I had died and been reborn as a bonafide breadwinner, a man of means.

I got to thinking about it while they were sewing

my thumb back on. The possibilities were endless. I'd get back on the job and quickly involve myself in another heinous mishap. I'd make sure to lose an arm or a leg this time, or break my back unloading a shipment of frozen butter beans. I'd strap myself to the sugar-tit of Workman's Comp and milk her for all she was worth. Gravytrain days from there on out. I'd lay home on the couch, letting the checks roll in and my gut grow round. I'd drink beer all afternoon, scratch myself, look at the walls, watch the Playboy channel, count my cash, burp and holler for a sandwich ...

But I didn't do any of that, of course. One so rarely possesses the courage to seize a dream. Especially if that dream entails serious injury. I was a big baby. I was afraid to lose a limb, I was afraid of pain, I was afraid of doctors, dentists, knives, needles, cancer, the common cold; I was afraid of cops, criminals, the rich and the poor, the middleclass; I was afraid of banks, checkbooks, credit cards, cash, having no cash, cats, flying insects, small children, doors with locks on them, doors without locks, off-white walls, blue walls, no walls; I was afraid of having a job I would hate until the day it killed me, I was afraid of not having a job ...

I'd grown up believing I'd been born for a life of unskilled labor. It was amazing what you could accomplish when you had the power of belief behind you.

I did try to weasel a week off—with full pay—out of Jack Philly. But Jack wasn't buying it. I had a feeling he wouldn't.

"Bullshit!" Jack said. "I'm a physical wreck, I'm falling apart, for Christsake. But I'm here every morning at eight. I should have retired after my heart attack. But you don't hear me complaining."

"My hand is killing me, Jack. I can't work this

way."

"Use your other hand then. Make do."

There was no arguing with him. He was the Boss, plain and simple. He'd stroke out over the meatgrinder one morning, loyal to his employer till the end.

So I made do. Primarily at the breaktable.

The girls had given me the sympathy vote. My little injury seemed to magnify their maternal instincts. For a while there, I was practically fawned over.

It only took a day before Jack caved in and joined me. We'd assume our positions at the break table out back. Newspapers in hand, coffee, cigarettes going. Good company men.

"Bring the boy a danish," Jack would say to one of the girls. "Bring me one too."

"And get a T-Bone for Kafka," I'd add.

Pretty soon, the girls were out there with us as well. The whole sorry lot of us lounging in the sun, eating, drinking, watching the fruitflies buzz 'round the dumpster, napping, fucking off, collecting our pay.

Inevitably, a customer would wander around back and find us out there. "Hey, does anybody work here?"

For a week or so, life was pretty good at the grocery store.

But I was rapidly losing what was left of my mind. I couldn't sleep, I couldn't eat, I couldn't bring myself to shower, shave, shit. All I could do was obsess over Tia Correlia, pace, pull my hair, spit nails, curse God and the men who had invented Him, curse myself for having let it all happen. *I should have seen it coming*, I kept thinking, *I should have loved her more.* I sure as hell loved her now that she was gone. Almost gone. She'd given me the summer to get my shit together. Come fall, she would decide.

For the first time in my life I was beginning to see the value of physical labor. My jobs kept me busy. Even if I had been able to sleep or think there wouldn't have been much time to. I worked at the grocery store from 11 to 5, Monday through Saturday. My hours at the bar were from 6 to 3:30 a.m., Tuesday through Sunday. My plate was full. I was always at one place or the other, most days both. I'd leave the grocery store and walk across the street to the bar. I'd suck down a pot of coffee, chainsmoke, change my shirt. Then I'd pick up a bar-rag and be assaulted by the dregs of humanity until last call. At which time all hell would break loose. Last call was something all drunks loathed, it meant the ride was over, the train had reached its destination—and those poor bastards just didn't want to step off, not now, not yet, not ever. By 2:30 all the liquor stores were closed, so if you hadn't planned ahead and laid yourself up a little stash you were finished, party over. All you could do was stagger home and feel the crash, the dream falling down around you, the roar of the world returning with all its piercing clarity, reality rearing its ugly, jagged head. A bitter pill to swallow, sure. I understood it completely, even sympathized, but it just wasn't my problem anymore. My problem was getting those pathetic sons of bitches out of the fucking bar so *I* could begin to drink. Which always proved difficult.

We'd eventually get them out, however—or rather, Angel would—and be faced with the task of cleaning the dump. By that time I'd be wound so tightly that the bottom of a bottle seemed the only real place to begin to unwind. We'd all have a few drinks while picking up the carnage, many drinks, getting drunker as the place got cleaner, dragging the mop around, picking up the stir-sticks and broken glass, getting the vomit out of the toilets and off the floor, trying not to touch or catch anything. Then we'd sit along the darkened bar and bitch about humanity, what worthless shits they were, how they would be better off dead and just how we would go about making them that way should they ever ask the favor—all the while counting out the tips they'd tossed our way, yawning, laughing, whining, stomping on the roaches as they zigzagged the floor and circled our stools ...

I'd get to bed around 5 or 6 a.m. most nights. Then at 9 the alarm would go off, a shrieking monster of sound. And it was back to the butcher's block. Parched, nauseous, aching, shaking, delirious. Hangover larger than God. Goodmorning world, goodmorning my fellow man, you ugly fuck. I'd raise the blade and hack away. I'd vomit.

But that wasn't the problem. The problem was Tia Correlia, being out of contact with her, having been cast out of Eden and into cold isolation, into the shitty barren lot next door, the place the poets were always wailing about—being forced to live there. And not knowing the way back, how to get there or if I ever would. That was the root of my sleeplessness. I'd been cut loose and was now tumbling, fumbling, falling, out of control, floundering ...

I began running into people who had Valium or Xanax, Codeine, Seconal, Darvon. I always ended up walking away from these encounters with a few pills in my pocket, or in my bloodstream, without even having to ask for them. These people seemed to sense that I was in need of sedation. It was an act of kindness on their part, like snuffing a horse after it snaps a leg. I found that these pills were far more effective when taken in conjunction with alcohol. I was aware of the danger there, but a voice deep inside told me not to worry, that whichever way the cards fell would be just fine. Besides, I wasn't blessed enough to be allowed to slip out of my mortal skin so easily. God would see to it that I died a slow, horrific death, whirls of cancer turning me inside out, flowers of pain forty feet tall, tearing the gut and the mind and the tincan soul, ripping, stabbing, the sword going in and out, the face of god as envisioned from the deathbed of Marquis de Sade ...

Well, it's amazing how dark a man's imagination can become when threatened with the loss of a good woman.

I took whatever drugs were offered me and tried not to think. I drank a lot. I had until fall to get my shit together.

***

It was a Monday. I didn't have to tend bar that night, so there I was, seated on the good side, drinking it up with the regulars. A local named Lugnut was pissing on the jukebox and another of Stillwater's finest was punching out the payphone. Angel had her hands full again:

"GODDAMNIT LUGNUT!—"

I was glad to be off the clock that night. This type of behavior had a way of upsetting the tourists. They'd bitch and complain and you would be forced to correct the situation, to comply to their demands. The fucking tourists. You'd think they'd never seen a guy piss back in anger at a jukebox before. Maybe they hadn't heard the sorry shit that was dominating the charts that year, every year. It was enough to push a man over the edge, especially after 10 or 12 drinks. Blame it on Whitney Houston. Blame it on Hammer.

The doctor had given me some excellent painkillers the day I took the top of my thumb off. They put you on a nice peaceful cloud, in a clean and happy place far from troublesome reality. I popped one, ordered another whiskey and water. Easy was out of the kitchen for a change and behind the bar. Aside from myself, Easy poured the strongest drinks in town. He set a tumbler of whiskey in front of me, a triple, with just the tiniest splash of water. I thanked him, laid a tip on the bar. I never had to pay for drinks anymore. Being an employee, it was all on the cuff. It could be a dangerous thing, at times. The best and the worst of all possible worlds.

There was a guy sitting on the stool next to mine. I'd seen him around town a few times that summer, probably in the bars. I'd never spoken to him. I didn't feel like speaking now, so I just stared into the mirror behind the bar and drank my drink and tried not to think too much about anything or notice how old and ill I looked in that bar-mirror: the Zen-Idiot approach. It rarely worked for me. My mind was a shrieking chatterbox of gibberish and cornered terror. But I was always trying to practice it nonetheless. I got the idiot part down pretty good. Most Americans did. Zen was for the older, wiser cultures. America was young, we were still spitting up on ourselves and rubbing shit in our hair. Not a bad state of affairs, apparently. We were envied worldwide.

"What's that you just took?"

It was the guy on the stool next door. He was white and he had a blonde afro. A cross between Bing Crosby and Jimi Hendrix, more Bing than Jimi. At first glance you would have thought he was wearing a wig. But when you looked closer you saw that it was real, which made it more ridiculous, somehow.

I didn't feel like talking to the guy. I rarely felt like talking to anyone, really. Purposeful silence, it was part of my Zen-Idiot plan. Or maybe I just didn't like most people.

I looked at that afro filling the mirror behind the bar, towering there, two circumvallating feet of permed madness. "Aspirin," I said.

"Looked like Vicodin to me."

"Yeah?" It occurred to me that he might be a narcotics officer. That may have explained the afro. Outdated undercover garb.

"I fucked up my thumb," I told him. It was still bandaged. I lifted it off the bar and waved it around. Dramatic effect.

"On purpose?" he asked.

"Sure," I said. I knocked back my drink and flagged Easy for another. I was playing John Wayne again, Humphrey Bogart, some asshole in a black-and-white movie.

"I did that once," the guy said. "I took a hacksaw to my pinky. I wanted some good drugs. I couldn't think of any other way to get them. What good is a pinky, anyway? What the fuck do you use it for?"

He held up his hand. Sure enough, there wasn't any pinky there. Another fucking nut. The world was full of them. It made you wonder if the insane asylums had locked up all the wrong people.

"You can find drugs on almost every streetcorner in America," I told him. "Why didn't you just score from someone?" I couldn't stop looking at that 3-fingered hand. Human aberration, the eternal curiosity.

"It never occurred to me," he said. "Besides, I don't know anyone who deals. And if I did, I wouldn't trust them. Dealers are scumbags."

"You trust doctors?"

"Sure. They're trained professionals." He reached into his pocket and took out a tiny orange pill, glanced around to see if anyone was watching, then ate it.

"Xanax," he said.

The jukebox music was making my crazy. I waved, Easy brought me a drink.

I'd been hooked on Xanax in the past, for a period of roughly eight years, along with a laundry list of other prescribed drugs. I had a quack shrink who used to give them to me by the sackful, "samples," he called them. I didn't even have to pay for the shit half the time. I knew I was in trouble the first time I came up short and ran out—which hadn't happened in years—because I was taking so much. I nearly went insane, then I began to get sick, deathly so. I puked all over the backseat of a taxicab trying to get to the guy's office during rush hour. First thing he did was stick a syringe full of Valium in my ass. Then he gave me a stack of free samples and wrote out a prescription for both Xanax and Restoril. I felt a helluva lot better after that shot. I was working at a cineplex at the time, one of those monstrous, 20-screen nightmares. I gathered my sanctioned dope and caught a bus back there. But my boss had already fired me. I'd walked off the job two hours earlier, jonesing for that good Doctor Robert dope ...

"So what'd you do this time?" I asked the nut with the afro. "Whack off one of your toes?"

"No, you need your toes for balance. Without the proper balance, a man is nothing. Besides, there aren't enough appendages on a human body. I'd be nothing but a stump by now, just my head would be sitting here." He pushed his stool back, knelt down and laid his chin on the bar. "Like this," he said. He sat back up and ordered a beer. Budweiser. He was a strange one. I'd never understood how anyone could drink that shit. Canned water, it seemed pointless.

"Why do you drink that?" I asked him.

"What? Beer?"

"No, Budweiser."

"I don't know. I've never thought about it." He held the bottle to the light, turned it around a few times, giving it some thought. "What's wrong with Budweiser?"

"It isn't beer." I felt it was only right to let him know.

"It's the KING of beers," he said. He looked a bit offended. It wasn't anything worth arguing about. Pitiful, but not worth arguing.

"Sure," I told him, "I've seen the ads."

He seemed satisfied with that. He had himself a sip. The Vicodin I'd taken was working its magic. My limbs felt loose, my spine was relaxed, no longer a steel rod of tension and pain. My thumb felt just fine. My thumb wasn't even there.

"So where do you get the stuff?" I asked. I was curious now. I was more interested in the pills themselves than wherever he may have gotten them. Old habits die hard, the ghost of the monkey is a heavy piece of baggage to shake off your back.

"What," he said, "are you a narc or something?"

"I was going to ask you the same thing." His afro seemed to get bigger every time I looked at it. Tall, round, blonde and bobbing. No wonder people were always staring into their drinks. To look at your fellow man was just too frightening, too ridiculous.

He tipped his Bud, his afro bounced. "Other than a doctor, where's the best place to find drugs?" he asked.

"A drugstore," I said. It seemed logical.

"One better than that."

"Fuck, I don't know—a hospital?"

"Exactly. A psychiatric hospital, in particular. They have the best shit, cutting-edge, the real mindbending stuff."

I could see his beer was getting low. I ordered him one, got another whiskey for myself. Al Green was on the jukebox, singing about love and happiness. He had a beautiful voice, that man. Lugnut and the payphone guy were pushing around a frightened tourist. The tourist had apparently been reluctant to give up his turn at the pooltable. Angel was over there in a flash, she'd had it—again.

"ALRIGHT YOU ASSHOLES!"

"So," I said. "You break into psychiatric hospitals? Or do you just get yourself committed from time to time?" The latter seemed most plausible. Hell, I'd been committed once myself. And I hadn't even been trying. This guy had sawed off one of his fingers just to get high. Well, Van Gogh hacked off his ear for a whore, so what the hell?

"Do I look like a fucking thief?" he asked.

I'd insulted him. I didn't know what to say. I watched Angel strongarm Lugnut and the payphone guy out the door. She booted the tourist too. She'd had it with everyone that night. Al Green was finished. It was Lynyrd Skynyrd now: "GIMME THREE STEPS, GIMME THREE STEPS, MISTER ..."

The pill freak said, "Do I look nuts?" He was grinning like a lunatic, rocking on his stool, afro bouncing up and down.

"Not at all," I told him. "But people are often committed for much less."

"I took it to the next level." He tipped his beer, put his head back to swallow, spilling half of it down the side of his face. "I got myself a job as an orderly," he said. "I'm a whitecoat, I keep the nuts in line."

"No shit?"

"Yeah. I'm the man with the keys."

He went on to tell me how he was in charge of

drug disposal. When a patient was admitted, whatever drugs they brought in with them—prescribed to them as outpatients—were taken away. They were given new drugs. The drugs they'd brought in were then disposed of. It was this guy's job to take them to the incinerator, he was the last person to see these drugs before they were destroyed. He became more and more excited as he told me all of this, just talking about it seemed to give him a hard-on. Well, I'd been there once myself.

"I'm not stealing the shit," he said. "It'd all be going into the incinerator anyway."

"Good set-up," I told him. "Sounds dangerous."

"I'm the last person to see the stuff. There's no way I can get caught. It's a perfect situation."

"That's not what I meant."

He leaned in close and lowered his voice to a whisper. Why, I don't know. The jukebox was loud enough to rattle the walls.

"You want some?" he asked.

"What, are you a dealer now?"

That pissed him off. His face turned red, he swallowed the last of his beer and slammed the bottle down.

"I'm no fucking dealer," he said. "Dealers are scumbags. Do I look like I need money? I *give* the shit away."

"Okay, okay. Relax. Let me buy you a beer."

I gave Easy the nod. He trotted a couple fresh ones over, Bud for the guy who kept the nuts in line, whiskey for me. On the cuff.

The guy who kept the nuts in line palmed me a handful of assorted downers: painkillers, tranquilizers, hypnotics; a deadly little potpourri he'd thieved from the madhouse. I put them in my pocket, thanked him. He was grinning like a fucking lunatic.

Between Easy and this Hendrix-looking freak,

my chances for survival that summer were growing slimmer by the minute. Tia Correlia was getting further and further from me all the time. But at the moment, I wasn't feeling it all that intensely. Behind the booze and the painkillers, I wasn't feeling much of anything, good or bad.

In times of crisis, home is often the worst place in the world to go looking for help.

Ask Jack Kerouac. Ask the Menendez brothers.

I was in the post office, checking my mail. I was always checking my mail. I'm not sure what the hell I hoped to find there. Checking the mail was always the best and the worst part of my day.

The box happened to be full. Good sign. I flipped through the stack, searching for traces of Tia Correlia.

But there was nothing, not even a postcard telling me to piss off.

Silence can sometimes be the cruelest sound in the world. The cold shoulder she was giving me was going to send me round the bend sure as shit. I was a fool. But there had been countless fools born into this world before me, and countless more would surely follow. They, too, would one day hang it all on a woman. Every man had his Helen of Troy. It was historical inevitability. So you watched and waited for her. You checked your mail.

My mail that day was mostly junk, as usual. There was a letter from a collection agency in cahoots with my mad surgeon. The guy had taken an allegedly cancerous lump from my neck that spring, shortly before I'd fled to Stillwater in search of work, love and a killing brand of kindness. I was supposed to have gone back to the hospital for a follow-up, but I hadn't even been able to pay for the first visit yet. I'd been under the knife roughly half an hour and it had cost me over three grand. A follow-up was out of the question. Better to risk the cancer. That guy's hourly wage was a lot higher than mine.

I opened the letter from his sinister henchman:

```
Dear Mr. Totten:
     Your account with Dr. Bledman has
been turned over to our agency. We are
fully prepared to take whatever legal
action is necessary to correct this mat-
ter. This is your third and final notice.
If this debt is not paid immediately we
will be forced to ...
```

I tossed that thing. Along with a Publisher's Clearinghouse Sweepstakes Notification, which I was instructed to open at once if I ever hoped to win that 10 million dollars and forever change my life for the better.

***

I couldn't sleep. I was worried about Kafka. He'd up and disappeared, I hadn't seen the mutt for more than a week. We'd hired a new bottle-boy at the grocery store, some snot-nosed kid from Hart. He worked in the basement, sorting the returnables, bagging the cans, boxing the bottles. I'd noticed Kafka had been spending a lot of time down there, more and more each day. Before the kid hired in, you couldn't get that dog anywhere near the basement. It stank like the bowels of a slaveship. It was dark, dank, dismal, hot and humid. Kafka wouldn't be down there unless he had a damned good reason. I had a hunch that fucking bottle-boy was pilfering company steaks and feeding them to my canine friend. Kafka had found a new master, another meat bearing object of love! I'd been made a fool, a cuckold! That goddamned dog had no loyalty.

Then again, maybe he'd been run over by a car. Maybe he was lying alongside a lonely stretch of road somewhere with his guts hanging out. I leapt out of bed and ran downtown. I started on Hitchcock Street and worked my way south. It was 4 a.m. I was in my underwear.

"KAFKA! KAFKA!"

I searched for close to an hour, calling his name over and over until I was hoarse. It was hopeless. I sat down at the corner of First and Rush. I put my head in my hands. I couldn't help it—my heart broke. I began to cry like a baby ... Then I jumped out of my skin. There were fingers in my hair. I wheeled around. It was the hunchback with the mystic three-cornered hat—the obsessive streetsweeper: Mr. Infinity.

"I do not mean to alarm you," he said, "but Kafka is dead."

"How do you know that?"

"He died in 1924. Everybody knows that."

"What are you talking about?"

"Kafka."

"Kafka's my dog."

"Kafka was no dog."

"Hey, listen—my dog is missing. I want him back. What do you know about it?"

"I don't know anything about your dog. But Kafka is dead."

"My dog is Kafka."

"If Kafka is your dog, then your dog is dead."

"You don't know what you're talking about, old man. Kafka isn't dead. He's just missing. It's that fucking bottle-boy's fault."

"What bottle-boy? Who's the bottle-boy?"

"The sonofabitch who lured my dog away."

"Kafka was a clerk. He worked in an oppressive little office all day. At night, he wrote. When he died, he left behind three unfinished novels and some of the greatest short stories of this or any other century. If Kafka is your dog, then your dog died in 1924. It was T.B. that got him—not the bottle-boy."

"I'm talking about Kafka—my *dog*. Not the writer."

"They're one and the same. You can't separate them. Who do you think you are—God?"

"You're crazy, old man. You're a nut-job. I have to find my dog."

"I'm crazy? You aren't wearing any pants! Why don't you put on some pants? You look like a fool."

"Oh, yeah? Well, you have a funny hat! It's ridiculous."

"At least I didn't lose my dog!"

"It's the bottle-boy's fault! That bastard's been feeding him steaks. He ran away with the bottle-boy."

"If your dog loves you, he'll come back. Love is intangible—you can't own it. Why are you out here torturing yourself?"

"Love? The goddamned mutt abandoned me for

a piece of meat. A Ribeye, for Christsake."

"That's a good steak."

"I know. That's how I got him. I found him prowling around behind the grocery store one day. I work there. He looked hungry. I started feeding him steaks. T-Bone, Prime Rib—nothing but the best."

"To feed and nourish another—that's one of the greatest virtues. It's heroic. It's all right there in the Bible."

"That dog has no loyalty. He was starving—I fed him, I gave him a name."

"Life can be cruel as well as kind. There's nothing fair about it. Kafka should never have been a clerk, he didn't belong in that office. He should have never worked there."

"What are you talking about? If he hadn't worked in that office, he never would have written those novels. Everything he wrote was ... Nevermind. You're insane. I don't know why I'm talking to you."

I started walking again. Faster this time. The old man didn't follow me. He stayed behind with his broom. He had a streetcorner to clean.

"I'll bet you forgot to feed him!" he shouted. "You got caught up in your crappy little life and forgot all about him! You, sir, are the one who killed Kafka!"

The hunchback was right. I'd forgotten to feed him. The bottle-boy had simply filled the gap. Hunger was the god. Kafka listened to his gut. He was a dog. That's what dogs did. A dog was only as loyal as his master.

I spun around, cupping my hands for volume: "Kafka's not dead! You don't know what you're talking about, hunchback! You don't know anything!"

"Yeah—well, neither do you, clerk!"

"I'm no clerk, old man!"

"Who are you then?"

I didn't feel like playing it out. It was pointless.

I started walking. I watched my shadow grow long, then short, then long again. I tried to step on my head.

"YOU'RE KAFKA AND YOU DON'T EVEN KNOW IT!" the hunchback screamed.

I ignored him. One more block and I wouldn't have to hear the crazy bastard anymore.

"YOU'RE KAFKA!" he laughed. "EVERYBODY'S KAFKA! YOU'RE A DOG, YOU FOOL!"

I cupped my hands again. "CAN IT, HUNCH-BACK!"

"PUT SOME PANTS ON! LOVE IS WILD, KAFKA—LET IT GO!"

"GET OFF THE STREET! STOP SWEEPING!"

"WHAT?"

I walked back half a block. I wanted him to hear me.

"Get rid of the broom," I shouted. "Stop sweep-ing!"

"I can't!" he wheezed.

I walked a little closer. "Well, that makes us even."

"Fair enough," he said.

***

There was to be an exhibit of my recent paintings at a gallery in Grand Rapids. The place was called The Severed Ear. It wasn't a bad gallery, really—which is to say, I liked what they hung there. Most galleries hung glori-fied nonsense and slapped an enormous price tag on it to lend the "work" an air of credibility. This sleight of hand seemed to fool people. *TURD #99 ($1200). Expres-*

sions in Excrement. The Kaka Series ... Shit sold. It had been selling for centuries. Even my shit sold, sometimes.

I'd been in various group shows The Severed Ear had put together in the past. In fact, I'd sold nearly fifty paintings through that gallery within the last two years. Not that I'd made any money to speak of. The Severed Ear was always raping its artists. All galleries raped their artists, it was standard procedure. Of every painting sold, the gallery took fifty percent. You had to pay a framer for *his* time and materials. You had to pay for *your* materials, and to factor in the time you spent *creating* these paintings would be to risk madness, suicide or murder. If a painting sold for $500 the artist walked away with $150 of that, sometimes less, depending on the quality of the frame and the medium he or she was working in. This was why the price tags were always so high and why it had gotten to the point where only the wealthy could afford to buy art. It was also the reason a person had to be a trust-fund baby, it seemed, if they were to be an artist and not be forced to work third shift in a gas station as well.

But there were those rare beings making money nonetheless. Some artists were raking it in hand over fist. I'd meet them and wonder how they pulled it off, what the secret was. People were always telling me that my prices were too low. But my prices were already so high that *I* couldn't afford to buy one of my paintings, which pissed me off to no end. I'd occasionally get drunk and give the fucking things away before they ever made it to the gallery, which in turn pissed the gallery off. The bastards couldn't take fifty percent of nothing, and without a painting to pretty up the framer was fucked too. Which is exactly why I would get drunk and give the shit away now and then. Petulant and ultimately self-destructive, sure. But it kept me sane and put a nice writhing little bug up the ass of my benefactors—which at least counted for something.

I decided to skip the opening. Openings were always embarrassing. If it was a group show, you were all there, *The Artists*, standing around like targeted idiots in a shooting gallery, to meet and greet, work the floor and play the game. Where did you study? What was your inspiration? What ism did you subscribe to? Why did you use this color or that? Question after question, all of them tedious, irrelevant, unnerving. I hadn't studied anywhere, I did nothing for any particular reason. If I ran out of blue I used green, if I was painting a horse and fucked up the legs I turned it into a mutant fish or a man or a woman or a spinning top with teeth and tongue and the face of Frank Zappa. I never knew what the hell to say to anyone about my work or anything else so I usually stood there mute, an imbecile with drink in hand. Most of the time, people had no idea that I was even one of the artists. I didn't look like an artist. I wasn't dramatic enough, I dressed all wrong. I looked like a janitor, a dishwasher, a service-station attendant. I'd hear people talking about my work. For whatever the reason, the compliments always threw me. They threw me more than the criticisms. I'd tune out, get drunk and pretend to be the janitor. A role I was able to pull off with remarkable believability.

And now I had a solo show coming up. Thirty-three of my paintings hanging from the walls like webbed insects. Being there for the opening was out of the question. I couldn't bring myself to do it. My life was full of enough bullshit as it was. I figured I'd send a clown to stand in for me, a juggler, a balloon folder, a fire-eater. Who would know the difference?

You see, I hadn't planned to be an artist any more

than I had planned to be a drunk or have green eyes. It just happened, it was just an accident, like the rest of my life.

I wondered if it happened that way for clowns and fire-eaters, too.

The Severed Ear had moved to a new and better location that summer. Much time and money had been spent. No shows had been held there yet. Mine was to be the first.

Send in the clown!

***

A week before my show opened, the owner threw a big party at her house; artists, collectors, newspaper and gallery people, all there to mingle and schmooze and jack each other off.

I decided to put in an appearance. I figured it would be the perfect time to tell Lydia Rykoff, the owner, that I wouldn't be making the opening. Besides, there would be a lot of free booze and I could always hide in the backyard if things became unbearable.

I had to work that night but I talked Angel into letting me off early. I told her I had to meet someone at the airport in Grand Rapids, suggested that it just might be the much-talked-about, bemoaned and now nearly mythic Tia Correlia. Angel was hip to this long-running romantic drama, I'd been crying on her shoulder about it since meeting her. I played the sympathy card. It worked.

I didn't feel like showing up at Lydia's alone. I needed some back-up, someone to turn to when I ran out of art talk—two minutes, tops—and was exposed as a fraud and told to trot drinks or take out the trash. Besides, I didn't own a car. If I couldn't find someone to

take along with me, someone with wheels, I wouldn't
be going at all.

So I hung around at the bar after getting off and
drank six or seven pints of Stout without pausing to
consider the fact that I had eaten nothing more than a
candy bar that day. Food had always been low on my
list of priorities. I just sat there bullshitting with the waitresses and getting stinko, watching the clock tick off the
hours and most of Lydia's party, which was now fully
underway and moving along just fine, most certainly,
without me.

One of the women I worked with got off duty
and joined me at the bar. Absolut on the rocks, she could
toss it back like a pro. My kind of woman. Her name
was Jenny. She was usually up for just about anything.
We drank and got to talking. One drink led to another
and she wound up driving me to Lydia's party. Alcohol, the great persuader.

I was well into the whiskey by then, still in my
work clothes, food and stout down the front of my shirt,
filthy pants. But I was drunk off my artistic, overly sensitive ass. So what the hell? Raze the house of cards,
raze the paper life, kick the can and see what's left come
morning. There seemed little else to do.

Grand Rapids was eighty miles away. Jenny's car was a
pile of shit and she was taking directions from a drunk
who had only the slightest sense of direction even when
sober. Braving serious radiator malfunction and my own
faulty navigational advice, we roared downstate along
I-96, toward high culture and free booze.

Remarkably enough, we made it to the party
without mishap. There it was, Lydia Rykoff's big brown-
stone, just where the map I'd been sent said it would
be. Nice crib. The Severed Ear had paid off, for Lydia,

at least. I was at the wrong end of the art world. I should have been running a gallery, lording it over a stable of lowly strokers like myself, filling my coffers with that 50 percent. Well, I'd missed the boat on that one. I was always missing the boat. And I was a lousy swimmer, to boot.

We rang the bell. Lydia opened the door, greeted us.

"Oh, I'm so glad you could make it!" she said. "Come in, come in!" She told us to put our coats anywhere we liked. We weren't wearing coats. She looked at Jenny.

"Tia?" she asked. Lydia knew all about the situation with Tia.

"No, I'm Jenny."

"This is Jenny," I said. "Jenny, this is Lydia."

"It's so nice to finally meet you," Lydia said.

Jenny said, "Likewise." She smiled. Jenny was a trouper. Nothing seemed to bother her, she just didn't give a shit. The world—*life*—actually amused her. If I hadn't already been terminally in love with Tia Correlia, I might have fallen for her then and there. One madness at a time, that's my motto.

"Everyone's in the livingroom," Lydia told us. She led us there and announced, "Everyone, this is Lupus and Tia. Lupus and Tia, this is everyone."

We gave them all a nod. It had gotten late, so there were only a dozen or so people there, which was a dozen or so too many, really. The rest had packed up their berets and gone back to their garrets and red wine or off to an all-night cafe somewhere to toss around stale philosophies and chainsmoke—well, no one seemed to smoke anymore so maybe they were just batting their philosophies back and forth while sucking on bottled water. The ones who had stayed for the finish simply sat there, still as stones, giving Jenny and I the once-over, staring at us without speaking. They all appeared to be wearing standard issue artist garb, swathed head to toe in tragic black, highcollared, rakish, aloof and knowledgeable, wine glasses held in thin delicate fingers of creativity. All women, all lesbian. Which might have been interesting had the party not been winding down. Purposeful boredom appeared to be the attitude now. It was the fashionable attitude to take at these events. Ironic distance, it was an artform. It required very little work. Sneer cynically and you were a genius, or might at least be mistaken for one.

We got a tour of the place, Lydia dragging us from room to room. I was glad Jenny was there. She held her own just fine, was savvy, witty, smooth; she knew the work of a particular painter from California whose soul Lydia had caged and hung from her wall. I, on the other hand, had transformed into an obvious horse's ass, legless, fumbling, dimwitted, stumbling around with a pricey bottle of Merlot I'd found on one of the tables and corked for myself. I grunted and mumbled, crashed into people and other objects, spilled wine on an Oriental rug, broke a glass, farted *faux pas* and apologies. Somehow, I even managed to spill a second glass of wine into the hot-tub out back, just walking past the fucking thing. I wasn't trying to play The Drunken Artist. Yet, there it was: The Drunken Artist, in all his imbecilic glory—the cliché at large. Well, as I've said, I never planned to be an artist. Drunk or otherwise.

We wound up in the kitchen, Jenny and Lydia and I, going over the details of my show. There was a nice spread of food in there, but I didn't eat any of it. It was too late for sustenance. My body would have rejected it as poison, as something contrary to the masterplan.

Jenny, however, helped herself to some baba-gnoush. Jenny knew what baba-gnoush was. She wore a crystal and was hip to all the New Age food groups. I leaned more to the school of cigarettes and coffee. I wore a medical alert bracelet. I liked Sweet-N-Low, bacon, pork rinds.

The show was going to be "a big affair," an opening for both myself and the new and improved Severed Ear. They were pulling out all the stops. Cards and invitations had been sent to collectors and the local press. There would be food and drink, a jazz band. Lydia had high hopes for its success. She expected to sell most all my paintings. I expected total rejection. I also expected to die penniless and anonymous at an obscenely young age—felled by cancer, struck in the head by a falling rock, shot in the face at a 7-Eleven for looking at someone the wrong way ...

"You're catching on," Lydia informed me. "People are aware of you." My name was becoming known throughout the free world. Right. That's why I was living with my mother in Northern Michigan, grinding hamburger and trotting drinks to any asshole with two dollars to wave in my face.

"You know," Jenny said to Lydia, "I didn't even know he was an artist until tonight. He's ashamed of it, I think."

"Nonsense," I said. But, in a way, Jenny was right. I did feel there was something shameful about being an artist. It was like walking around with a load of shit in your pants. You tried not to advertise it, but the stench gave you away.

"He's a natural," Lydia laughed. "Don't let him fool you."

I noticed my zipper was down. I hadn't thrown a piss since we'd left the Sause Box, which meant the goddamned thing had been down all evening. Another sophisticated entrance, another indelible first impression. I turned to Jenny, fly wide open: "Why didn't you tell me my zipper was down?"

"I hadn't noticed," she said.

I was about to zip up when an odd little woman crept into the kitchen. Waifish. Sexless. Skull-faced. Gaunt. She took me by the arm and whispered: "Welcome to our blessed home. From the very moment you open the door and behold the beauty of every treasure we have collected from different parts of the world, we pray that it will bless you and minister God's presence of love to you."

Oh, for Christsake, a born-again cross-fetishist! A flower child! Her eyes shrieked Acid Casualty. I could see her dancing around in a robe at an airport somewhere, babbling the teachings of Baba-Gnoush. I was always running into these types, they'd attached themselves to me my entire life. Every time I so much as left the house, there they were, lying in wait. If I stepped onto a bus, the maddest person aboard would invariably change seats and snuggle up to me like a long-lost friend. I was flypaper for the insane. I'd been born and bred for it.

The skull-faced woman drew me closer, pulled me forward and down until our noses touched. She stared deeply into my eyes, searching for something there, it seemed. All at once her eyes widened and her mouth formed an O. She dug her painted nails into my arm, crossed herself and ran screaming from the room. Off to San Francisco, perhaps—with serpents in her hair.

I zipped up, then turned to Lydia: "Jesus, who was that? Does she live here with you? Is she your girlfriend?"

Lydia wrinkled her nose. "No. I like my women

a little meatier than that. But she buys a lot of art. She owns at least a dozen of your paintings. She heard you were coming tonight and wanted to meet you. She's a bit off ..."

I was feeling a bit off myself. The Merlot wasn't sitting too well on top of all the beer and whiskey I'd sucked down before arriving. I had to close one eye to avoid seeing double. Never a good sign. Lydia seemed to sense my distress.

"Wait right here," she said. "I'll get you a cigar." She crossed the kitchen, opened a drawer, pulled out a fat Havana or whatever the fuck—something big and expensive. She stuck it in my mouth and fired it up with a fancy silver lighter. Then she fired up one for herself, exhaled into my face while my stomach rolled. "Fifteen dollars a pop," she laughed. "Enjoy." She offered one to Jenny but Jenny demurred. Jenny's intelligence far exceeded my own.

"Thanks," I said. I was smoking that thing like a cigarette. Inhaling, exhaling, inhaling. I was the Marlboro Man. I didn't know dick about cigars. Maybe Lydia was trying to kill me. Death always increased an artist's market value. As your soul scurried off to hell, your prices shot skyward.

Lydia turned to Jenny: "So, you've never seen any of Lupus's work?"

"Not a thing," Jenny said. "I only know him as a bartender."

"Follow me," said Lydia. She spun round on her heels and disappeared in a cloud of cigar smoke. Jenny followed. I went along, too. I was afraid the Skull-Faced Woman might find me again and force communion or some other variety of voodoo on me.

Lydia led us down an avocado hall to her bedroom. I managed to trip over an end-table and break a vase along the way. I apologized for that. Also for the rug I'd ruined and the glass I'd shattered in the hot-tub.

"Don't worry about that," Lydia said. "It wasn't an original."

"What about the rug?" I asked.

"Let's not talk about that," she said.

Her bedroom was enormous. Hardwood floor. Vaulted ceiling. A plush, outsized bed at the heart of it all. You could have thrown quite an orgy on that thing. The fantasy played through my mind, sure—stereotypically male, hackneyed, universal, erect. Jenny, Lydia, and a few of the other women at the party, all of them groping and groaning, licking, sucking, sliding and rolling around down there—me trying to work my cock into that, throbbing, aching. Me being rejected by all. Me being put on trial and pronounced GUILTY. Me being strung from the rafters, dying for the sins of every man who had ever pinched a waitress's ass since the time of Adam. Jenny, Lydia and the others dancing around my limp, lifeless body in a state of crazed Darwinian glee ... My psyche was such that I couldn't really enjoy myself even in idle fantasy without serious repercussion.

Hung on the walls were paintings of every school, movement and style. It was Lydia's private collection. It was better and more extensive than most minor museum collections. Once again, it became clear to me that I was at the wrong end of the Art Animal. Lydia was the devouring mouth, I was the unattractive yet essential asshole, pooting out factory parts.

She had a few of mine hanging in there. She'd bought them two years earlier, when she'd first taken me on at the Severed Ear, for next to nothing. At the time, I was more than happy to have made the sale. They were the first paintings I'd actually gotten money for.

When I received the checks for these paintings I noticed that she'd taken her usual fifty percent—a hard-earned commission for having had to sell herself the fucking things. I thought it was amusing—at the time. And it did keep me in cigarettes for a few weeks.

The largest of these paintings was currently hanging above Lydia's massive bed. She pointed it out to Jenny: "Now this painting here is, I think, one of Lupus's finest. Everyone who sees it seems to fall in love with it." Jenny moved in for a closer look. This is what she saw: A tall, mythically impressive goddess done in blues, greens, violets and swirling yellows. The goddess was naked. She wore a headdress of writhing, primordial reptiles. There were fish wriggling through the air surrounding her, primitively rendered, and a blood-red, menstruous moon hung in the upper lefthand corner of a deep, fecund, algae-colored sky. The goddess stood slightly hunched, her left arm bent at the elbow, her palm outstretched. In the palm of her hand sat the tiny head of a man. The goddess was peering into the manhead's eyes as if studying a small weed-like flower she'd recently plucked from a crack in the sidewalk. The manhead was wearing a dunce cap. The goddess appeared bemused, eyes alight, the suggestion of a smile upon her lips, the reptiles of her headdress grinning madly. The manhead's expression—stoic. And not altogether unhappy ...

"I LOVE IT!" Jenny shrieked. "The little man— he looks like you, Lupus."

I made no comment in regard to that observation.

"Oh, it's wonderful, isn't it?" Lydia said. Jenny agreed. I had a big female following. Considering the content of my work, that wasn't surprising. "You'd think a woman painted it," they concluded.

My eye wandered from the rear ends of Jenny and Lydia—they both had nice ones—to a small Picasso. One of his crazed, sloppy, primitive late period wonders. I couldn't quite believe it. Lydia owned a Picasso—and she had the fucker hanging in her bedroom. Amazing! I staggered over to it for a closer look, bottle in one hand, cigar burning in the other. I stood there before it, weaving back and forth, staring at that immortal signature with my rolling cyclopian eye. It didn't take Lydia long at all to pull me away from that thing.

"I think we'd better get back to the party now," she said, taking me by the arm. Jenny thought that was a good idea too. We made for the door, Lydia on my left arm, Jenny on my right. Goodbye, bedroom. Goodbye, Goddess and Dunce Cap Man. Goodbye, Picasso, you beautiful monster of art and darkly mad delight.

Down the avocado hall we went: *Two Goddesses Shepherding a Fool. Oil on perishable flesh. $19.95.* Something came over me while passing through the kitchen. The walls seemed to suddenly tilt and tail-spin, the floor changing places with the ceiling, rolling, rolling, rolling. The cigar wasn't sitting too well with the wine, which in itself wasn't sitting too well with the beer and whiskey. I watched the floor chase the ceiling 'round and 'round. This is it, I thought: Nirvana—then fell into space, cracking my skull against a corner of the kitchen counter on my way down.

Goodbye, consciousness.

***

When I came to I was slouched in Jenny's car, shotgun. We were racing up the highway, muffler roaring, windows open, wind whipping. There was a bloody bandage wrapped around my head.

"What the fuck is this?" I asked.

"You fell," Jenny said. "You'll live."

"That's good. I guess ..." I checked the rearview mirror. It looked like somebody had stuck a red and white tie-dyed turban on my head—mostly red. I'd died and been reincarnated. The man in the rearview mirror was mystic, knowing, deep. I turned to Jenny and screamed: "I AM THE GREAT BABA-GNOUSH! I AM THE GRAND WAZOO!"

"KEEPER OF THE MYSTIC SCROLLS!" Jenny fired back. Losing control of the car, grinding along the guardrail, sparks flying ...

After a short curiosity stop to check the damage inflicted upon the car—a deep gouge running the entire length of the driver's side—we got to talking about the party. Lydia. The house. The people who'd been there. The absurdity of it all.

"I had a good time," Jenny said. "Lydia's nice. A little odd, but nice."

"I like her too," I said. "There's nothing wrong with being odd." I'd decided to forgive Lydia for constantly robbing me blind. Everyone was robbed in one way or another—usually by those closest to them. It seemed to be one of the sacred laws of Man: Fuck thy neighbor. Let someone else bend over for the soap— and carry a big stick. It was only human, sadly enough, and it was nothing new. I didn't want to spoil Jenny's world view, so I didn't inform her of Lydia's more conniving tendencies. Accentuate the positive. People were always saying that. It was hard sometimes ... Well, hell, maybe Lydia would make me rich and famous some day. Then my accountants could rob me blind.

"Of course not," Jenny said. "Most people are odd."

I shook my head, a bit too violently, judging from

the pain it caused toward the top of my turban. "No. Most people aren't brave enough to be anything but identically dull. And look at the pile of nothing they collectively create."

Jenny tipped her cigarette out the window. The wind sucked the cherry away. "I didn't know all the women there tonight were going to be lesbians. You got a light?"

"You didn't know I painted, either." I re-lit her Virginia Slim.

"Some of those women were okay. They were interesting."

"They probably were. I don't remember."

"You were too busy getting drunk. You were also knocked out for quite a while." She threw me a playful little wink, smiled and put her eyes back to the road. "A sleeping worm misses the bird," she said.

Jenny was alright. It occurred to me that I might have missed something good, something a whole lot better than that late period Picasso Lydia had on her wall. There was a can of beer rolling around at my feet. I reached down, cracked it. Budweiser.

"I'm never comfortable at those kind of parties," I confessed, as if it weren't already obvious. "Artists, gallery people ... I always feel like an idiot."

"How come?"

"I was raised in a trailer park. Those people at Lydia's tonight, they're educated, they know things, they go places. I work in a grocery store. I tend bar at the Sause Box. I don't know a damned thing about art. I'm untrained. When I paint, I don't even know what the fuck I'm doing."

"Sure you do—or else you wouldn't be able to do it. Fish can't tell you squat about water, but they live in it, they know it."

"So I'm a fish." I wanted to ask Jenny if she'd ever read *As I Lay Dying* but decided it was irrelevant.

"Yes, you're a fish," Jenny said. "You have instinct. Your paintings are beautiful. Maybe those people just pretend they know what they're doing. Maybe they just talk about it a lot. Maybe having half a dozen degrees doesn't matter."

"Maybe ..."

"Maybe shit. I saw some of their work tonight. It wasn't that great. Yours had more soul, Lupus. Especially that one above the bed." She jabbed her Virginia Slim in my direction to help punctuate her point. The cherry fell off. It landed in my lap.

"Thanks, Jenny." I brushed the cherry off my crotch. It wasn't really true, what Jenny was saying. She was over-estimating my talent. (Tia Correlia often did the same thing. Personal bias, it made you unable to see straight.) But it made me feel good nonetheless.

At least she knew what she liked.

"Most of those people were pretentious," Jenny barrelled on. "It was like they were dressed for a play. Like they were playing at being artists, making a big production of it. It was silly. I kept expecting a director to jump out from behind the curtains and yell *cut* or something. A few of them were downright obnoxious, Lupus."

"Everybody plays at being something," I said. It was true. Terrorists played at being terrorists. They grew the beard, donned the beret and the guerrilla garb. Bankers dressed like bankers. A plumber looked like a plumber. Ronald Reagan was an appropriately costumed handpuppet. Gandhi copped his wardrobe from Christ. "I'm sure a lot of those people tonight thought I was just as obnoxious. I try real hard not to come across as an artist. It's like I play at it," I confessed. It hadn't really occurred to me before.

"You were pretty rude to some of them. Breaking that glass and bleeding all over the kitchen didn't help. Do you always drink like that when you're nervous?"

"I always drink like that, period. A psychologist once told me I was overly sensitive. He said I was the fragile type."

"Well, your head is pretty fragile—I'll give you that. You should've seen it. There was blood everywhere. We had to get a mop!"

"I'm a bleeder. It's true."

"Maybe you're a lesbian artist trapped in a male bartender's body," Jenny mused. She could make me laugh. I liked that about her. I hadn't been able to laugh much that Summer. It felt good to do a little laughing just then. Even if I did feel mostly like dying.

"I really wish Tia could have been there tonight," I said, apropos of nothing.

"What? My company isn't good enough for you?"

"That's not what I meant."

"I know. You really miss her, don't you?" Jenny, like everyone else I worked with, had heard my sob story a thousand times that Summer.

"She's the one," I said. "Everything seems pointless now. If I lost her for good, I think I'd crawl into a hole and die. I couldn't deal with it, I'd lose my mind, I think. I'd probably drink myself to death."

Jenny was good enough not to articulate what we were both thinking in regard to that. I found a few more runaway beers in the backseat. I reached back there, made the snag. Cracked one for Jenny, one for myself. We turned the radio on, got a good soul station out of Detroit. The Chi-Lites came crooning from the speakers, those great voices filling the night, the dark landscape rolling by, the void in which I lived. The song was "Oh, Girl"—of course, what else? I turned it down a notch. These things did not occur by chance. God timed them. It was all designed to drive you mad.

"Listen, Jenny, do me a favor," I said. "Don't go telling everyone at the bar that I'm a painter or a fucking artist or something. They'd laugh me out of town, I'd never hear the end of it. I get thrown enough shit from those drunks as it is. I don't need to be tarred and feathered."

"Don't worry," Jenny laughed. "Your vile secret is safe with me, Picasso."

"Thanks, Jen. I think I love you." "Oh, Girl" had drawn to a weeping close. Now it was the Spinners: "Mighty Love." Don't get me wrong, I liked soul music, I loved it. But goddamn, it was pushing me toward the noose, the razor, the cocked revolver. I had a few more paintings to do before I blew my brains to the wall—so I spun the dial. And landed on some vintage AC/DC. "Highway to Hell." I turned the knob to eleven—for the benefit of those about to rock. Namely, me and Jenny.

"Let's pick it up!" I screamed. "If we hurry we can make last call!" Jenny put her foot to the floor. We roared up I-96. Back toward lowbrow culture and drinks on the cuff. Back toward the world to which we'd grown accustomed.

"Hey!" Jenny hollered. "Have you ever read *As I Lay Dying*?"

I was feeling nauseous. "What the fuck does Faulkner have to do with anything?"

"I'm not sure," Jenny said.

I stuck my head out the window and vomited into the void. The wind unravelled my turban. And

My show opened the following week. I didn't make it. And Lydia didn't seem to mind one bit.

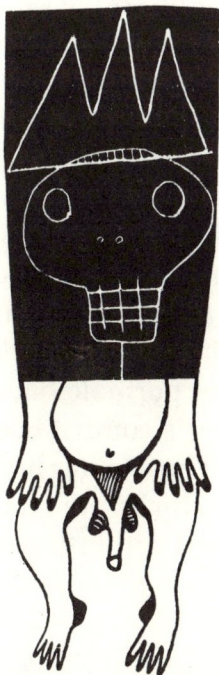

***

I decided to open a savings account. I'd been squirreling my money away in a pair of my father's old combat boots. I'd found them in the room I rented from my mother—in the attic, to be more accurate. My room had a tiny door cut into one of the walls, a kind of square porthole fitted with a plywood cover. You pulled this cover away, climbed through the time-hole and there you were, in the attic. I wormed through there one night hoping to find some long lost family treasure—something worth pawning, in other words. But there wasn't while I was at work, rooting around for rent past and present? What if those fucking wires finally chose to blaze up and engulf the place? My nest-egg, my sole means of escape, would burn right along with it. I'd be fucked. Those boots were good, but they weren't that good. I didn't like banks. But my mother's shack housed a far greater potential for disaster.

So I opened a savings account—my first. The days and nights and paychecks blew by in a haze. I soon lost the bankbook they'd given me to keep track of my deposits and withdrawls, so I wasn't really sure anymore how much money I had in there. It must have been plenty, though. I never took anything out and I was always making deposits. My egg was growing fatter every day. Come Fall, I wanted a nest-egg impressive enough to hold up the pants of the Paul Masson-era Orson Welles. I tried to get by on next to nothing, pinching every penny, obsessed with it. I smoked the cheapest generic cigarettes you could buy and drank almost exclusively at the Sause Box, because at the Sause Box the employees drank free of charge, whether they were on the clock or off—same with food. I also ate for free at the grocery store, in addition to making off with steaks and other perishables every day. I'd use what little free time I had to mow a lawn or paint someone's porch— even pocket change got squirreled away as rocket fuel for The Great Escape, the Red-Eye back to Tia Correlia. Any fool could see I'd lost my fucking mind.

All I thought about was money. Making money, saving money, making more money. I probably would have rolled it all into stocks or savings bonds, but I didn't think I'd ever live long enough to collect on something as farsighted as that. My mother would wind up with it all. She'd cash them in to pay for my funeral or a trip to Miami. I was only thinking short-term. Build a substantial nest-egg and be back on my feet by September. Catch a bus to Chicago. Patch things up with the beautiful Tia Correlia. Show her that I was a man of means, hard working, resourceful—a breadwinner. Then take it from there. Of course, there was the small issue of whether she still loved me or not. But I tried not to think about that. To think would have derailed the entire undertaking. It would have instilled doubt. And doubt was not an option. Doubt would have knotted the noose.

So I staggered forward on auto-pilot. I went to my jobs, got paid, made my deposits at the bank. I wrote several hundred love letters, as many as three a day, licking the envelopes, dropping them into the box— waiting for an answer. All the while making detailed plans for some hoped-for future. A future that could not possibly come to pass, I felt, without the lovely Tia Correlia. A five-foot-two, Portuguese-Irish woman living on the northside of Chicago, Illinois. And going about that life without me.

***

I'd been stalling my mother's demands for rent. It was all a part of my savings obsession, another way to cut a corner and get back on my financial feet. A temporary means to an end. My mother didn't quite see it that way. She gave a flying fuck what my ultimate ends were. All she knew was that she was getting the shaft. Smart lady.

In the beginning, it had been necessary. I was broke then. I had no choice but to hem, haw and stall. But I was making good money now. I'd skated by on the cuff for more than nine weeks. I'd been laying stolen sirloin and unmarketable works of art at her feet in lieu of coin—transparent offerings to stave off the inevitable. She didn't mind the steaks, but the paintings were another thing altogether. You couldn't eat art.

"These are crap!" she'd say. "People aren't yellow and purple! Their heads and bodies don't look like that! You paint pictures of freaks—your people are monsters, they're ugly! What am I supposed to do with these things? I can't pay my light bill with them! I can't cash them at the bank! Why don't you paint something constructive?—like the HOUSE!" Then she'd make a big show of dragging them out the back door. Presumably to the trash.

Well, my time had come to cough it up.

She climbed the stairs one day and began beating my door with a broomstick. 7 a.m. She rose with *The Today Show* every morning. I laid the blame on Bryant Gumbel. She considered that jackass a golden boy, the successful son she'd never had. I just didn't measure up.

"OPEN UP! GET OUT OF THAT BED, YOU BUM!" She was beating the hell out of my door with that broomstick. End of the world, sure as shit. I told her to hold on a fucking minute but she couldn't hear me above the thunderous music she was making. I'd fallen into unconsciousness two hours prior to this assault. Now I was lying there awake on my thin, shitty little mattress—beneath the weight of a hangover the size of the Chrysler Building. I was hoping the electrical wiring would go up crazed and blazing and engulf the both of us—so I could forget about the whole silly business of getting out of bed each day. My luck wasn't worth a barrel of cat piss, however. I was going to have to open that door—or go deaf with the pounding. I threw the lock and in she stormed. Hurricane Annie. And I wasn't wearing a stitch.

"WHY DON'T YOU COMB YOUR HAIR! YOU LOOK LIKE A MADMAN!"

"WOMAN, YOU HAVE *DRIVEN* ME TO THIS

MADNESS!"

"PUT ON SOME CLOTHES! THIS ISN'T A NUDIST COLONY!" I was holding a pillow over my crotch. The woman had always been prone to exaggeration. I let the pillow fall to the floor:

"THERE, NOW IT'S A NUDIST COLONY!"

"PUT THAT PILLOW BACK ON!"

"I GOTTA BE ME! I GOTTA DANGLE AND BE FREE!"

"YOU'RE SICK! YOU NEED HELP!"

"I'M FRANK SINATRA! I'M ALLEN GINSBERG!"

"YOU SHOULD BE LOCKED UP! YOU'RE ILL!"

It *was* a bit odd. I reached down and put the pillow back in place. There was a pile of cash sitting on my dresser. She was all over it in a flash.

"DON'T TOUCH THAT!"

"YOU'VE GOT A FORTUNE HIDDEN AWAY IN HERE! I WANT MY RENT!"

"HELP YOURSELF!"

My fortune amounted to 87 dollars and change. She'd swooped down and counted it with amazing speed. All singles. She waved them in my face."

"EIGHTY-SEVEN DOLLARS! YOU OWE ME SIX HUNDRED!"

"I HAVE GIVEN YOU *AT LEAST* SIX HUNDRED DOLLARS WORTH OF MEAT THIS SUMMER—ONE HUNDRED PERCENT GRADE A!"

"MEAT WON'T PAY MY LIGHT BILL!" The woman was obsessed with that. I'd been hearing her scream it all my life. It seemed as if the light bill represented to her the tedious, unending burden of survival itself. Technically speaking, she was right. You really couldn't hand the electric company a T-Bone and call it a done deal.

The bank was closed on the weekends, and that's when I made the majority of my money at the bar. People got paid on Friday and spent the next two days pissing it away. It was Monday now. I had a couple hundred singles stuffed into the toes of the old man's combat boots, which I planned to deposit later that afternoon. The boots were sitting on the floor. I pointed to them:

"TAKE THE BOOTS! PAY YOUR GODDAMN LIGHT BILL!"

"THOSE BOOTS AREN'T WORTH BEANS! I CAN'T PAY MY LIGHT BILL WITH—"

"INSIDE! INSIDE!"

She turned them over, gave them a shake. Out tumbled the green. She totalled it:

"NOW YOU OWE ME THREE HUNDRED DOLLARS!"

"I'LL TAKE IT OUT OF THE BANK TODAY! DON'T WORRY!"

"NO! DON'T TOUCH YOUR SAVINGS! YOU'LL SCREW UP THE INTEREST! JUST SET YOUR TIPS ASIDE! YOU CAN PAY ME THE REST THIS WEEKEND!"

"WE AREN'T ARGUING ANYMORE! WILL YOU STOP SCREAMING ALREADY?"

"WHY DO YOU KEEP YOUR MONEY IN THOSE BOOTS? IT'S STUPID! ANYONE COULD WALK RIGHT IN HERE AND STEAL IT!"

"LEAVE! VANISH!"

"GET DRESSED! COMB YOUR HAIR! MAKE SOMETHING OF YOURSELF!"

I had no choice but to drop the pillow again.

"I'M KING OF THE NUDIST COLONY!" I screamed.

"YOU'RE SICK! YOU WERE BORN SICK!" She stuffed my money in her bra and made for the door. I slammed it behind her. Climbed back onto my bed of nails. Pulled the sheet up over my head.

"ONLY AN IDIOT KEEPS HIS MONEY IN A BOOT!" my mother screamed.

I had to get the hell out of that house. After a certain age, shacking with your mother became obscene. It was a first-class embarrassment. It was also a sure-fire way to lose your mind. Besides, for the kind of rent she was asking, I could certainly afford a dump of my own. Problem was, I didn't plan on staying in town much past September. There were no boarding houses in Stillwater, no rooms for rent by the day or the week—unless you counted the exorbitantly priced Bed and Breakfast joints, which existed solely for the raping of tourists. I couldn't afford to bend over that far. My only option was an apartment—and the landlords all wanted the same thing: for you to sign away a full year of your life. They wanted a commitment, a guarantee. I couldn't guarantee squat. I was only projecting as far as Tia Correlia. All thought, all plan, came to a halt right there. And if that fell through, well, there was always the shotgun blast to the head—Papa style. Anyway, my credit was such that no landlord in their right mind would ever rent to me. Those bastards stuck together. My previous slumlords would blow the whistle on me. My mad surgeon would be more than delighted to trumpet *deadbeat*, as well.

I was against the wall. I'd been there before. I'd been there so many times that being against the wall felt more natural than not being against the wall. I'd learned the terrain, how to operate there. If life had suddenly thrown me roses rather than dogshit, I probably wouldn't have known how to react. I'd grown accustomed to dogshit, to the smell and the feel of it. Roses were a mystery to me.

Well, I had to give it some thought before making my next move. Careful consideration was called for. So I kicked my feet up a while longer. My back against that fabled wall, the familiar smell of dogshit filling my nose—feeling normal, feeling miserable and most at home. Thirty-years-old. Thinking it through ...

    The old lady and I continued to fight like mountain lions. I wasn't dreaming up my next move as quickly as she'd have liked. But she was emptying my combat boots on a regular basis. So we had moved on to arguing about bigger and better things—more personal things, more biting, more cruel. It was the nature of our love for one another, the only way we knew how to express it anymore. I'd noticed long before that the world seemed to be full of people just like my mother and I. It wasn't a very comforting observation.

4. LISTS

4. LISTS

4. LISTS

4. LISTS

4. LISTS

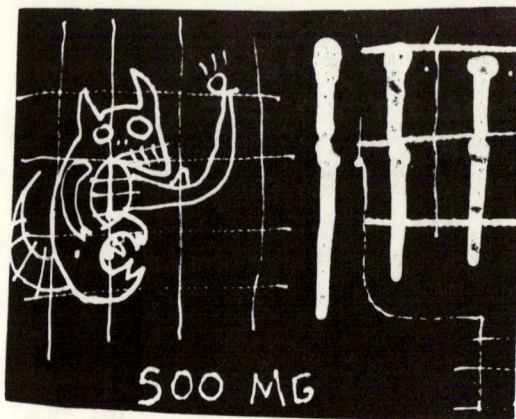

500 MG

F*!#IN' UP

I needed to get out of the suburbs, out of my mother's house. I was eighteen and my life wasn't progressing well. You might say it wasn't progressing at all. I'd just been released from the state psychiatric hospital—nine months of Thorazine, electro-shock therapy, moon-white walls and lunatics. Now I was holed up in my mother's basement, killing time and feeling like an alien. I had no idea where to go or what to do. I seemed incapable of making a move. I'd gone through a long Frances Farmer phase and was just waking up. The fog was still thick. I couldn't see much further than my next sedative, the cigarette trembling at the end of my arm. And what little I could see didn't look any better than the madhouse I'd just been spat out of. So I lay low for a while, waiting for the fog to lift. I began a journal, filling notebook after notebook with obsessive, chemically neutered gibberish—sailing each of these purgings into the trash upon completion, then beginning another. I found an old typewriter and made a religion of pecking out formless narrative poetry every night—most of it autobiographical, most of it bad. I read the classics. I sat on an old couch, staring out the window. I slept for two or three years ...

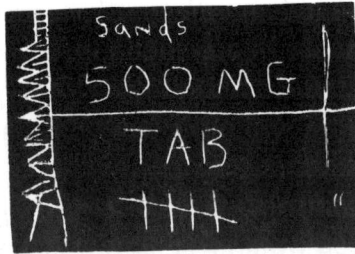

Well, the fog never really lifted (it may have been the medication). But the time had come to make a move. Any move. So I made it blindly. I wasn't sure whether I was moving forward or backward. It didn't seem to matter. But it broke my mother's heart. Like my father, I left without saying goodbye. She was alone now. My little brother had drowned himself in a plastic swimming pool at the age of seven. He tripped over a horseshoe stake while tearing through the backyard one night. He fell into the pool. The water was only two feet deep. But he'd left one of his Tonka Trucks in there. An old green pick-up, just like the one my father drove. That's when my father went from being a drinker to a drunk. Three years later, he was dead. I found him on the couch, the TV glowing, his green eyes fixed on the ceiling. A glass of bourbon in his hand. My brother's eyes were blue. Like my mother's. He didn't say goodbye, either.

Lansing seemed to be as good a place as any. It was the state capital. I remembered going there once on a field-trip back in grade school. I remembered how beautiful I thought it was. What the hell, I figured, why not live next to the Capitol Building? Maybe I could get a job mopping the floors ...

I'd worked very little after being released from the psychiatric hospital. The few jobs I did have, I quickly lost due to apathy and insomnia—as well as glaring incompetence. I was just about unemployable. And broke—which goes without saying, I suppose.

One day I came across an ad in the classifieds. Upjohn was looking for volunteers to take part in an investigational drug study—guinea pigs. The pay was fifteen hundred dollars. A seven-day stay. I made the call. Then got a ride to Kalamazoo to find out whether or not I qualified. I was used to controlled environments. Hospital gowns. Doctors. Nurses. Beds with rails. Barred windows. Shatterproof glass. The stench of disinfectant. Clocks slowed to a crawl ...

Exploit your strengths.
I'd read that somewhere.

***

The hospital was large and white, my room light and airy. There were plastic flowers by my bed, the food was excellent. It was a far cry from the state insane asylum. I thought maybe they were going to hang me come dawn—but they never did. The nurses shot me full of some space-age, previously untested elixir three times a day. The nurses looked good. They wore tight-fitting uniforms and were always bending over to examine this vein or that, their breasts often brushing my face as they jammed the needles in. I didn't give a fuck-all what they were injecting me with. It could've been strychnine for all I cared. I just kept my famished eye on all those breasts and legs and wide white asses. I was in heaven for a week.

After six days of being poked, prodded and tortured, a doctor came to my room and said, "The drug we have been giving you this week has been known to enlarge the hearts of cows. How do you feel?"

"Just fine," I told him. It was true. I'd just finished putting away a Porterhouse. Rare, the way I like it.

"Hmmm—that's odd," the doctor said. Then he scratched his head and left the room.

I climbed out of bed and made for the cafeteria. According to the intercom, it was snack-time. I hadn't eaten so well in years. I made the best of it. Those cafeteria babes could really work the ladle.

There was another day of blood-draws and electrocardiograms and bountiful bouncing bosoms. Then it was over, the study, the good meals, my seven-day erection. They released me—along with a check for fifteen hundred dollars. And, presuming the tests had come back correct, no enlarged heart.

I cashed the check less than an hour later and bought a one-way ticket to Lansing. I bought a bottle of Wild Turkey and rode the bus and drank and watched the land and the buildings and the people bleed by in the rain-streaked window—a show that was only slightly more interesting than the shit I'd been watching on television all week. I closed my eyes and got to thinking about the nurses back at the hospital. Those nurses had been kind to me. I'd fallen in love with those nurses. I thought maybe I'd found my true calling, a reason, a way. The Sweet-N-Low rats had never had it so damned good. Lupus Totten: pampered, well-paid warrior in the battle against death and disease. Modern medicine's own little Jesus Man ... I dozed off, thinking about those sexpot nurses and their youthful, heavenly cleavage.

The bourbon jammed between my legs, my experimental drug money folded thick in my left shoe.

The guy sitting next to me was an ex-con, just out on parole. He had a bottle, too.

***

I got myself a room right next to the Capitol Building. The area surrounding the Capitol Building was one big slum. Poor blacks, poor whites, poor Mexicans, ugly blank-faced houses squatting along streets with names like Pleasant View and Sunnybrook, porno and pawnshops, liquor stores on every corner, the people all on welfare, riding the heavily advertised malted Bull and beating their women. So much for stately beauty. Memory was a damned funny thing.

I sat in my room for a few days and drank and thought about things. I was living at the Jack London Hotel, an old dilapidated flophouse on Michigan Avenue, directly across the street from a rehabilitation center. So I would drink and watch the drunks drying out, doing lawnwork all day, sweating and shaking and praising their higher power. I'd gotten myself a goldfish. I'd turn away from the drunks in my window and watch the goldfish now and again. I kept him in a fruit jar at the foot of my bed, so the fish really didn't have much room to swim. It just sort of hung there in the water, stricken, paralyzed, in a kind of claustrophobic state of shock. Every now and again the fish would turn round the jar in a slow, lethargic circle, looking me up and down, it seemed—only to quickly lose interest and look away. It wasn't a particularly happy or dynamic creature to look at so I didn't look at it much.

I tried to find a job. But there seemed to be no real jobs in the city of Lansing. Lansing was mostly colleges and bad restaurants—the rest of it an urban wasteland. I was no student and I certainly didn't look like a waiter at the time. I didn't look much like anything—except maybe a serial killer. Landing a job was like landing a part in a play. You at least had to *look* the part. The employers didn't want me because I didn't quite look like a WORKER. They had a keen eye, those employers. Even the hobos who panhandled up and down Michigan Avenue night and day wanted nothing to do with me—I didn't look like I had any pocket-change to palm out, and yet I didn't quite look like a bum. You apparently had to look like something in a CAPITAL way. If you were somewhat lowercase, people didn't know what the hell to take you for. That was one of the reasons I remained unemployed and spent the majority of my time alone. The other reason? I couldn't stomach human beings and I loathed the Work World.

I handled the job problem the same way I handled my affairs with the opposite sex—I stuck my head in the mud and sat around waiting for a miracle to arrive. The employers didn't come scratching at my door any faster than the women did. Go figure.

Every now and then, I'd make a half-hearted attempt. I'd hop on a bus and make the rounds, filling out applications for unskilled labor, leaving most of the questions blank. I didn't want much. And I didn't get it.

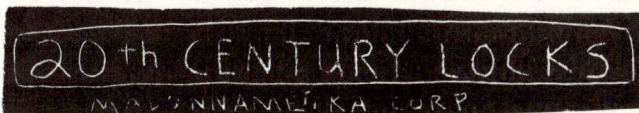

20th CENTURY LOCKS

I went through my drug money quicker than gooseshit. I was popular at the bar for a while. I'd go to a place called the Elbow Room, drink myself into oblivion night after night—the only condition in which I could stomach my fellow man—and buy rounds for all the regulars. But then the money ran out and I was a pariah again.

I lay in my room at the Jack London a lot, shades pulled, staring up at the water-stained ceiling and drawing parallels between myself and the common cockroach. I considered suicide but seemed to have neither the nerve nor the energy for such an undertaking. Rustling up a gun, stringing a noose, locating a razor to open the wrists—it required a determination and a willfulness I apparently lacked. It was too much fucking work, just another JOB. Hell, I could have committed just as effective a suicide by taking work as a janitor or drill-press operator. A form of self-murder sanctioned by all.

I wound up going to the bloodbank twice a week. But the nurses weren't anything like the nurses back at Upjohn. They were mostly male and it was hard to like them. They seemed to enjoy putting the spike to people, they seemed to get a kick out of it. They looked well-fed, maniacal, educated, bored. I'd sit in the chair and watch my blood drain into a plastic bag and fantasize about mowing them all down with an M-16. The sign on the door read:

EARN 8 DOLLARS. SAVE A LIFE. AND WATCH TV.

But I was a mercenary. I was only in it for the money.

All they ever played on the TV were tits and ass and war pictures. I'd fall asleep with the spike in my arm and one of the male nurses would come along and pound on my chair with a broomstick: "NO NAPPING!" I'd open my eyes and watch the tits and the ass and the carnage for a while. Then nod and begin dreaming about mowing everybody down with the M-16 again.

The bloodbank was called AMERICAN PLASMA. There was a take-out store right across the street—ONE THOUSAND AND ONE LIQUORS. You'd see all the donors over there after the draws were finished and the cash had been passed around. I'd be over there, too. Picking up booze, cigarettes and bean soup— the three essential food groups you traded your life-blood for twice a week. I was always more than happy to make the trade. It kept me going throughout a Winter that might have otherwise buried me. And don't forget: I wasn't only making money. I was also saving lives and watching TV. How many CEOs can make that claim?

The Jack London was not exactly a magnet for the well-heeled. *Jack London—Hotel of the Damned* would have been a more descriptive name for the place. It drew an all-inclusive gruel of lowlifes. Petty thieves. Third-rate prostitutes. Con-men. Winos. Paper-hangers. Bookies. Welfare frauds. Gangbangers. Child fuckers. Defrocked priests. Hardcore alcoholics. Heroin addicts. Crack addicts. Religious fanatics. Tragedy mongers. Mumblers. Mental cases. Crackpots of every stripe, the downtrodden and indigent, the lost and the damned— Dostoyevsky's people. Well, I had a bed there, and that was that. Money didn't mean a goddamned thing to the Dalai Lama. But I was no Dalai Lama.

The people living above me were named Tom and Angie. Tom and Angie had two kids, a girl and baby boy—so they were up there too, jumping up and down on my ceiling sixteen to eighteen hours a day. The little girl was four, the baby was pushing two. He appeared to be catatonic, a cipher. He never cried or made a sound. Always silent, always staring stone-still into space, into the shimmering black beyond—a shell-shocked little soldier. I felt an instant kinship with him. The little girl still smiled now and then, even talked on occasion. But the baby boy knew better, the baby knew the score, the baby wasn't smiling at shit. He was just lying in the damp foxhole of his diaper, heart and soul and ass retracted turtle-like—wet, raw, itching, inflamed—watching the world scream itself blue and waiting for the inevitable big bang. Tom had once been in the Army but he'd lost that gig—dishonorably—so now he drank and fought at home. Angie didn't work either. Welfare paid twice as much as McDonald's and didn't require you to wear an idiotic uniform and smile at people you would just as soon kick in the teeth. Tom and Angie were both nineteen. They'd grown up together, one door apart. They started dating in Junior High. They fucked, Angie got knocked up, they married. Now they sat around all day watching the soap operas and drinking beer—fighting, taking pot-shots at one another, playing it out. Tom beat both Angie and the kids, continually. It was a horrible thing to live beneath. When the weather was nice, I sometimes sat out on the front stoop and drank with them. They seemed all right out there. But an hour later they'd be at it again, Tom beating Angie's head against the wall, the little girl screaming, the baby boy strangely silent—Angie crying for Tom to stop, Tom screaming "WHORE!" and pounding away, Angie throwing things, the other tenants banging the walls and screaming at them to shut the fuck up. It got so bad sometimes that small pieces of plaster would fall from my ceiling.

On one occasion, Tom tried to stab Angie with a carving knife. He missed and skewered the waterbed. Fifty gallons of stagnant water came pouring down through the ceiling—3 in the fucking a.m. I sat there, soaking wet, wondering what the fuck they were doing with a waterbed in the first place. My room hadn't come with one.

The night finally came when I thought he was going to kill her—and the kids. I walked up the street to a payphone and put in a call to 911. There was only one rule of etiquette at the Jack London, and that was to MIND YOUR OWN FUCKING BUSINESS. But you had to draw a line somewhere. The voice at 911 didn't sound too thrilled—overworked, bored, jaded, fed up. On the corner, two aging yet alarmingly buff leather boys were leaning against a green Cadillac, holding hands—and leering at me. They could have been linebackers. They began to whistle.

I whimpered into the phone: "I'm calling from the Jack London Hotel. I'd like to report a murder in progress. I think the guy on my ceiling is killing his wife. More importantly, I think I'm about to be raped."

"Are you sure? We get calls from that dump all the time. We send out a cruiser and by the time they get there everything's fine—there's no one to arrest. Sending out cars costs money. You can't be calling us over every little family spat you hear. Why do you think taxes are so high?" All of this within the space of a yawn. I'd dialed 911 about this shit on at least a dozen or more occasions in the past. She was right—by the time the Man got there, there was no one to arrest. And even when there was, no one would want to press charges. I'm talking about Angie here, but it was the same all over America. The wives and the girlfriends were insane. The people at 911 were insane. The husbands and the boyfriends and the fists were sure as shit insane. We were all insane. Fucked, plucked and married—to madness. Of course, when I made this observation, I was only eighteen. Call it instinct. Call it a day.

"HEY, LISTEN!" I screamed into the mouthpiece. "THERE'S A WOMAN AND TWO SMALL CHILDREN BEING BUTCHERED! IT'S A FUCKING BLOODBATH! YOU WON'T BE DISAPPOINTED!"

"Where did you say you were calling from?"

"THE JACK LONDON HOTEL? MICHIGAN AVENUE, RIGHT NEXT TO THE CAPITOL BUILD-ING!"

"This better be for real, buddy. Or you're gonna have some questions to answer—it's gonna be your ass."

"Hey, it's gonna be my ass if you people don't get here soon! There's two Spartacus-looking freaks circling me like sharks—leather boys, *get it*?" They were moving closer and closer, moving in for the kill. Studded G-strings and chaps, biker-boots, collars—*cowboy hats!* It was the most ridiculous thing I'd ever seen. And the most primally terrifying.

"I thought you were calling about a domestic violence case."

"That, too. But I think I'm about to be buggered, as well."

"We'll send someone out. This better be for real."

I slammed the phone down. Fuck it, it was time to move along. I started back to my room—nervous, white, homophobic, justifiably paranoid. Well, maybe it wasn't justified. But I wasn't about to second-guess anything ... I looked back. The Texan galley slaves whistled and cat-called, shoved out their tongues and grabbed their G-strings. I bolted—I wasn't going to be anybody's bitch. The few gay friends I had were nothing like these freakish motherfuckers. Imagine gay fratboys gone mad. Imagine fratboys, period.

I ran a few blocks, then stopped and caught what was left of my breath. I hadn't been followed. There were a group of kids playing stickball in the street. High-topped tennis shoes, whoops and hollers. 3 a.m. A school night. One of them walked up to me, banging his stick on the pavement. He looked about twelve-years-old.

"Hey, mister—there's somebody gettin' kilt in that building over there." The kid pointed his stick toward the Jack London. There weren't any cops there yet. Angie was screaming like a banshee. Tom was screaming. The little girl was screaming. They had a room facing the street. Their window was open. You could hear them screaming from a block away. Nearby, a dog was barking and someone was screaming at the dog to shut the fuck up. It was hard to get any sleep in that neighborhood.

"It sounds like somebody gettin' kilt," the kid repeated. The others were zig-zagging around with their sticks, whacking the road and passing a jug of wine back and forth. It looked like pretty good wine. "I think you might be right, little man."

The kid shrugged. He whacked his stick against the pavement. Pulled out a cigarette. "You wanna play, mister? We one guy short. We need another guy."

"Naw. I got a bad back."

"Okay," he said.

***

I was eating a can of string-beans (French Cut), combing through the classifieds, listening to Tom and Angie shake the ceiling. My goldfish had gone belly-up that morning—something in the water, perhaps—and had he been any bigger, I might have stuck a fork in him. I'd blown that week's bloodmoney at the bar. The next draw was two days away. I'd become *The Hunger Artist*. I needed to find another line of work.

CLERK WANTED.
BOOKSTORE. $5/HR.
1115 MICHIGAN AVE.

What the hell. I was starving. I went on down.

The place was just a few blocks from my room, sandwiched between a stripjoint and a gay bar called *Members*. It was a horrid little hole in the wall—graffiti-scrawled door, broken glass, foil-covered windows. Typical whack-off parlor.

THE PLEASURE NEST
adult books   mags   peepshows   massages

I filled out the application, leaving most of the questions blank. The guy behind the counter was Iranian, thin, dark, unsmiling. He stood there with his arms folded across his chest, watching me push the pen around the page. The pen was attached to a chain so you couldn't run off with it. Inside the pen was a tiny naked lady, cupping her huge pink breasts, smiling, licking her lips. When you tipped the pen a certain way, her panties disappeared and she gave you a seductive little wink. American ingenuity.

I signed my name, pushed the application across the counter. The clerk looked it over. While he was doing that, I wandered around a bit. It was absurd. No matter which way you turned, you saw a cock—a dildo, a massive rubber monstrosity. They were everywhere, on the counter and above the counter, on the walls and under glass. All of them enormous, idealized, exaggerated, idiotic. Like America itself. Big cars, big hair, big wallets, big mouths, big missiles—big dicks. And, of course, big breasts. Along the walls of Triple-D titty mags leaned a buxom array of inflatable dolls—blondes, redheads, brunettes, blondes and more blondes—mouths open wide, parted legs and vibrating pussies, racks like cream-colored mountains. They had names. Dirty Debby. Hot Helen. Virgin Mary (who was reputed to be a very horny young housekeeper—"She'll wax more than your floor!" proclaimed the manufacturer—but painfully shy). Some of the dolls were still in their boxes, deflated, their names and measurements clearly labeled, their faces mooning out from behind small cellophane windows, lifeless, marble-eyed. The one named Dirty Debby was a deluxe model. She had flaming red hair, projectile breasts, and a round white ass—she also had a string you could pull, which made her talk, in case you were the sensitive type and wanted a bit of friendly banter before getting down to the business of coming in her mouth. Debby was pretty spendy, but the rest of the dolls cost around $59.95, which was slightly more than you'd pay for a flophouse hooker—but, unlike a hooker, you could stick it to a latex doll any time you pleased, day or night, rain or shine, cash or no cash, seven days a week. A sound investment, a gift that just kept giving ... And you knew damned well that there were people buying these things. It was a frightening thought.

"Lupus?" the clerk asked. "Like the disease?"

"Yeah. Like the disease." I was going to hear that my entire life. My old man's idea of a joke. He had to have been drunk at the time. He was a fucking card, that guy.

"Ever run a cash register, Lupus?"

"No."

"Ever been arrested for, or involved in any way

with prostitution?"

"No."

"Do you use narcotics or have a drug problem of any kind?"

"No. Just television now and then. Bogey films, mostly. *Baywatch*."

"What do you think of John Wayne?"

"Repressed homosexual."

"Do you drink?"

"I'm unemployed. There's nothing else to do."

"Do you work for any law enforcement agencies, local or otherwise?"

"I'm unemployed."

"Newspapers? Magazines?"

"I have no job. I haven't worked in over two years—I'm clean."

"Do you like people? Do you like working with people?"

"Not especially."

"Do you mind working nights?"

"Nights are good."

"Weekends? Holidays?"

"Whenever—I'm not going anywhere."

"Would you consider working for minimum wage?"

"The ad said 5 an hour."

"Yeah, but would you consider working for less?"

"Less is okay."

"Great," said the clerk. "You're hired. We've got a guy quitting in two weeks. You can start the day he leaves."

"Great," I said. I was screwed. I'd starve for the next two days. "Hey, listen, do you think I could get a cash advance to carry me through till then? I'm broke."

"Are you fucking crazy?"

"Probably." I wasn't quite sure.

Later that afternoon, I gave it some serious thought, sitting in a chair at American Plasma, watching my blood drain down into a plastic bag—having conned them into letting me donate a third time that week.

I jacked off a lot. It was a way to pass the hours, and it helped drown out the sound of the atrocities being committed upstairs and across the hall. I'd spent ten dollars on a secondhand typewriter shortly after taking up residence at the Jack London, so when I wasn't jacking off, I was writing short stories—another form of masturbation. I hadn't caught the painting sickness yet—or Tia Correlia, who bought me my first box of oils and brushes—but I often filled the margins of my fledgling manuscripts with pathological doodles, tiny drawings of madmen and their mad, bullet-breasted women— coins, coffins, crosses, handguns, blackjacks, dogs, rats, nooses, nighthawks pissing gibberish from the wing.

None of my stories had women in them. They were all about little men in tiny rooms, watching the walls and going insane with it; waiting for something to happen, something eventful and violent—for life to close in for the kill, quicktight and tiger-like, to take them out of it swiftly and without regret. They drank and smoked and cursed and waited on time. They thought about women, dreamed of, longed for, and even worshipped them—but the women were nowhere to be found. All of these men were potential geniuses—of course—who had never been given a fair shake, born in the wrong place at the wrong time, born into the wrong skin, the wrong species, on the wrong planet altogether. Great men in small cages. They were always right, always victims of the system, it was never their fault and society was always fucked, always and forever wrong.

I thought my stories were pretty good—raw, but interesting. Far more interesting than the shit I'd had shoved down my throat in highschool. But no one else seemed to think so—certainly not the boneheads behind the *Paris Review*, which, I suppose, was reassuring in a way (almost everything they published put me to sleep). Then again, every writer had an inflated sense of self-worth, their work was always better than the next guy's—to think otherwise could instill serious self-doubt, and doubt could shut you down, completely. A touch of self-delusion was necessary, it was more necessary than talent, and second only to discipline—but talent was important, too. In all likelihood, my efforts were as equally dismal, just as half-baked as the rest of the drivel being wanked off as literature. Still, to be rejected by magazine after magazine, week in and week out, pissed me off, if only mildly.

It worked that way with a lot of things. I seemed out of step, a gimp in an allegedly healthy land—true enough, perhaps. But then again, maybe not. It could have just as easily been the other way around. Who's to say? Galileo Galilei was labeled a nutbag, too—and maybe he was. Either way, the earth became round and I, Lupus Totten, was born into something entirely distasteful. I hated fluorescent colors, they pained my eyes and increased the throb and horror of my hangovers, yet every third person I passed in the street seemed bent on wearing them. I loathed Lite Metal but that was about all I ever heard on the radio. I tuned into the small, public-supported stations, but they talked too much and were always asking for the money I didn't have and they went out of business and off the air. I didn't like

Julia Roberts, the current cultural icons, or movies in general. The media was a nightmare and I disliked Warhol even more now that he was dead. I enjoyed paging through *Playboy* but every time I did so, it depressed me. I'd look out my window and watch the neighborhood women wriggling by, and that depressed me, too. I found them *all* beautiful. Too beautiful. They seemed beyond me—unattainable, even the not-so-beautiful ones. My confidence, never large to begin with, dwindled further. I gave up writing and went back to jacking off full-time. I sat in my room with the shades drawn. I stared at the walls. I went to the bloodbank twice a week, traded my plasma for booze, cigarettes and bean soup...

I was sure many great men had suffered worse. But I never seemed to meet those men.

***

A thousand wide-eyed women, cocks in their mouths and up their asses, staring into the camera lens, staring out from the magazine racks ...

My job was to run the register, push the movies and the mags, count inventory, and introduce the girls who gave the massages. The girls were called "models." They were kept corralled in a parlor upstairs. The stairs consisted of seven short steps, with a length of cheesy velvet drawn across the top—a demarcation line separating the simply curious from the seriously deviant—roughly fifteen feet from the cash register, the cockrings, the dildos, the love lotions, and me. The parlor was imitation turn-of-the-century whorehouse, and the models were not to set foot from it. If the models left the parlor for any reason other than business in one of the private, backroom "boudoirs," where the massages and the handjobs and the officially unspeakable took place, they were fired. They weren't allowed anywhere near the cash register for fear of theft. The models were not to stray, the models were to stay put, the models were not, under any circumstances, to be trusted. Their job was to lounge in the parlor, salivate, and attempt to look sexy. They could go to the bathroom if bowel or bladder called, but they couldn't dally in there, they had to hurry back to the parlor and resume their lascivious poses for the customers, for the buyers and the browsers. They were allowed to smoke—smoking was phallic, and phallic was good. They smoked incessantly. They were excellent smokers. They could really work their lips up and down those filters ...

They were all off-limits to the clerk.

The Iranian guy trained me.

"Lupus, these women are she-devils. They are whores, they will sell their pussy for a dollar. Do not let them fool you. They will do anything to get you fired. They will prey upon your weaknesses. They will toy with you. They will offer you the blow-job, Lupus, they will pretend to be kind and caring. But do not believe it, do not accept. If you allow them to perform the blow-job, if you allow them to touch you—you will be fired. You will lose your job. The she-devils *want* you to lose your job. They love nothing more than to see you take the fall. It makes them feel they have the power. The she-devils have come to believe they are running the store. They believe they are indispensable."

"Well, they are, aren't they?"

"Of course. But you must never let them know this. You must always make them believe they are expendable. That you are doing to them a great favor to allow them to sit naked in our parlor. And do not forget to curse them on occasion. Show to them their place.

Show to them who is in control. If you do not do this, the she-devils will believe you to be soft. If they believe you to be soft, the she-devils will seize the power, they will grind into you their high pointy heels. You will be fired of your job. Do you understand what I tell you?"

"I understand." He didn't seem too convinced.

"You must be certain of this. The she-devils are ingenious. The temptation to touch them will be great and unending. Your will must be iron. You must never weaken. Never. If you weaken, you will be fired. The she-devils will have beaten you."

"Never touch the she-devils, I got it." I glanced toward the parlor. There they sat, the she-devils, in varying degrees of undress—a blonde, a redhead and a brunette. All three were sprawled upon fat velvet loveseats, legs scissored high, stilettos dangling, nubile breasts spilling out of satin bras, or no bras at all. G-strings, crotchless panties, garters, garishly painted eyes, mouths smeared with lipstick, widened with wine— sexy, lascivious, maddening. The sort of harpies who were forever calling sailors to their doom. The brunette had a sucker in her mouth. She winked at me. My cock rose. Instinct would be my undoing.

I found myself moving forward, one step, two steps, three—pulled toward her as if by a magnet, zombie-like, erect.

The clerk caught me by the collar, wheeled me around. "Do not look at them!" he warned. "Do not think of them! Look upon the she-devils only when necessary, only when introducing them to the swine and the perverts. And then you must quickly look away. If they speak your name upon their vile lips, you must cover tight your ears as well as your eyes! You must not listen to their song!"

"They're beautiful," I said.

"They are she-devils!" the clerk insisted. "You must not weaken!" The guy was a fucking nutbag. If these women were the taloned concubines of the damned, then hell wasn't a bad place to be. Had Satan suddenly appeared waving a contract, I would have signed away my soul without a second thought.

"They're beautiful," I said. "The she-devils are beautiful."

"Beautiful, yes. And you are a fool."

Fair enough.

He showed me how to work the register, run the credit-cards through, record video rentals. I didn't catch most of it. I couldn't concentrate knowing that twelve feet away those magnificent she-sluts of Hades were letting it all hang out, dangling the apple and the dream and to hell with Eden.

"I'm not too good with these sort of things," I said.

"I will show you again. You must get it right. If you are a penny off, they will fire you."

"Okay."

He went over it with me again, from the beginning—including his word of warning concerning the she-devils.

"Do you understand?" he asked.

I nodded.

"You must be certain," he said.

"I got it. No problem." I could see that naked brunette in the round surveillance mirror above the clerk's head. Also the blonde and the redhead. The blood kept rushing from my brain to my cock, skewing all hope of concentration.

"Good then," the clerk said. "I am out of here."

"How's that?" I wasn't sure what he meant. I had

an idea, though.

"I am out of here. I am gone. I am quit."

"Oh," I said. "Okay ..."

He grabbed his hat, stared brazenly at the she-devils, crossed himself then bolted for the door. There was a flash of sunlight. Then the door banged shut and it was dark and cave-like again. I stared at the door. That fucker wasn't coming back.

I looked at the lovely she-devils. The she-devils looked at me. I cleared my throat:

"Hey, do any of you girls know how to run a cash register?"

Three hours later, I was fired.

It was the brunette's fault.

***

The ad said I could make $225 a week—all I had to do was help save the planet. I was having a hard enough time saving Lupus Totten. I couldn't see carrying the goddamned planet on my back, as well. But that $225 sounded good. It could help save me.

So I got myself an interview. Next thing I know, I'm a canvasser for *Clean Water Action*. I'm saving the planet. I weigh a hundred and twenty-five pounds. I'm shacking at the Jack London Hotel, hiding under the bed at night with a bottle of whiskey while the crack dealers shoot it out in the hallway and the pimps bitch-slap their whores. But I'm helping to patch that hole in the sky. UV rays, they were hazardous to human health.

They'd pile us into a van, drive past the city limits, and drop us off in various godforsaken neighborhoods. Eight hours later, they'd pick us up again and we would fork over whatever donations we'd been able to coax from the guilty, frightened masses. We always went out just before dinner—better to catch the breadwinners at home—and by that time the temperature had usually dropped to around zero. If I was lucky enough to be dumped in a neighborhood that had a bar or coffee shop, I'd camp there half the night for fear of frostbite. The coat I owned was just a rag. Seeking out a coffee shop or bar was more a matter of survival than sloth. And I did pound on a good number of doors. You had to make quota. If you didn't bring back at least $125 in planet donations per night, you were given the boot. Canvassers were expendable. The planet they lived and died on was not. Maybe we were saving it for the cockroaches ...

I knocked on a door one night, not giving a good goddamn about the hole in the sky or getting any cash to patch it up—just having to shit so badly I thought I was going to die. I was in a suburb somewhere: all money and no trees. Nothing to squat behind and discreetly drop a load without risking arrest. All the doors in this neighborhood screamed money. I was only interested in the toilet facilities. I pounded on one. There was a rent-a-cop cruising the street. High in the hole-punched sky, a commercial airliner hummed through the dark—two-hundred-fifty passengers eating peanuts and gulping overpriced drinks, ogling the stewardess, making the long narrow walk to the rear of the plane, throwing a piss or dropping their excrement over a weary, television-addled America.

The person behind the door took their time in opening it. I stood there, freezing in the porch-glow, the shit halfway out of my ass. I stared at the door, trying to think of other things ... Two times two was four. The first jet to break the sound barrier was the Bell X-1. Four times four was 16. The Manx had no tail. 16 times 16 was 256. Belladonna was a berry best eaten when depressed. 256 times 256 was too much. The Great Blue

Heron laid a beautiful egg. Bears shit in the woods. Men shit in the woods—when they were in the fucking woods ...

The door finally opened, gloriously, mercifully— a hinged miracle of modern convenience, right up there with the crapper in terms of human achievement. To hell with the space program.

"Hello," I said, voice quivering from the cold, bowels about to burst. I was looking at Tokyo Rose, badly aged. An ancient Japanese woman, old-world, who spoke not a word of English. I went into my scripted song and dance. No response—confusion and a puzzled stare. She turned and shouted something in her native tongue. A man who I took to be her husband appeared in the door. He spoke two words of English: Yes and Yes, each followed with a question mark. He bowed. He straightened and disappeared. I stood there. The mean diameter of the earth was 12,760 kilometers. The Manx had no tail and neither did I. A young girl appeared, the grand-daughter, perhaps. "How may I help you?" she said. Bingo.

I introduced myself. I talked about the end of the world. Global warming. Skin cancer. I talked about aerosol cans. Freon. The ozone. The second coming of the Stone Age. I talked about toxic fish. Three-headed calves. Sideshow freaks. The Elephant Man. I wondered what it would be like to shit my pants in front of Tokyo Rose and her slim-hipped, thoroughly Americanized granddaughter. I cut to the chase. I began talking about the toilet. They had one, the girl informed me. She showed me where it was located. I made a run for it, sat down, and took care of business momentarily more important than the salvation of the planet. It was amazing how fast life's trivialities fell away when you were denied a proper bowel-movement and about to implode. In the end, life came down to shit, pure and simple.

I was in the home of strangers, so this moment of relief and revelation wasn't as enjoyable as it might have been. There was no time to meditate. So I wipe, I flush—and the fucking toilet overflows! It's everywhere. I bend to the task of mopping it up—with toilet-paper. I was in there forever, it seemed ... Two times two was four ... The earth was round ... Four times four times forever was a 16-year-old Japanese girl with a flat ass but a bosom glorious enough to bring the world to its knees ... The ostrich and the zebra were beautiful freaks of nature and Lupus Totten laid an ugly egg.

There was a knock at the door. I had no choice but to open up, to expose the atrocity, to explain it. I drew the door back, cautiously. It was Tokyo Rose. I tried to explain myself but she cut me off in Japanese. You would have thought I'd dropped the bombs on Hiroshima and Nagasaki all over again. She was scream-ing at me, four feet tall and flying into a rage down around my waist. I sought out the grand-daughter, told her the story. She explained to me that the old woman was under the impression that I had clogged the shitter deliberately—because she wouldn't fork over a fiver to help save the planet. The old woman didn't believe in handouts. The grand-daughter, however, was hip to the nature of my call. She'd read all about Greenpeace and this environmental holocaust crap on the back of an R.E.M. album. She was in love with that band. She thought the singer was cute ...

I walked out of there with a handful of piggybank change and a phone number that could have landed me a statutory rape charge.

I fell about a hundred and some-odd dollars short of my quota that night. Down came the axe, up came the boot. A familiar ballet.

Two days later, the Ugly American was working as a pizza cook in a seafood restaurant. Then as a beer trotter at local sporting events. Then a third-shift janitor, on my knees before an infinity of urinals every night, scrubbing row after row of toiletbowls, spittoon-like sinks, piss-stained floors and tampax boxes ...

Before long, I was back on the bum. Going to American Plasma twice a week, collecting my bloodmoney, trading it for booze, cigarettes and bean soup.

Shortly thereafter, I moved back into my mother's house. I was in the suburbs again. In the basement. On the couch. Reading the classics. Staring out the window. Watching the walls. Trying to figure my next move. Thinking it through ...

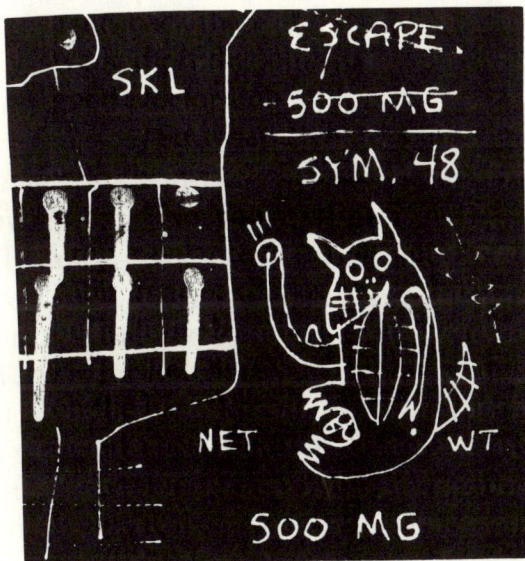

elvis aron presley
1958-1977

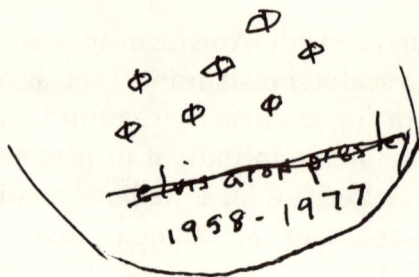

ROUND AND ROUND

Lance Barley had moved into a ridiculous little trailer on the outskirts of town. This trailer was worse than the one I'd grown up in, no child would have ever survived this monstrosity. It sat in a blighted, weed-choked field behind a last-chance gas and liquor store called *The Wish-U-Well*. Dark, claustrophobic, decaying—it possessed the unmistakable stench of desperation, of death and universal defeat. The trailer had no electricity, no running water, its walls had given way to rust and gaping holes. Someone had obviously abandoned the fucking thing decades earlier. The Manson Family, perhaps. Barley had staked his claim, however. Being rent-free, it fell within his budget. As far as he was concerned, the place was perfect.

He had an old sun-bleached American flag planted out front by the door. He was a vet, he couldn't let that shit go. The first time I saw it, I told him he'd be better off taking the fucker down and using it for a bedspread or a couch-cover. It attracted too much attention. I was pretty sure he was breaking more than a few laws shacking there. In addition to a laundry-list of healthcode violations, that tin can was sitting on government property—Uncle Sam's land—and that fascist weasel didn't want any patriots planting a personal flag in his dying, weed-wasted fields.

"You've gotta be insane to live in that thing," I told him. "It's like living in Hell. This is Satan's outhouse. What are you thinking?"

Two weeks later, I was trudging through knee-high weeds, dragging my brushes and paints, my typewriter and a small suitcase—asking myself the same fucking thing.

The moon was out, bright and mad. The stars were out and God was rumored to be dead.

The light in Barley's trailer was out. But I could see the dark, huddled shape of it in the moonlight, the squat and the moan of it. I could see that faded American flag hanging limp in the redneck night. I dropped my possessions to the ground and began beating on the door. I heard a rustling inside, the sound of a glass falling to the floor, a smoker's cough. I pounded on the door again. I felt a bowel-movement coming on.

"IF YOU'RE FROM THE COLLECTION AGENCY YOU CAN PISS OFF!" Barley screamed. He was up to his ass in debt, so his paranoia wasn't altogether unjustified—just a little extreme. The Army had given him a truckload of money to go to college with after he'd gotten his walking papers, the only stipulation being that he *finish* college. But he never finished, he'd dropped out halfway through. Now he owed them two years tuition money and was squatting on government land in a tin hovel unfit for even the beggars of Calcutta. Had he completed college, he wouldn't have owed Uncle Sam a dime. But a voice deep inside told him to hang it up at the halfway point. He never told me about this voice himself, but I had an inner-voice which often instructed me to make similarly idiotic moves, so I figured Barley had one too. It was an intuitive thing.

I kept banging away at the door. I really had to shit. "OPEN UP, YOU JACKASS, IT'S ME!" Barley was a clumsy fuck due to his extreme height. I could hear him falling around in there, crashing into things, knocking bottles and cans over, swearing loudly. The shit was barely hanging on. I was about ready to break the door down.

"IDENTIFY YOURSELF!"

"BARLEY, IT'S ME, YOU ASSHOLE! OPEN THE FUCKING DOOR!"

There was a moment of silence, then the door came flying open with such explosive force you'd have thought a grenade had just gone off in there. I leapt, practically soiling my pants. Barley thrust his head out into the moonlight. He had a Coleman lantern in one hand and a shotgun in the other. His hair was smashed to one side as if he'd been hit in the head with a paddle. He was a bonafide fucking lunatic but I loved him, and vice-versa. Or so I hoped—the s.o.b. was pointing a shotgun in my face. It took a moment, but his eyes slowly widened with recognition. He smiled. I'd been identified.

"Hey, what's up?" He put the shotgun down and gave me a hug. "Where you been, bro?"

"On the cross." I pushed past him and into the trailer. It was a coal mine in there. I couldn't see a fucking thing.

"Hold on a second," Barley said. "Let me give you some light." He followed me in with his Coleman, hung it on a hook, lit a second one. They did the job. What they illuminated, however, was a horror show. There was junk laying all over the place. Beer bottles, cans, garbage, food, half-eaten meals crawling with maggots, condoms, dirty laundry. Your typical bachelor shack. I didn't waste any time taking a tour of the place.

"Listen," I said. "I have to shit like a madman. Where's your crapper?"

"Outside. Go anywhere you want—but make sure you do it away from the trailer."

"Oh, for Christsakes!"

"And don't forget to bury it."

***

I mounted a major clean-up operation the following morning before heading off to the grocery store and punching the butcher-block clock. That trailer was as chaotic as my mental state. I figured if I cleaned and organized the trailer, it might help to put my thoughts back in order, or at least on a rail running in that general direction. "Tidy house, tidy mind." I'd read that in a book somewhere—*Dhammapada*, or *One Hundred and One Zen Fables Further Condensed to Accommodate the American Attention Span*. Maybe I'd read it on the back of a cereal box. Either way, I'd never tried it before. I'd always been too lazy. I was still as lazy as a zoo ape, but that trailer was the heart of darkness, an inanimate manifestation of insanity itself. I was afraid if I didn't create a bit of order right then and there, that first morning, I might allow myself to go with the flow—and be swept even further down that fabled Conradian river than I already was. There was one hell of an undertow at work beneath that frayed American flag Barley had flying out front.

By the time Barley woke up, I had most of the organic and/or biodegradable garbage piled into a small fly-frenzied mountain just beyond the front door. I'd been hurling it out of the trailer for a good forty-five minutes. I planned to dig a hole later that night and bury it all, or just torch it, the way the Europeans had torched their dead during times of plague. I had a second pile going alongside the first. This pile consisted of nothing but beer bottles and cans, returnables, each worth a dime. There must have been at least eighty dollars there.

Barley finally came outside to see what all the bang and clatter was about. He had to stoop to fit through the door. The sun was coming up. He stood there in his underwear, scratching his head, a bent cigarette stuck to his lower lip.

"What the fuck is this?" He stepped away from the trailer and threw a piss. He zipped up. "What the fuck?"

"It's the fallout of your existence. You're disgusting. I was forced to take action. Check it out—you've got about eighty dollars here."

"Where?"

"The cans, the bottles—look at that pile!"

"I'm not returning those fucking things."

"Why not? It's money."

"They'd think I was an alcoholic. Besides, that stuff'd make my car reek." Barley had an old black Cadillac. You could get those secondhand gas guzzlers fairly cheap at the time. It was Barley's pride and joy, he kept the thing immaculate. Drove it around without a license or proper registration. Like a lot of people in Stillwater, he'd had his driving privileges revoked, more or less permanently. Yet he still needed to get to work, drive back and forth to the bar, etc.

"They already know you're an alcoholic!" By *they*, I assumed he meant the people who ran the Wish-U-Well or any other liquor store in town. Barley was in and out of those places two to three times a day, his slur growing more dramatic with each visit.

"Only bums return cans, they dig through the trash for that shit. They'd stink up my car. Forget it."

"Barley, I dug them out of your fucking trailer— you were sleeping in them!"

"Forget it."

"How much money you got in your pocket?"

"None of your business."

"There's eighty dollars here. I'll take it as my cleaning fee."

"Fuck you, the trailer isn't even worth that much."

"Good help is hard to find these days. You're getting off cheap. Before I got here you couldn't tell the trailer from the trash."

"So?"

"So I think I'll take that eighty and go up to the Nickerdown Inn tonight. Get a filet mignon and some of those fifteen-dollar fruit drinks."

"Fruit drinks? With filet mignon? You can't do that—you'd ruin the whole meal! When you're eating steak, red wine is the only way to go. Don't be a fool."

"I'll get a bunch of fruit drinks *and* a bottle of red."

"Goddamnit, it doesn't work that way!"

"FRUIT DRINKS!" I screamed.

"YOU'RE INSANE! YOU DON'T KNOW ANY-THING!"

I got in his face. "ORANGE CURACAO! BA-NANA LIQUEUR!"

He put his hands over his ears. "SHUT UP!"

"I'LL GET A STEAK SOAKED IN CREME DE CACAO! I'LL MAKE THE CHEF PUT A CHERRY ON TOP!"

"SHUT UP! SHUT UP!"

He turned and made for the trailer, slammed the door. I could hear him digging around in there. Maybe he was looking for a book on wine, or the Ten Commandments of Upscale Dining. Barley had a food obsession, everything he ate had to be just so. He'd been a gourmet chef at one time, but he'd gotten himself fired from place after place for drinking on the job and berating customers. Now he painted houses with a crew of alcoholics and had a boss who was too brain-damaged by the toxins of the trade to notice that his employees were tipping brown bags all day and staggering across the scaffolding in a way that was less than professional.

The trailer door burst open—Barley. He was holding a box. He threw it at me. Trash bags. *Hefty*. Extra Strength.

"Okay," he said. "Let's bag 'em up. Make sure you double-line everything. I don't want my car getting fucked up, I don't want any stink."

"No stink," I assured him.

"You're goddamn right. If there's any stink, it's your ass."

"We'll trade them in at the grocery store. I need a ride there anyway."

"You working the Box tonight?"

"No, I'm off. Fuck that place."

"Good. I'll make reservations at the Nickerdown. And you're not ordering any fucking fruit drinks."

"We'll go with whiskey. When the grub arrives, we'll get on the red."

"Steak on a whiskey gut—that works. Bushmill! We'll get there early and drink the good Irish shit. We'll sit on the deck and terrorize the tourists."

"Hell yes. We've got the cash, Barley—we're Bushmill men. We'll lay out a fat tip the minute we get there—then send the wine back half a dozen times and abuse the waitstaff all night."

"Shit, let's ditch work and buy a bottle right now, get a jump on things."

"Forget it. Jack would fire me."

"So what? You're living rent-free now. And we have all these cans—look at that pile!"

"Are you insane? I'm trying to get out of this town, remember? I have to think ahead. Chicago's expensive."

"You think she's gonna take you back?"

"Not if I chuck my job for a pile of fucking beer cans."

"Okay, forget it. You're in love. I understand."

"I don't think you do."

"You're in love. It's hell—I'm hip."

"It's like a knife in my gut. It's killing me."

"Listen, I'll swing by the grocery store at 5. We'll go to the Nickerdown, get loaded, eat some steak—you'll feel better."

"Christ, I wish I didn't have to work today. I hate that fucking place."

"Look upon the world as a bubble. Regard it as a mirage."

Barley, too, had gleaned a bit of Eastern philosophy here and there. Not much, but enough to justify his existence somewhat. These philosophies came in handy when you were living below the poverty-line in the most prosperous nation on the planet.

"Fuck it. It's a bubble," I said.

"Damn straight," Barley coughed. He tossed away the cigarette he was smoking. "Shit, these things are killing me. I'm a dead man."

"Look upon cancer as a mirage."

"It doesn't work that way," he said.

We spent the next twenty minutes bagging that reeking mirage of beer-bottles and cans, loading them carefully into Barley's imaginary Cadillac, so as to avoid any spills, leaks, or worldly stench.

It was a day of unparalleled insanity. It would have meant nothing to a Zen Buddhist. A Zen Buddhist would have smiled at it all, peace, love and acceptance oozing from his pores. But I was no Zen Buddhist. I was an uncentered American with a bleeding ulcer, sweating alcohol and ill-will ...

The tourists were out in droves, swarming the streets and storming every establishment in town—insectile, frenzied, unstoppable—loading up on food, beverages, beer, bugspray, towels, tanning oil, sungoggles, umbrellas, hats, condoms, charcoal, paper cups ... anything and everything they could conceivably drag to the beach. Sun, sand, water—it boggled people's minds, it made them crazy, transformed them into imbeciles, trained seals, spending machines. I could never see what the appeal was. To me, the beach was an overcrowded, hot, gritty oven. Nature's frying pan, God's melanoma factory. The sand stuck to your back and balls, some jackass was forever stepping on you and the wind always blew the cherry off your cigarette.

The grocery store was a fucking zoo. The animals were clearing the shelves at an unbelievable rate. We were running to the stockroom every five minutes to fill the void, but there was no keeping up, the stuff was gone the moment we replaced it. I'd always thought the store would have run a lot more smoothly without customers. They got in the way. Their primary function was to cause headache and nausea. I stalked around the place trying to do my job, sneering, pushing people out of the way. These fools were tripling my work-load—couldn't they see that? We kept selling out the shelves left and right. The announcement of each of these sellouts was their cue to pitch a collective fit. You'd have thought the world was coming to an end. Maybe it was. Maybe it should have been. I wouldn't have minded one bit.

I got a call from the Sause Box. Angel. She needed forty pounds of ground round. The tourists had seized the place and eaten everything in their path, it was pandemonium. I was more than happy to get out of the grocery store. If I was lucky, the place would blow up while I was gone, leaving no survivors.

I ran the meat through the grinder, bagged, weighed, and walked it on over to the Box.

The bar was piled to the rafters with middleclass couples and their screaming hellspawn—all of them demanding to be fed and watered that very instant. The Pope was an idiot. What we needed was *more* birth control, a worldwide mandatory birth-control program to be put into effect immediately—for the rich, poor, and middle classes alike. God was dead, alright. And humanity was a sack of shit. The Pope obviously didn't get out much.

Angel met me at the door. I had the meat slung over my shoulder. She cleared us a path, shoving people aside, trying to get me to the kitchen before the sack split and the meat spilled to the floor—*Out of the road, assholes! The provider is plowing through!*

It was ancient Rome, Nero's rule, the golden jaded days of unbridled madness, the far-side of idiocy. As we pushed our way through the throng and the morons caught sight of the meat, they began to whistle and shout, catcall and salivate—you'd have thought it was a stripshow. I had half a mind to drop it all down on some waste of sperm and egg's head, or simply walk it over to one of the All-American families, toss the sack onto their table, slice it open, and pass out forks. That's what capitalism ultimately was: tossing meat to dogs with dollars in their jaws.

Well, we made it to the kitchen without mishap. Which is to say, before I snapped and acted out one of the afore-mentioned fantasies. It was disappointing. To snap would have felt so good. I just didn't have it in me, or didn't have the balls to let it out. I was all blather and smoke. It was a depressing realization.

"Thanks a lot," Angel said. "It's been crazy here today."

I threw the meat down. "It's been crazy every-where. The sun's shining. It draws them out from un-der the rocks. They turn off their TVs and seek other forms of entertainment."

"It'll be even worse tonight."

"I'm glad I'm not going to be here. I'd rather die and go to hell."

"I don't blame you. People suck."

"They're shit."

"They're worse than shit." She glanced around the room, chewing her nails, taking it in. My poor, beau-tiful Angel. As manager, she had the thankless task of making it all run like a well-oiled machine. She was re-sponsible for it all, and it was all madness, a pile of noth-ing—less than nothing.

I saw Easy back there slaving over the grill, thirty or forty food tickets lined up, another being put in ev-ery other minute. I gave him a wave. He didn't wave back—he had no time to. He'd fallen so far behind there was no catching up anymore, it was hopeless, he was

fucked. The waitresses were complaining, the customers were complaining. The waitresses were hating the
customers, the customers were hating the waitresses—
and all of them were hating Easy. Easy looked about
ready to have a meltdown, say *fuck it*, pick up a gun
and call it a day—EAT THIS, MOTHERFUCKERS! He
was moving like a madman, but it wasn't enough, it
was never enough. I watched him pop a handful of am-
phetamines and take it to the next level, go from fast to
flying—expedient but insane—The Danger Zone. In the
service industry, drugs were a necessary tool. Without
them, your life was hell, you just couldn't keep up—or
even begin to find the deluded nail that kept you hanging there. Easy was a pro. He'd have it all under control
soon enough. By the time his shift was over he'd have
to drink half an ocean of whiskey just to get back down
and feel remotely human again—assuming he didn't
have a heart-attack first. I'd been a short-order cook
myself. I knew the drill all too well. You did this atonal
death-dance night after night until you were finished,
used up, burnt from the inside out and the other way,
too, coked, cooked, and eaten alive by it. All for five
dollars an hour and no benefits whatsoever. And by the
time you quit or were fired, you were definitely in need
of medical attention—a surgeon, a shrink, a nightmarish trip to rehab. Then you turned around, held your
nose, and dove back in—got another job in the service
industry. If you snapped, that meant you'd been there
awhile, and after awhile, the service industry was all
you were qualified for. You were locked in the cage. You
were back on the cross. Your stress level skyrocketed.
You upped your drug and alcohol intake and your disgust for humanity deepened, parallel to the disgust you
felt for yourself. You became intolerable to be around,
people outside the service industry couldn't understand

you, you were alien, they were alien. You spent your off-hours alone, or with other service industry workers, people whose hatred for humanity ran as deep as your own. Then, given time, even they became too much to stomach, intolerable, all of them. You stewed alone, solitary, the only complete man in the industry, the last of the sound and sane. You were a lifer, a pro. Maybe you keeled over while turning a cheeseburger one day, found it pleasant, more appealing than facing the endless days to follow, and allowed yourself to be pulled through the death-door—goodbye orders up, hello oblivion. Maybe you climbed the TV-tower or walked into the nearest McDonald's carrying a 30-ought-6 and a Gideon Bible to usher in Endtime for all those present. Maybe you thought you were doing them a favor. Maybe you got smart and chucked it all before you reached that point. Became an artist or a panhandler. Or, the success rate of artists being what it was, both.

"If it stays like this," Angel said, "we might need you tonight."

"You have my number," I said. I neglected to tell her I'd taken up residence elsewhere and that the number she had was no longer worth a fuck. She could go ahead and call it. I'd be up at the Nickerdown, knocking back Irish whiskey and lecturing Barley on just what was wrong with humanity, how we were doomed and why nothing could be done to correct it short of letting the missiles fly.

Jenny was working the bar. A sight for sore eyes, that woman—just like the song. I squeezed through the crowd to say hello. Actually, I needed a drink. But it was always nice talking to Jenny. Almost as nice as ... well, drinking the drinks she poured.

She saw me coming and had a shot lined up even

before I got there. I thanked her.

"My pleasure, Picasso. You're lucky you're not working today. These people are disgusting."

"It's the same at the grocery store—they're not used to clear skies and open space. It rattles their bells, they go apeshit, they can't relax. I think Angel wants me to work tonight."

"God, how can you stand it? I'd lose my mind working two jobs. I'm losing my mind just working here. I can only take people for so long—after that, forget it, all I wanna do is disappear."

"I'm sick with love, remember? The booze helps."

"Have another," she said. "You'll need it." She grabbed a glass, tipped the bottle high. There were thirty or forty people trying to get her attention, but she ignored them for the moment.

"Thanks, Jen."

"So, maybe I'll see you around tonight?"

"Maybe. I don't know. I sort of have plans."

"Well, stop in for last call. That way Angel won't be able to rope you into working."

"She'd put a broom in my hand before I got the glass to my mouth."

"We could go to my place. You could meet me there. I have some beer ... We could talk, get to know each other better. I hardly know you."

I was beginning to feel uncomfortable—why, I don't know. Jenny was a friend. You should know your friends. I knew her as well as I knew anybody. Maybe I didn't know anybody. Maybe I didn't want to. I gulped my drink. Jenny stood there, smiling. She had a great smile. She had a great everything.

"Hey, listen," I said, "I have to go. You don't have any speed, do you?"

"God, yes. Sally was passing it out this morning.

Employee incentive. You gotta love the perks around here." She dug into her pocket and came up with a handful of blacks and yellows, also a few colors and shapes I'd never seen before.

"Two of these," she said, "and your hair will stand on end. You'll be Superman."

"What are they?"

"Hell if I know. Open up."

I opened up. Jenny took aim and fired them into my mouth—bullseye. I washed them down with a shot, gulped, gagged, and got the hell out of there. I was afraid Jack would send out a search party if I lingered any longer. Besides, the look I saw in Jenny's eye was unnerving. She'd never looked at me that way before. I hadn't seen Tia Correlia for close to three months. The flesh was weak. I was weak. That look meant nothing but trouble.

When I got back to the store, Jack was bitching. I'd been gone too long. The checkout-lanes were backed up. I reeked like a barrel of whiskey. There was anger in the air. But I worked with such speed and efficiency I made everyone else look inept. Jack wound up giving me a twenty-five cent raise. I'd unwittingly set a new standard of performance. A standard by which, in the future, we could all be measured—and fall miserably short of. Unless Jack wanted to spring for pharmaceuticals every day.

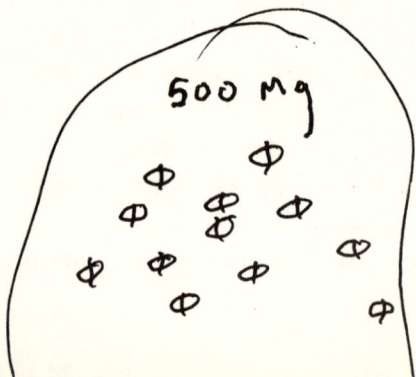

***

Linen napkins, cut crystal, comfortable chairs, the sun setting over the lake, cigars, subservient waiters, cool breezes, candles, ease, table after table of the well-dressed, pompous elite ...

Barley and I had cashed in our beer cans. Now we were out on the deck at the Nickerdown, sipping Irish whiskey and looking conspicuous. I picked up one of the menus the waiter had left with us.

"Barley, look at this—twenty-five dollars for a piece of fish. Fuck that, I'd rather starve."

"Check out the appetizers. Ten bucks for a plate of sauteed mushrooms. They're good, though."

"For ten bucks they'd better be hallucinogenic."

"Let's get another drink."

"Right."

I waved the waiter over. They made the poor bastard wear some sort of turn-of-the-century monkey suit—Batman's Alfred, trotting drinks to Bugsy Malone and his cronies at the Brown Derby, circa 1930. I'd seen him roll his eyes the moment we walked in, passing judgement, no doubt, on *our* work-clothes. Now he was rolling them again as he made his way across the deck. Our drinks were mostly ice, they looked bigger than they really were. We'd been keeping him busy.

"Are you ready to order, gentlemen?" He had his pen out, tapping it impatiently against the palm of his hand. Like any sane waiter, he hated us. Seeing that, I could forgive him for agreeing to wear that ridiculous uniform.

"I'm sure that the food here would sicken even a dog," I told him. "The rotgut, however, is superb. My compliments to your bartender. The time has come for another round."

"Not according to *my* watch," he said.

Ah, a bit of fire, a bit of spark and flame. I liked that. Nothing made me sicker than an ass-kissing waiter without balls or self-esteem, mouth agape, crouched low so as to better swallow your shit.

"Well," I said, "your watch is obviously slow." I handed him a fiver to give to whomever it was pouring the drinks. I put a second one into his vest pocket, then another for good measure.

He turned and made for the bar.

"Are you crazy?" Barley said.

"Hey, he's a brother. Us service people gotta look out for our own."

"That money you're giving away is half mine."

"Relax. We're loaded."

Our waiter returned with fresh drinks. They were better this time, less ice, the tumblers filled to the brim. I thanked him.

"See how that works, Barley?"

"I'm hungry. I haven't eaten all day." He still had drywall dust in his hair, paint on his shirt. Barley often worked through his lunch-break while his boss hit the nearest McDonald's. It was tragic.

"We'll get something later," I told him. "Drink up."

We had several more rounds. Then several more after that. For every other round the waiter brought us, I tipped both he and the bartender. We were getting every other round on the house—I assumed. It worked that way just about everywhere, it was standard etiquette. Waiters and bartenders were free agents. It didn't take much to get them to fuck over their employers.

"This is good shit," Barley said. "The Irish know what's what."

"You ain't kidding." I was well on my way. The

good stuff was so smooth it almost went down like water. The danger there was obvious. But the cost usually kept you in check. Sooner or later, you had to switch to something cheaper.

"I wish I could drink like this all the time," Barley said. "How much is this stuff, anyway?"

"I don't know. We should probably get on the cheap shit soon."

I flagged our waiter. The sun had fallen into the lake. The crickets were fiddling Dixie and I was drunk.

"How are you gentlemen doing over here? Another round?"

"That depends," I said. "How much are these fucking things?"

"Six dollars."

"Oh shit ..." Twelve bucks a round. I checked my wallet. I'd already handed out close to 40 dollars in tips, without even realizing it. There were only two twenties left. We were in trouble. The waiter stood there. Barley spilled his drink trying to light a cigarette. The waiter whipped out a rag and a lighter. I tried to do some quick addition in my head but had no idea how many rounds we'd had.

"Could I see our tab, please?"

It was ridiculous. The drinks ran the length of two Guest Checks. None of them had been on the cuff, apparently. What the hell was the service industry coming to? This was a violation of etiquette, a betrayal of the Brotherhood, a slap in the face to bartenders everywhere— blood betraying blood. Well, fuck.

The total came to $96. We were mathematically buggered.

I knew Barley didn't have any money.

I had to think. The waiter was hovering over me.

My liver hurt.

"We'll have another round," I said. I had to come up with something. They only let you wash dishes in the movies. You couldn't settle up that way in real life.

"How much do we owe?" Barley asked.

I didn't say anything. I couldn't think—the crickets were making too much noise. An atonal Schoenberg concerto. Latter-day Coltrane madness.

"Oh, fuck, you gotta be kidding me!" Barley said.

"Don't worry. I'll think of something ..."

Then I had it. The tab wasn't computerized, it was antiquated pen and paper—scratched upon the outdated honor-pad. Which meant it couldn't be accurately accounted for. If the waiter were to lose it, that would be that.

"Goddamnit," Barley said. "I can't believe this! I knew we should've never returned those fucking cans."

Our waiter was on his way back with another round. We'd passed the hundred-dollar mark.

"Relax. We owe him a hundred and two dollars now. We might be able to get around it though."

"You asshole!"

"Be quiet, he's coming. Let me work."

The waiter set our drinks down. He picked up our tab, did the math. Unless he was on the hustle, we were fucked.

"Listen," I said. "We have a little problem here. My associate and I have gone over the figures and it appears that this bar-tab exceeds our combined worth. I got forty dollars in my wallet. If you were to misplace our check, that would leave me just enough for a tip."

There was a moment of awkward silence. Neither of us said anything. Barley was looking at his shoes, mouthing the word "asshole" over and over like a mantra—trying to find his center.

I reached into my wallet, laid the bills down by my drink.

The waiter glanced around the room to see who might be watching—sly, casual, discreet. He was a player. We were in the black again. With one swift sleight of hand he scooped the money from the table, slipped it into his pocket and balled up our tab. A pro.

"Thanks," I said.

"Don't mention it, bro."

"Listen, I tend bar at the Sause Box. Stop by sometime. I'll hook you up."

"Right on. Thanks."

He went back to his job. Barley and I finished our six-dollar drinks. The crickets played away, legs rubbing legs, in insect time. The service industry was full of disgruntled employees just like that waiter and myself, the whole disgraceful mob of us sticking it to the Man every chance we could. It was a wonder anyone was able to stay in business.

"Let's get the hell out of here," Barley said.

"Right. We can make last call at the Box."

"We're broke."

"So what?"

I woke up on the ground, about five feet from Barley's ailing American flag. I'd been too drunk to make the trailer, apparently. My head felt like a bag of broken glass. The birds were chirping madly, my stomach was in my mouth. Somewhere in China, a monk was carefully washing his ricebowl ...

I puked, rolled over. I put my face to the sky, closed my eyes.

The flag flapped back and forth.

An image of my father came to mind, something I'd

never been able to shake. I was probably 12-years-old at the time. It was Summer, late July or early August. It was hot and I hadn't been able to sleep all night. My room was upstairs, my window faced the street. I was sitting on the floor, my feet hanging out the window, sneaking a cigarette and watching the sun come up, listening to the birds sing. As I was sitting there, my father drove up in his old green truck, a relic that his father had once wheeled around town in—drunkenly. The thing was a fucking wreck but my old man wouldn't scrap it. He always said he was going to restore it some day when he had the time and the money. But he never had the time or the money. So he just kept driving it, the truck falling further into ruin each year. When he pulled up in it that morning, it looked like some ghostly monstrosity resurrected from an auto graveyard operating out of a lot just south of Hell. I remembered watching him kill the motor, pull the keys from the ignition, lay his head against the steering wheel. He sat there the longest time, slumped like that. Then he got the door open, staggered out and began kicking the shit out of the thing, caving in the front corner-panel, the rust and the swearwords flying. As he was doing this, he lost his balance and fell backwards into the gravel. He reached for the doorhandle, tried to pull himself up, fell again. He kept doing this over and over—staggering to his feet, falling, pulling himself up, falling again. Finally, he gave it up—just lay there in the gravel like a dog, on his hands and knees, his forehead bleeding. He was in as bad a shape as that fucking truck. I remember the shock I felt at seeing him kick it. He loved that old piece of shit. If anyone else had kicked it, he would have thrown them through a wall.

I don't know how long he lay out there. After he fell, after I saw that he was bleeding, I shut the window and got back into bed. I slept most of the day. When I woke up, he wasn't out there anymore ...

Anyway, I thought about that as the birds chirped the sun up and Barley's flag moved in the breeze above me, casting its mad American shadow.

***

I hadn't had a shower in more than a week. My scent was even getting to me. I hitched a ride into town and stopped by my mother's place before punching the clock at the grocery store and giving them another day of my directionless life. No one in Stillwater ever locked their doors. My mother was no exception. I got one foot over the threshold before she accosted me.

"WHERE HAVE YOU BEEN? YOU LOOK LIKE A WINO! YOU HAVE BLOOD ON YOUR FACE!"

"I'm sick. Leave me alone." I was too exhausted to get into it with her. These arguments never led anywhere. A two-headed dog chasing its tail round and round—year after year after year—barking, scratching, and pissing upon the family tree—all of it pointless.

"YOU STINK! YOU HAVE VOMIT ON YOUR SHIRT! LOOK AT YOURSELF!"

"I've looked. I'm tired. I have to go to work."

"WHERE HAVE YOU BEEN?"

"Lance Barley has a trailer. I'm living there."

"HE DOESN'T HAVE A SHOWER?"

"No shower, no stove, no TV ..."

"LIVING LIKE A BUM! YOU ENJOY IT!"

"Yes, that must be it."

"WHAT KIND OF PERSON DOESN'T HAVE A TELEVISION?"

"Are you finished? I have to go to work."

"YOU STINK! YOU NEED A SHOWER!"

"That's what I'm here for." I tried to get around her, but she blocked the hall. I knew what was coming next. It was in the script, we'd played the scene a thousand times.

"I HAD NO IDEA IF YOU WERE DEAD OR ALIVE!"

"I'm sorry. It didn't occur to me."

It was funny. Whenever I was living in another city, neither one of us ever wrote or called. An entire year would pass without either of us making any effort to stay in touch. But if I was living with her and disappeared for ten days, all hell broke loose.

"YOU COULD'VE BEEN DEAD! I WOULDN'T HAVE KNOWN!"

"UNLESS YOU ARE NOTIFIED OTHERWISE, CONSIDER ME ALIVE!" There, I'd done it, I'd raised my voice. These exchanges never came to an end until I snapped and began screaming at a volume equal to her own.

"TAKE A SHOWER! YOU STINK!"

I made for the bathroom. My mother set herself down in front of *The Today Show*. Bryant Gumbel was on—her golden boy—telling the nation what was what about breast implants and other hard realities.

That shower felt good. I let the hot water pound down and work its magic, melt my spine and wash the week away. I was in there a full fifteen minutes, eyes closed, breathing the steam, allowing my mind to go blank. I let loose an involuntary Om. I'd never done that before, I had no idea where it came from. I did it twice: "OMMMMMM ... OMMMMMM ..." I was in Tibet. I was having tea with the Dalai Lama. I was a man bowing down before stone. I was the flower and the bee, the root and the tree.

Then my mother began beating on the door.

"YOU'VE BEEN IN THERE AN HOUR! YOU'RE WASTING MY WATER!"

I pretended not to hear her. It was too nice in there. I didn't want it to ever end. I thought I might just stand beneath that showerhead for the remainder of my life, let the water flow, forget I'd ever been born. Goodbye sad and soiled world. I'm swimming into the womb again.

"TURN THAT WATER OFF! GET OUT OF THERE, YOU BUM! I KNOW YOU CAN HEAR ME!"

The spell had been broken. It was no longer peaceful in there. I turned the water off, killing the Om, spilling the tea. I'd been yanked again. My mother kept banging away. She was probably out there waving a pair of forceps. My entire life up to that point had been one long breech-birth. Why should it work any differently now?

I toweled off. The mirror was fogged with steam. I couldn't even see myself—I couldn't see anything. I liked that. The world beyond the womb was overrated. Amniotic fluid was where it was at. People were loathe to admit it, but any damn fool knew that it was true. Man's idea of Heaven was just a dim recollection of the womb—swathed in baptismal robes rather than placenta. The only way back was through the death-door. But most of us were afraid to die. It was a combination of instinct and simple observation. The lip of the grave looked a hell of a lot less inviting than the fleshy, living lips of the vagina. Clearly, they were two radically different doors. That's where religious mythology came into play, I guess.

I went up to my room to see if I'd left any clean clothes behind. I found a Famous Faces t-shirt—a caricatured

Hemingway with an insane shiteating grin—and a pair of corduroys that didn't quite fit. I put them on, tossed my dirty stuff into the attic, sealed the little door back up. Maybe I'd father a son before I died. Maybe he'd find those filthy clothes some day and consider them a clue to my existence, an insight into who and what his old man had been. Blood. Vomit. A penny for each eye...

I laced my combat boots and stomped down the stairs to poke around in the refrigerator. The thing was packed with leftovers, most of them going bad. I grabbed a chicken wing, got it to my mouth. Before I could bite into it, my mother's radar went off. She came raging down the hall:

"PUT THAT CHICKEN BACK!"

"I'M STARVING!"

"THAT'S *MY* FAULT?"

"YOU'VE GOT FOOD ROTTING IN HERE!"

"IT WOULDN'T BE ROTTING IF YOU'D COME HOME FOR DINNER!"

"I'M HOME, I'M HERE! I'M EATING THIS CHICKEN WING!"

"OH NO YOU'RE NOT! I WON'T HAVE YOU WASTING IT!"

Further argument was futile. We'd long ago crossed over into the realm of the insane.

I bit into the chicken wing. It was shit.

"PUT THAT BACK!"

She looked like a rabid dog.

I put it back. I could always grab a donut at work.

My mother returned to the livingroom to see what Bryant Gumbel had to say. I sat at the kitchen table and lit a cigarette.

"DON'T SMOKE IN HERE!"

"I HAVEN'T EVEN INHALED YET!"

The woman had some sort of sixth sense when it

came to cigarettes. If someone lit up in Idaho, she knew about it. Her father and six of her brothers had died of cancer. My father's family had a history of it too—that and heart disease. They'd all died before the age of fifty. I'd had a lump removed already. We all smoked like active volcanoes. Except for my mother, who planned to live forever simply to say I told you so.

"YOU'RE GOING TO GET CANCER! YOU'RE GOING TO KILL US BOTH!"

I didn't want to kill her. I ground it out and added a minute or two to both our lives. We'd be able to argue that much longer.

"I'LL FINISH IT OUTSIDE!"

"YOU'LL END UP DEAD! JUST YOU WAIT!"

Well, that was all anyone could do. Short of suicide.

I hadn't noticed when I'd come in, but during the time I'd been away, my mother had hung the paintings I'd given her that summer, the ones I thought she'd tossed to the trash man. There were two of them hanging in the kitchen, three in the hallway, a large one in the diningroom. They looked pathetically out of place. It was a horrible thing to see, somehow. And it broke my fucking heart.

I had every intention of walking into the livingroom and telling her all the things I'd never told her before. But all I did was walk out the backdoor. I hated goodbyes.

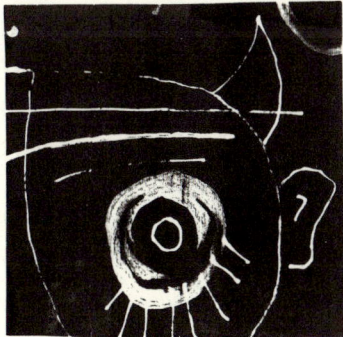

MR. SOUL

I stopped by the drugstore for Mylox and cigarettes. I was late for work, but what the fuck? The body wants what it wants.

I ran into Jenny. She was buying a box of Tampax and a chocolate bar. She looked as hungover as I was. But not as unhappy.

"Hey, Jen—what's up?"

"Lupus!" She threw her arms around my neck, gave me a big kiss.

"What was that for?"

"Last night," she said.

I was too hungover to think back that far. I'd obviously gotten ahold of some bad ice.

"What was last night?"

"You don't remember?"

"I'm not sure. Did I see you at the Nickerdown?"

"No, it was the Sause Box. I was working. Some tool at the bar was throwing me a bunch of shit. He was getting really nasty, he kept calling me a whore or whatever—maybe it was cunt. Anyway, you freaked! You pulled him right off his stool. You put him on the floor and let him have it!"

"I hit him?"

"No, you gave him this crazy lecture on how to

treat a lady. You defended me—you know, my honor. You told him I was your wife. You declared your love for me to everyone in the bar."

"Oh, Christ. I'm sorry, Jen."

"No, don't be. It was sweet. You climbed on top of the pooltable and announced it. You even made a toast. You were so cute."

I stared at the bottles behind the counter, the cork-screws, the condoms, the party-hats. I had a bad feeling. Something in the pit of my gut was sounding an alarm.

"You really don't remember?" Jenny asked. "I mean, if you do, you can admit it. It's nothing to be embarrassed about."

I shrugged. She really believed I was lying—I could see it.

She kept looking at me.

"Sorry, Jen. I really don't remember."

"Well, you were great. I'm glad you were there. That guy was a jerk. Thanks for standing up for me. It was a sweet thing to do, Lupus."

"I was drunk."

"Drunk or not, it was sweet of you."

"Not all blackouts are ugly, I guess."

I put my Mylox on the counter, my cigarettes, a pack of Tic-Tacs. The clerk rang it up, bagged it. I took the Mylox out. I had a pull, Jenny had a pull. I took the cigarettes out, put them in my pocket. I took the Tic-Tacs out, balled up the bag and sank it into the waste-basket behind the register.

"Nice shot," the clerk said.

"Thanks, bud."

As we were leaving, Jenny said, "So, you wanna come over again tonight?"

"Your place? Was I there last night?"

"Of course—you have to remember *that*." I didn't say anything.

Jenny stopped walking. I turned around.

"Goddamnit, Lupus! I can't believe you!"

"What?"

"You're such a JERK sometimes!"

"What? What did I do?"

She stormed across the street, throwing things from her purse as she plowed through the early morning tourist traffic—Kleenex, coins, hairclips, pens, make-up, crumpled Guest Checks, candy wrappers, coasters, lottery tickets, flattened cigarette packs ...

I stood there—dazed, incredulous. A war criminal.

"Jenny, wait! What did I do? I'm sorry!"

"DON'T WORRY!" she screamed. "YOU DIDN'T DO IT VERY WELL!"

"Jenny, I'm sorry—I didn't know!"

"I CAN'T BELIEVE I LET YOU COME IN MY MOUTH!"

She got her keys out, unlocked the Sause Box, slammed the door. I stood there. The door came flying open. She ran to the curb and flung her purse at me—it landed in the street. She stomped back to the bar, slam, bang. She stormed out again, picked up her purse, ran inside.

The tourists had all paused to gawk.

"Take it somewhere else!" one of them said. A moron wearing a Hawaiian shirt and a sunvisor. He had his wife and kids with him. They were all identically dressed.

I pointed West: "THE BEACH IS THAT WAY, RUBBERNECK! GO FRY ON IT!"

I called in sick to the bar that night. It was no fabrication. All afternoon, while cutting steaks, I'd had to fight an urge to bring that butcher's knife down on my hand. I even considered shoving my arm into the meatgrinder—an act of penance serious enough to absolve the sin. Guilt was a powerful emotion. I was sick alright ...

***

I went back to the trailer and lay on the floor like a gutshot dog. I told Barley all about it—the blackout, the Jenny debacle, the lure of the blade. He seemed to think I was overreacting, he didn't see the tragedy.

"I not only humiliated Jenny and myself," I told him, "I humiliated Tia, too. I betrayed her. I'm a piece of shit. I deserve to die alone in a madhouse."

"Well, stick your arm in that meatgrinder and you might get your wish."

"I've got it coming to me. I deserve it."

"Tia doesn't even know. Why are you so worried? You don't have to tell her a damn thing. Shit, she hasn't even written you. It's been three months—she's probably sleeping with one of her old boyfriends by now."

"I have to tell her—I can't lie, not to Tia."

"I don't know what to tell you," he said. "You romanticize everything."

"Christ, I've betrayed Tia, and now Jenny hates me too."

"Jenny's cool. She'll get over it. So you blacked out—big deal."

"Blacking out is one thing. I had my dick in her mouth and I don't remember it—to her, it's a big deal."

"She'll get over it. She always does."

"What's that supposed to mean?"

"It means what it means."

"No, you're wrong—Jenny's not like that. Don't talk about her that way. It isn't fair. I don't like it."

"She's okay."

"She's great. I think I'm half in love with her—that's the worst part of it all. I love them both. My mother was right—I'm a fuck-up. I should have been aborted, I should have been snuffed in utero."

"You got a blowjob—that's not really sex. Besides, you don't even remember it. You didn't really betray anybody."

"I'm not even going to address that—but for the record, I think something more took place than just a blowjob."

"You were blacked out. You don't know what the fuck happened."

"When I woke up this morning I had blood all over my face. I didn't have any cuts anywhere. It was spooky. I thought I'd killed somebody."

"So—what was it?"

"I don't know ... I mean, I'm not sure. When I ran into Jenny this morning she was buying Tampax ..."

"Too drunk to fuck! Nice work, cannibal!"

"Go ahead," I told him, "laugh."

***

My old man had a little brother. He was still alive. He was the last of the last, the only member of his family who hadn't bought it yet. But he was 49, so his number was just about up. His name was Fritz. His friends called him U-Boat. His ex-wives called him Asshole. I called him Uncle Bone. The ex-wives were right—he was an asshole. But he was my uncle.

He lived about a half mile from my mother. I hadn't seen him in years. I knocked on his door.

"WHO'S THERE?" he screamed.

"Fritz, it's me. Open up."

"WHO THE FUCK'S *ME*? I DON'T KNOW ANY *ME*!"

"GODDAMNIT, BONE, IT'S ME—LUPUS!"

"LUPUS WHO?"

"YOUR BROTHER'S SON! HOW MANY LUPUSES DO YOU KNOW?"

"WELL, GODDAMNIT, THE DOOR'S UN-LOCKED—COME ON IN! YOU KNOW HOW TO OPEN A DOOR, DON'T YOU?

I walked in. He was sitting at the kitchen table with a syringe stuck in his belly.

"Hey there, Shag, what's happening?" He always called me Shag—it had something to do with my hair, I think.

"You need a fucking barber," he said.

"Probably."

He had a fifth of Popov on the table. The seal hadn't been broken yet. It was almost noon. His hands were shaking like a motherfuck. First stage D.T.'s. If he didn't have a drink soon, he'd be foaming at the mouth.

"Listen, Shag: If you help me get this shit injected, I'll let you have some of my vodka."

Bone was diabetic. He needed his insulin. He needed that vodka, too. He needed it just as much as he needed the insulin.

"I'm not too good with needles," I told him.

"Come on, chickenshit—all you gotta do is push the plunger down and pull the needle out. I can't do it—look at me. I'd break the fucker off before I got it out of my belly."

"Alright—but if I fuck it up, don't bitch."

"You won't fuck it up. Don't worry."

I sat down. The syringe was hanging from his gut. The needle was thin, it had a bit of bend to it, some flexibility. When he spoke, it bounced up and down. I was afraid to grab it.

"Stop talking," I told him.

"Alright—just do it, get it in there!"

"Okay—here we go, Bone. Hold still. You ready?"

"FUCK, YES! HURRY UP!"

I grabbed it, closed my eyes, pushed the insulin in, yanked the needle out.

"Okay, good job—give me that vodka."

I cracked the seal, put the bottle in his hand, guided it to his mouth, held it there while he gulped and gagged.

Visiting relatives was always a joy.

Bone kicked back in his wheelchair. He'd lost another leg since I'd seen him. It was the diabetes and the

booze—they didn't mix. Every year he lost a little more
of himself—a toe, a foot, a finger, a leg.

"Goddamnit, Lupus—where the fuck have you
been? You're looking tired, kid. You look just like your
old man. Christ ... I miss him. What happened to you?"

"I don't know. I'm okay—just kicking around.
Chicago, mostly."

We were sitting at the table, passing the vodka
back and forth. The shades were drawn. There was crap
scattered everywhere—clothes, bottles, cans, car parts,
tools. The place was tiny, one room with a roof over it.
Bone slept on the couch. Next to the couch, he had an
engine up on blocks, motor-oil dripping into the car-
pet.

"What the hell's in Chicago?" he asked.

"A woman."

"A woman? That city's a fucking sewer. What
happened—you get sick of it?"

"No, she kicked me out."

"I could never live in the city. I hate cities."

"I'm moving back there. I'm gonna marry her."

"They whacked my other leg, kid—check it out.
Got a couple fingers, too."

"You've gotta stop drinking so much."

"Don't get married, Shag. You'll never be the
same. Why'd she kick you out?"

I started laughing—I couldn't stop. Bone was
territorial about his booze. I had the bottle between my
legs. It was all he had in the house—he was getting nervous.

"Stop hogging the vodka, Shag—you finish that
and I'll crawl out of this wheelchair and kick your ass!"

I handed him the bottle. I was still laughing.

"What's so funny?" he asked. He had to squint
to see me—I hadn't noticed it earlier. He faked it well,

but he was going blind.

"I'll get you some more," I told him. "Don't worry."

"Goddamn right you will."

"How are your eyes, Bone?"

"My eyes are fine. Are you going downtown?"

"Yeah. I have to go to the bank."

"Get me a half-gallon—Popov. I'll give you the money."

"Are you sure your eyes are alright? Can you see?"

"Fuck it—it's the sugar. I see okay."

I gave him the bird. "How many fingers am I holding up?"

"I'm fucking blind!—what difference does it make? When are you going downtown?"

"I can go right now, if you want me to."

"I want you to. Take some money—my wallet's by the couch."

"Forget it, Bone—it's on me."

"What are you—a big shot now?"

"Yeah."

"Well, don't bring back any of that cheap shit. No Popov. I want the good stuff—Absolut. You hear me, boy?"

"I hear you."

"You oughta get yourself a haircut while you're down there, too."

"How do you know I need a haircut, Bone? You can't even see me. I have a crewcut for all you know."

"Bullshit. You've needed a haircut your whole fucking life—why would it be any different now? Your old man, he wore the same suit for fifteen years. People stay the same more than they change, Shag. Don't you know that by now?"

I got up and walked to the door. I hadn't written Tia yet. I tried to write her every day. The mail went out at 4—I had to get going. The door had a peephole. I pressed my eye to it and looked outside.

"Bone, what was my Dad like?"

"What do you mean?"

"I don't remember him anymore."

"Sure you do."

"No—I don't. I remember *things*. I remember that suit, I remember his hat and the truck he drove, I even remember what his coffee cup looked like—but I don't remember *him*. Who was he, Bone? Just a drunk?"

"What the fuck kind of question is that? He was my brother! You had a brother too, once—remember?"

"Fuck you, Fritz." I was looking at the school across the street.

"HE WAS MY *BROTHER*, YOU LITTLE SHIT! HIS NAME WAS CHARLES! HE LOOKED OUT FOR ME!"

I shut the door and walked away.

He could buy his own fucking booze.

***

It was payday. I stopped at the Sause Box to pick up my check. Easy poured me a drink and slid it across the bar. It was nice out so the place was empty—the undesirables were all at the beach. I looked around for Jenny, but I didn't see her. It was just me and Easy. I dropped some money into the jukebox. I had some paper in my back pocket so I sipped my drink and listened to Billie Holiday and started writing a letter to Tia Correlia. Billie Holiday sounded good, but my pen was running out of ink. Billie finished her song and the John Coltrane Quartet started playing "Chim Chim Cheree." I sailed the pen into the wastebasket behind the bar.

"Try this one, it works."

I turned around. It was Jenny. She'd been working in the back. She handed me her pen.

"Thanks ..."

"What are you writing?"

"Nothing. Just a letter."

"Tia?"

I didn't say anything.

She sat down. She took off her apron and put it on the bar. Easy brought her a drink.

"So, you're still talking to me?"

"Listen," she said. "I'm really sorry about the other day."

"I'm sorry too, Jen. I didn't mean something like that to happen."

"You were drunk. We were both drunk. It happened. It wasn't anybody's fault."

"I feel fucking terrible about it."

"Don't. Shit happens, right?"

"Shit happens. That's a bumper sticker."

"Well, it's true."

"I'm a fuck-up, Jenny."

"Not always," she laughed. "Only when it counts."

"Did I ever tell you I had a brother?"

"No. Really? Does he have a girlfriend?"

"He's dead."

"I'm sorry ... I didn't know."

"He drowned in a plastic swimming pool. He tripped—he hit his head on a fucking Tonka Truck. He was seven. My parents were out of town. I was supposed to be watching him."

Jenny didn't say anything.

"I had some friends over. We were drinking my dad's beer and listening to the Rolling Stones. We were

twelve, that's what we listened to. My little brother liked
the Beatles. He kept bugging me to play the fucking
Beatles. He was driving me nuts. I told him to go outside. He wouldn't go, so I threw him in the backyard
and locked the door ..."

"Lupus, come on—you were only twelve."

"I was his brother. I was supposed to be watching him."

"It was an accident."

"He thought I was so cool. He used to follow me
around like a dog, he imitated everything I did. He
looked up to me. I was his big brother ... I wasn't shit."

A couple of regulars walked in. There was a blast
of sunlight, then the door swung shut again.

"Fuck it," I said. "Shit happens—let's get drunk
tonight, Jen."

"Let's get drunk right now." She walked over to
the jukebox, dropped a handful of quarters down the
slot. The Beatles came blaring out—"Back in the
U.S.S.R." *The White Album*, first track. Easy freshened
our drinks.

"Here's to your little brother," Jenny said.

I raised my glass.

Jenny was alright.

***

I was in the post office. I could see that my box was
full—there were envelopes of all shapes and sizes in
there. I was going through my pockets, trying to find
my key. Whenever I'd lost it in the past, the woman
behind the counter was always good enough to waive
the rules and hand me my mail. But she was gone. They
had a new guy back there now—and he was a petty
little power-mad prick who played it strictly by the
book: no key, no mail. The world was full of these types,

they were worse than medflies and twice as thick. Every year there seemed to be more of them. You couldn't even throw a piss at a gas station anymore unless you knew the secret password—CASH—and could prove beyond a shadow of a doubt that you weren't there to steal the crapper.

So I stood in line, along with half a dozen senior citizens and their contagious senility, rooting around for my mail key. There was an odd stench in the air, an admixture of cabbage and bedpan. I felt a hand on my shoulder. I wheeled around—combat stance. The last few months had made me jumpy.

"Lose something?" It was the Guy Who Kept The Nuts In Line, the one who'd whacked his finger for a pharmaceutical high.

"Yeah," I said, "my fucking mind."

I lowered my fists. His afro looked even more ludicrous in the light of day. It was almost frightening. It made you wish you were packing a gun—just in case you'd run into him on the day he'd gone off the deep-end.

"You dropped this," he said. He had my key in his hand, the gimped one. He put it in my palm, winked. It smelled like he had a load of shit in his pants. But then, I often smelled the same way—maybe it was me.

"Thanks," I said. "I'm always losing that thing."

"Of course you are."

I have no idea what the fuck he meant by that. He kept staring at me with a mystic-idiot gleam in his eyes. Acid. He was probably on his way to work.

"You look nervous," he said.

"I haven't been sleeping."

I turned to open my box, but he got his claw on my shoulder again before I could put the key in the hole.

"I can help you with that," he said.

"No, I'm alright." The guy had been laying drugs on me all Summer, every time I turned around there he was with some new and improved pill to ease my troubled mind. I kept waiting for him to just cut to the chase and offer me a lobotomy.

"What are you afraid of?" he asked.

"Listen," I told him, "I don't need to get hooked on that shit again. Wait till you try to quit—it's living hell."

"Why would I quit? Besides, I rotate. I do downers for a while, then take a few days off—switch to speed or just trip. That way, I don't get addicted, see? I've got it all figured."

"Nice work. Where you getting the acid? They don't still experiment with that shit on patients, do they?"

"None of your business. You want some?"

"No thanks. It's not a very good cure for insomnia."

"Suit yourself ... Let me give you some Xanax." He reached into his pocket and pulled out a sandwich bag full of tiny orange pills, hundreds of them.

"Put that away," I told him.

"What? I've got more Xanax than I know what to do with," he said. "My apartment's full of the shit—my cat's even on it now. I eat it like candy. It doesn't get me high anymore."

"Will you put that shit away!"

The old folks were shooting us some fearful looks. They'd seen people like us on TV—we were usually being led away in handcuffs, sirens whirling, dogs barking, a body being bagged.

"Do you want some or not?" he asked.

"Okay, sure, I'll take a few. Wait till we get outside." Every now and then, I'd take something he'd given me, usually when I couldn't sleep or was about to go off on a customer at work, or when I was just too wracked with heartache and worry to sit still for more than a minute. Mostly, I just stockpiled the stuff—why, I don't know. I guess I figured that if Tia Correlia decided to quit me for good come Fall, I'd have something to turn to, a door to open, a fire exit, an out. You had to cover all your bases when dealing with a thing this big. Love either saved your life or it killed you. God had set it up that way. God was a fucking joker sometimes. Check Adam and Eve. Check the holes in the hands of the Son.

"Take them all," said the Guy Who Kept The Nuts In Line. He was high, he didn't care who saw us. He dumped the entire bag on me. I shoved it into my pocket, quick-like, before one of the old folks in there decided they'd like to see me on *America's Most Wanted*.

"Thanks, asshole."

"You're welcome," he said.

I turned to get my mail, then turned around again. He was still there.

"Do you ever get the feeling that there's something drastically wrong with you?" I asked him. "Like maybe you have a problem?"

"No—why?" He seemed puzzled, as if the question itself was insane.

"I always feel like I have a problem," I told him.

"With what?"

"With everything."

"Take some Xanax," he said. "You'll feel better."

He scratched his balls and disappeared, back to whatever *Mod Squad* episode he'd escaped from.

I pulled my mail out of the box, shut the door.

There was an old man standing to my left, struggling to hold himself up with his walker, glaring at me.

I was glared at a lot in Stillwater. I'd almost gotten used to it. But I thought I'd address it this time. You had to take a stand every now and then if you wanted to retain any self-respect.

I looked the old fart in the eye: "You got a problem, mister?"

"I can't find my key," he said. "That sonofabitch won't give me my mail! I've been picking up my mail here for 35 years!"

"So why you looking at me? I'm not running things, I don't make the rules."

His face flushed red, he tightened his grip on his walker. "You could help me find my key!" he screamed.

"Where'd you put it last? Have you checked your pockets?"

"Goddamnit, I can't reach down that far!"

Oh, Christ—the guy wanted me to fish around in his pocket for it. Where the hell was his family? Why did they let him wander around without an escort? It was insane—the guy could barely walk. He probably lived alone, had no contact with his kids. No one gave a fuck about the elderly anymore, the world was moving too fast, no one had the time to give a fuck.

I put my hand in his pocket. I figured I had the time.

"LEAVE THAT MAN ALONE, YOU CREEP! STOP! STOP!"

I yanked my hand back.

It was a gaggle of old crones, all of them in as bad a shape as the old man, all of them pointing at me in alarm—a withered lynch-mob. I was Bigger Thomas. I was one of the "evil people" they'd seen on TV time and time again.

I backed away. The power-mad prick behind the counter came running out. He was in his late 20s, short, balding, thirty or forty pounds overweight. He huffed and puffed his way across the lobby, hitching his pants as he bridged the gap, his face the color of a hothouse tomato.

"WHAT THE HELL IS GOING ON HERE?"

"I WANT MY MAIL!" the old man screamed.

"NO KEY, NO MAIL!" the clerk shouted. "THAT'S THE LAW!"

"I WANT MY MAIL, YOU SONOFABITCH!"

Soon the old women were screaming too.

"GIVE THE MAN HIS MAIL!"

"YEAH, GIVE HIM HIS MAIL, YOU!"

They'd forgotten all about me. Now the clerk was the Bad Guy. No wonder postal workers were always going off the deep end. They had to operate under a nightmarish amount of rules and regulations, make insane deadlines, deal with the public. All we wanted was our mail. We didn't give a shit what it took to get it to us. And I thought the way I made *my* money was absurd.

I got out of there. I had to throw a piss.

I walked across the street to the Sunoco station and asked the attendant for the key.

***

Well, I'd left the post office with a stack of mail under my arm and only 90 percent of it was junk, so the trip hadn't been in vain. I also had enough tranquilizers now to drop an elephant. But I was trying to stay away from that stuff.

I cracked a beer and flopped down on the floor of Barley's pigsty to separate the junk from the non-junk. It didn't take long. I tossed out the *Publisher's Clearing House* garbage, tore up the offers from *Playboy*, set aside a *Leisure Products* catalog for the hammerheads at the bar, pitched another notice from the collection agency. That left me with four letters, a postcard, and the latest issues of *Verbal Abuse* and *Shit Diary*. Not bad. After weeding out the junk, I was usually left with nothing.

I had this game I played when it came to personal mail. I could always tell by the envelope whether a letter was personal or not, but I wouldn't look at the return address—I just turned them face down and set them aside while weeding through the rest of the shit. Sometimes, I'd even go so far as to open all the junk mail and read it top to bottom before tossing it. Personal mail was often just as big a letdown as junk mail. I liked to prolong the suspense, savor the anticipation, and postpone the disappointment ...

All I was really looking for that summer was a word or two from Tia Correlia—good or bad. Day after day, I waited for that. And when I didn't get it, my day was done, shot, destroyed. There was nothing more to do but drink and toy with the notion of suicide. Suicide was a comforting thought, at times—but it really wasn't an option. My hope was such that it negated self-annihilation. Or maybe I was just a coward. Mostly, I drank. Drinking was a form of suicide, but it was slow, and unlike a shotgun blast, it was forgiving and allowed you time to think. Your head usually hurt the following morning, but at least it was still there—you were always afforded the luxury of reconsidering your position. Of course, I was sharing a trailer with Lance Barley—the king of unregistered firearms—so the possibility for disaster had increased exponentially. Having guns lying around when you were drunk half the time was never a good idea—even if you weren't prone to suicidal thinking.

Anyway, I didn't want to be disappointed just

yet, so I set the letters aside and took a look at the magazines. I checked the tables of contents and saw I had a sonnet in *Shit Diary*. I'd given up writing, more or less, but like the pills I'd once been addicted to, it was hard not to dabble. I wrote poetry now and then—just to keep my finger in the pie. It required less time than fiction, it was direct and to the point, and I could hack it out between paintings. This one was old, I'd written it two years earlier. It was called *Wave a Severed Tongue in Jism Starved Vaginas of Nowhere*, one of my more lyrical pieces. I read the first three stanzas. Then yawned and fell asleep ...

I dreamed I was Dylan Thomas. I was in the White Horse Saloon, roaring drunk, reading poetry from atop a barstool—shouting it, screaming it. The local rummies were cheering me on. There was a knockout brunette at the end of the bar—it was Tia Correlia—she was the one I was reading for, no one else. But she wasn't cheering, she was sneering. With every word I read, she seemed to grow more angry. She lit a cigarette and blew the smoke in my face. I kicked it from her hand. She lit another, inhaled, exhaled—amused, contemptuous. An uncontrollable rage surged through my veins, dark, animalistic, unforgiving. I leapt from the bar and landed on her, toppling the stool, dragging us both to the floor, a million miles down: the final fall ...But when we hit bottom, it was only me, landing on myself.

I pulled the Eight Star out from under the couch, poured myself a tall one, gagged and knocked it back. At six dollars a bottle, Eight Star wasn't the finest of whiskeys, but it was affordable and it got you where you wanted to go just as well as the good stuff did.

I had the radio on. The Cowboy Junkies were

singing a slow, hypnotic version of "Sweet Jane." The radio ran on batteries and the batteries were just about cooked, so the Cowboys were sounding even closer to narcosis than they normally did.

    I sat there on the couch and drank my Eight Star and listened to the Cowboy Junkies drawl and didn't think about anything. Just stared at the wall and let it all glaze ...

I was pissing into a beer bottle when Barley walked in. He'd just come from work, there were flecks of blue paint on his face, drywall dust in his hair. He had a couple six-packs with him, Tall-Boys, one in each hand. He saw the Eight Star sitting out:

    "No letter from Tia today?" He flopped down on the couch, cracked a beer. Budweiser. Those ads were powerful. But no pretty girls appeared.

    "I don't know." I pointed to the letters. They were lying on the floor by the couch, face down. "I'm afraid to look." I'd figured I'd save them for later. Get drunk now and face whatever pain they might inflict from the bottom of the bottle—like putting on a flak-jacket before taking a bullet. I didn't waste any time getting started.

    "My day was shit," Barley said. "Rob's gone insane, I think he's lost it."

    "Rob lost it a long time ago, Barley."

    Rob was Barley's boss. He'd spent the last 25 years inhaling toxins, ingesting lead and god knows what all. It had affected both his body and his mind. I'd met the guy. Every time I saw him he was singing the praises of the house-painting trade, growing more and more excited as he talked, extended monologues so powerfully passionate they seemed almost sexual. He'd often lose his balance while speaking to you, fall over backwards, pick himself up and go right on talking as if nothing had happened. It got to be disconcerting after awhile.

"He's getting worse," Barley said. "He doesn't even work anymore. He just stands under the scaffolding shouting instructions. Nothing's good enough for him. He walks around bitching and screaming all day about what a bunch of fuck-ups we are. He actually grabbed a brush out of my hand today and told me I was holding it wrong. I've been painting houses for three years!—what the fuck? The guy's a freak, you can't get any work done when he's around—and he's always around! I swear to God, every time I walk off to take a piss I think he's gonna follow me to the crapper and tell me how to hold my cock."

"It's all those paint fumes," I said. "He's been in the business too long."

"He *likes* the fumes! Whenever we work indoors he shuts all the windows. We'll be choking on varnish, spraying the shit, but if one of us tries to open a fucking window he freaks out. He's a goddamn junkie and he doesn't even know it—he says he likes the *smell*. If we ask for masks he just laughs, he thinks it's funny. That asshole's gonna give us all brain damage."

"Maybe you should quit."

"I can't quit. What the fuck would I do?"

"Go freelance. That's where the money's at. Bid on the jobs, then pay some chumps five dollars an hour to do the work for you—like Rob does."

"No way, he's got the market cornered. Stillwater's too small. He's the fucking king, there isn't room for anyone else."

"Well, shit, buy yourself a gas-mask then. Go to one of those military surplus stores in Muskegon."

"Those things are too uncomfortable. Besides, I

spent four years in the fucking Army. I'd be having flashbacks every morning—forget it."

"You risk brain damage with any kind of job you take. It's the price you pay for security, it's inevitable."

"What are you talking about? I don't have any security."

"Well, you know what I mean."

"Ah, fuck it. Who cares? Give me some of that Eight Star, Homes."

I rolled him the bottle. The sun was still up, falling golden through the holes in the walls. I didn't have to tend bar that night, which meant I didn't have to deal with any tourists or local drunks. And there was still a chance that one of those letters lying on the floor was from Tia Correlia, telling me she loved me and that all was forgiven.

Barley tossed me a Bud, rolled the Eight Star back.

In a pinch, Budweiser made a pretty good chaser.

"We're gonna need more whiskey," Barley said. He stood up, grabbed his car keys. I threw him some money.

"Get a half gallon," I told him. "Something good—none of this Eight Star crap."

"I'm gonna need more money then. I'm broke."

I told him to stick with the Eight Star.

By midnight we were legless. Barley had gotten some fresh batteries for the boombox and he was playing it at an ear-splitting volume. He was a big Neil Young fan. He kept playing the same song over and over again, something called "Everybody Knows This Is Nowhere." I'd never heard it before and I was already getting tired of it, but it was a great song and it seemed to speak to me in a way most rock 'n' roll songs did not. Most rock 'n' roll seemed to miss the mark, it just didn't work for me. Neil Young was different. There was real passion there, a rawness behind his singing and playing, a damaged quality that I identified with and couldn't help but respond to. It wasn't all just "Louie Louie" and fast cars and trying to bang some chick under the boardwalk. There was something great about all of that, of course, given the right mood, moments when "Louie Louie" hit the spot like nothing else around, times when you wanted to be blinded by a beat, thrust your crotch forward, shake your hips, let go of the wheel and let your libido do the driving. But Neil Young dug deeper than that, he went beyond the crotch, dug his fingers into your ailing heart, clawed at your soul. His music was an exorcism, and like all good blues, it was also a celebration of the human spirit—it brought you up, it elevated you, made your blues universal, put a smile on your face.

But I was too drunk. The music was having the opposite effect. It was bringing me down. I was already down. Too much booze, too many blues. I needed some crotch-rock, I needed some funk.

"THIS IS A GREAT FUCKING SONG!" Barley kept screaming. He'd rewind it and play it again. "ISN'T THIS A GREAT FUCKING SONG?"

"PLAY SOMETHING ELSE!" I told him. "PLAY SOME JAMES BROWN."

"WHAT?"

The boombox was shaking the walls, rattling my teeth, blasting my skull apart.

"SEX MACHINE!" I screamed. "PLAY SEX MACHINE!"

"FUCK THAT SHIT!"

I was so drunk it really didn't matter what the hell he played. I could have listened to crickets fuck and found some sort of sad social significance in it, some deep lyric to drink in and weep along with.

But Barley finally did change the tape.

He played *Arc*, a 35-minute exercise in sonic noise which sounded like the end of the world. Atonal guitars, shrieking feedback, apocalypse. Neil Young gone mad.

I grabbed a can of spray-paint and staggered outside. The stars were out, lonely, cold, lovely that way. I was seeing double so there seemed to be twice as many that night. I wanted to believe that my old man was up there somewhere—looking out for my little brother. But I had never bought the notion of heaven or an afterlife. I wasn't even sure if this world was real, let alone the next. Either way, the old man wasn't in it anymore. Neither was my little brother. They were beyond it all. And they couldn't tell me a thing.

I stood outside in the dark for awhile, looking at the trailer, thinking *this is where I live*, thinking *this is where I've always lived*. I could hear Barley in there, screaming along with the guitars and the feedback, totally in tune with it all, understanding that, at home with that. He'd keep his sanity, he'd survive in this world.

I shook the paint can, listened to the rattle, laughed at the sound of that little ball and went to work:

EVERYBODY KNOWS THIS IS NOWHERE

Tall blood-red letters scrawled across the face of the trailer, the world, the universe.

I stepped back, watched them drip and run.

Pure poetry, no doubt about it.

The stars winked down from the heavens, cold and insipid. I gave them the finger, laughing. Fuck it, I was drunk with the blood of the Father, flush with it. I was a painter and a poet, alive and writhing. The stars were nothing more than dead points of light, long extinguished, non-existent. I was immortal. I was Rimbaud, Gauguin, I was Jesus and Hitler, Buddha, Stalin, and Lupus Totten—I was everyone who had ever been or ever would be. The world was nowhere and it was mine and no one could take that from me, I was heir to it all and it was all so fucking funny I just had to dance a little victory dance right then and there for the amusement of those deaf and dumb stars, those long-dead points of light.

I raised my leg and gave myself a spin, whipping round and round in pirouettes of mad joy, fast, wild, whirling, the stars and all that lie beneath them a blur, a smear of light and dark, a smile. Round and round it all went, the whole mad planet, a whirling carnival of impartial motion—and I screamed and I screamed and I screamed—despair, delight, despair, delight, delight, delight ...

But dancing had never been my forte', unfortunately.

I tripped over my immortal feet, fell into space and split my head on an old hubcap.

The stars blinked out. My day was done.

***

I opened my eyes. My head fell apart. It was dawn, the sun was coming up, the birds were beginning to sing. Familiarity breeds opera.

I got off the couch and walked outdoors to piss and yawn. Did that, zipped up, puked, and went back to the trailer. I looked around: bottles bled of their liquor, tossed into trash-strewn corners, half-eaten meals, Christ hung dead on a wall, back against the rust to cover a hole, garbage bags bulging, rat-chewed, guts spilling to the floor, forks, spoons, fly-infested fish, the fruits of sloth ...

It occurred to me that there might be a Heaven after all—and I had died and gone to Hell the night before.

Barley was sleeping in a lawnchair by the boombox, bottle of beer between his legs, head tipped back, mouth crocodiled, snoring like a chainsaw: Survivor Type.

I was sporting another turban, an old t-shirt, torn into strips for medical purposes, wrapped a little too tightly. Barley had apparently found me lying in a meat-heap the night before, dragged me out of the starlight and into the trailer, patched me up. A regular working class Mother Teresa. I saw my reflection in Barley's Jack Daniels mirror. Spirit of '76. I looked fucking ridiculous.

I had to vomit again. I stepped outside and let it go.

My mail was still lying on the floor. I opened it.
There wasn't anything from Tia Correlia there.
But Lydia had sent me a check for three grand.
My show had been a success.

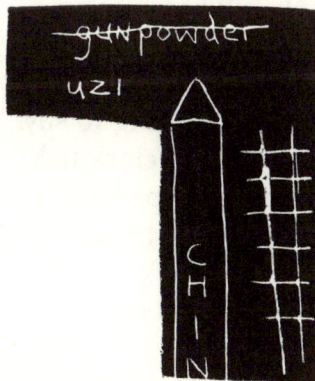

***

I punched the clock.

Linda Lee was eating a longjohn. She had some sort of pastry goo running down the front of her blouse, but aside from that, she looked professional enough.

"You look like hell," she said.

I thanked her.

"You're bleeding," she said. "What happened to your head?"

"I need some coffee." I walked over to the coffee-maker. There weren't any customers in the store yet. That they wouldn't come in at all was too much to hope for, but I was hoping nonetheless. I just wanted to lay down in the milkcooler and sleep for five or six years.

"Maybe no one will show up today," I said. "We'll just kill the lights and go home. Besides, I came into some money today. I'm rich—I don't need to be here."

"You should take that rag off your head. You'll scare the customers away."

"Good. Where's the sugar?"

She didn't say anything.

"Hey, where the hell's the sugar?" I said.

"Jack had a heart attack last night."

"What?"

I turned around, looked at her. She wasn't joking.

"It's his second," she said. "I guess there was a lot more damage this time."

"Christ ... Is he going to be okay?"

"He's in critical condition. They don't know yet."

There wasn't anything to say. I sat down, stared at the wall, listened to the clock tick.

Linda Lee unwrapped my head. She found the wound, cleaned it up a bit, put some iodine on it. She gave me a kiss on the cheek.

Then she wandered off.

I put in some extra hours at the store, trying to cover for him. Jack didn't do as little around that place as he appeared to. I began going in earlier and earlier each morning, just to get a jump on things. I'd punch in around 6 a.m., I'd grind hamburger, cut steaks, run the register and unload delivery trucks till 5, then head over to The Sause Box to tend bar and deal with tourists, waiting on many of the same people I'd waited on at the grocery store during the day. I felt like an indentured servant to some of these morons. The mere sight of their faces was enough to make me sick. But I had to do more than just look at them, I had to listen to them, too. And they all loved to tell me things—their troubles, for the most part. They also liked to tell me about their sex lives, their likes and dislikes, their fetishes, their favorite positions, who they were fucking, who they'd *like* to fuck and why, how their wives wouldn't suck cock, how their husbands wouldn't eat pussy—or how they would, all in great detail. I was a captive ear, they had me trapped there behind the bar, and they knew it. I never said anything, never responded in any way. They may as well have been talking to themselves. I suppose they were. I'd nod now and then, that seemed to be enough. They weren't looking for conversation, just a wailing wall. I'd trot them their drinks and listen to their bullshit all

She looked real good from the waist up, Barbarella type. When she stood and wriggled her way to the drinking fountain I saw that the rest of her was just as fine. What was it about those uniforms? They drove me mad. I could have been involved in a head-on collision and pulled wood on the emergency table the minute a nurse entered the room. Maybe all men were that way. Or maybe I was just a sick bastard.

I got into the elevator, pressed the button, went on up.

I took a wrong turn, doubled back, got lost, wandered the halls for twenty minutes—then found Jack's room. The door was open. I could see him lying there on the bed, tubes running in and out of him. He looked the way I thought he'd look: like a guy who'd just had a massive heart attack.

I tapped the door, walked in.

Jack had the TV going. He turned the volume down and gave me a wave. There were flowers everywhere, on the nightstand, on the windowsill, in vases on the floor, the sickly-sweet stench of love and illness in the air. The guy in the bed next to Jack's had a sheet pulled up over his face. I couldn't really tell if he was dead or not.

Jack raised a smile. "Hey, punk."

I smiled back. "Hey, old man. Good to see you. I didn't bring any flowers ..."

"Good. Any more and I'd probably puke."

"They look nice."

"Yeah. The old women I wait on, they love me."

"Why wouldn't they? You're the Meat Man."

"Shit yes ..."

I pulled up a chair and sat there alongside the bed. Neither of us said anything. The clock ticked, the lights hummed. We were strangers, more or less. It was the first time we'd seen one another outside the grocery store. It was awkward, disorienting—we had no point of reference, no common ground. It was a sad thing to realize, even sadder when I thought how that was the way in which I knew most everybody.

Well, I could sit there like a rock just as long as any man. I listened to the clock tick, looked at the wall. The nurses were making their rounds. I could hear the clack of their heels as they walked the halls. I watched one wiggle by and disappear. I looked at the guy with the sheet over his face and wondered again if he were dead or not.

Jack apparently couldn't stand the silence any longer. He broke.

"So, how are things at the store?"

It was the obvious thing to ask. It mattered less than nothing, but I was glad he'd thrown it out there.

"Everything's fine, Jack. I've been covering for you."

"You mean it's a disaster then."

"Business as usual—right."

"You're a real comfort, Totten."

"I wouldn't worry about it, Jack. Same shit, different day."

"Everything's a mess."

"Of course. What difference does it make?"

"Well, how is everybody?"

"They're okay. Donnie Lynn got the other cheek of her ass tattooed. She's been showing it to just about everyone who walks through the door."

"Oh, for Christsakes!"

"It's a little rocketship or something. The customers seem to like it—the men, anyway."

"Oh, my God ..."

"Is that a healthcode violation?"

"Shut up. I don't wanna hear anymore."

"Okay."

"What the fuck is wrong with her? She's insane— why don't you stop her?"

"*You* never did. What the hell am I supposed to do? I tell her to cool it and five minutes later she's got her ass in the air again."

"You're gonna have to fire her—that's it, she's out!"

"Jack, look—the nurse told me not to upset you. I'm sorry I brought it up."

"I've been shitting in a bedpan for two weeks— I'm already upset!" He was sitting up now, pulling at the tubes in his nose. Not good. I was going to kill the poor bastard with smalltalk. An army of nurses would storm into the room, the accusations would fly, Jack would go to the morgue and I would go on trial and be shot by an angry old woman while being led from the courthouse to the hoosegow, Oswald-style.

"Listen, I'd better go, Jack. You're supposed to be resting."

"I can't rest in this fucking place. Look at all these flowers—it's like a funeral parlor!"

"Pretend you're in a garden. Pretend you're Miss America."

"I hate gardens. All I can think about when I see a garden is the goddamned Bible."

"The Bible?"

"Yeah—Adam and Eve, all that stuff."

"Really? I always think of horseshit, the crap people throw around to make the flowers grow."

"You're strange, Totten."

"No, think about it. You throw shit around and roses grow, everything grows. A farmer spreads cowshit in a field, corn comes up, you eat the corn. You pick a flower, stick your nose in it, and it smells good. But it all comes out of shit. Everything is shit. It's disgusting."

"It's the nature of things! It's not just shit that makes things grow. You bury a dog or a cat and you get mushrooms. It's the life-cycle, fool—that's how it works."

"It's disgusting."

"Nature isn't disgusting."

"I'm not talking about pets buried in the backyard, Jack. I'm talking about excrement being tossed around, about the world being nothing but a big ball of shit."

"What?"

"Nevermind, forget it ... There's shit inside those dead animals, you know—it's just like spreading manure around."

"What difference does it make? It's all organic, it's all the same shit!"

"Exactly!"

"So what's your *point*?"

"I'm just telling you: Gardens make me think of shit. They sure as hell don't make me think of Adam and Eve."

"What—you an atheist or something?"

"I don't know. I don't think I'm anything."

I glanced at the guy in the next bed. He still looked dead. It was driving me crazy. I couldn't pretend he wasn't there anymore.

"Jack, that guy over there, he has a sheet over his face—what the hell?"

"I don't know," Jack said. "He hasn't moved all afternoon. I think he might be dead."

"What the fuck? Why don't they move him?"

"Is he breathing?"

"I can't tell."

"Maybe he's sleeping. Maybe he's a deep sleeper."

"Maybe ... I don't know. He hasn't moved a muscle since I've been here."

"Oh, Christ. What the fuck am I doing in this place?"

"Want me to call a nurse? They'll know what the deal is."

"I'm scared, Lupus."

"I know. It's okay, Jack."

It was amazing how fast the horseshit fell away when death presented itself. Death was always there, of course, lying in wait for all of us, and it could come at any time. But unless it was directly in front of your face, or lying just a bed away, you managed to push it from your mind—it just didn't exist, at least not for you. Even when it was tearing at your chest, it was an impossible thing to accept.

I didn't know what to say to Jack that would make him feel any better. Maybe there wasn't anything to say.

"I don't wanna die here, Lupus."

"Then don't," I told him. "You're an ex-cop, you're a tough sonofabitch, remember?"

"Yeah ... maybe."

"Maybe, hell—you're big as a mountain, Jack. You're solid rock."

"Fuck it, you're right. I'm not gonna die, not in this fucking place."

"There you go—just say NO. I say no to just about everything. Except drugs and alcohol."

"You're gonna regret that, Totten."

"Gonna? Hell, I already do."

"Why don't you stop? That shit's gonna kill you."

"I don't know. I can't think of anything else to

do. Maybe I need a hobby. Maybe I should take up golf or something."

"Golf? You're not the type, Totten."

"What do you know about it? I could be a *great* golfer."

"You'd have to set your drink down for five minutes, you'd have to put your cigarette out—it'd never work, golf's not your game, kid."

"Yeah ... I should probably stick with the drinking. I'm good at aiming a glass."

"You can say that again, rummy."

"Hey, you're the one in the hospital."

"Don't worry, you'll be here soon enough."

"This conversation is getting depressing, Jack."

"Wanna watch some TV?"

"Sure."

Jack hit the remote, got *The Beverly Hillbillies*. Ellie May was running around the cement pond in her tight little cut-off shorts, her haltered breasts bouncing up and down. Ellie May might have been an airhead but she had the best ass in Beverly Hills.

Fuck death.

We kept our famished eyes on Ellie May's wide, inviting ass.

But then the show ended and Ellie May's ass disappeared and Jack wanted to talk again. About God. The God thing seemed to be nagging him. It was understandable enough.

"Lupus, you really don't believe in the Bible? Adam and Eve, all that?"

"You mean God? No, not even when I was a kid."

"Really?"

"I have a theory about Adam and Eve, though. Wanna hear it?"

"Sure. What the hell, I'm not going anywhere."

"Maybe you should take a nap or something. The nurse told me you needed your rest."

"Fuck the nurse. I've slept enough—I've slept half my life away. I'm not gonna nap away what's left of it."

"Hey, listen—I'd *like* to fuck the nurse. Have you seen her?"

"I've seen her, asshole. That's all I need—a fucking bombshell walking around here giving me a hard-on while I shit into a bedpan."

"You've got a point there."

"Tell me about Adam and Eve. What's your theory?"

"Okay, first off—they weren't kicked out of that garden by God. They left voluntarily—that's what *I* think."

"Why would they do that?"

"Well, shit, they were stuck in this garden, this little patch of paradise or whatever. There wasn't any war or pain or disease or death—and there wasn't any *sex*. If there's no such thing as death, why procreate, right? So there they were, lying around in this garden, nothing to fight for, nothing to strive for or aspire to, no goals, nothing to build, nothing to create—not a goddamned thing to do but smell the flowers and sit around looking at each other all day. And there was *no fucking* allowed, no recreational sex. Who could live like that? You'd go stark raving mad! Adam and Eve were *bored*! They couldn't take it anymore. So they sprouted wings from the sides of their heads and they flew the fuck out of there. God had nothing to do with it, aside from putting up the NO FUCKING sign."

"That's the craziest goddamn story I've ever heard."

"You keep taking the Lord's name in vain. That's a sin, Jack—you'd better watch it. You're at the edge of the abyss, remember."

"It's stupid! Why would they grow wings out of the side of their head? It doesn't make any sense—where would their ears be?"

"What do you mean *where would their ears be?* The wings shot out from their temples, their ears were right where they always were!"

"That's fucking ridiculous!"

"Jack, the Bible has a talking snake crawling around like Elvis—trying to get Eve to eat a forbidden apple! Why is my version any more ridiculous?"

"It's insane! Why wouldn't the wings be on their back? Why wouldn't they sprout from their shoulders where they normally would? Nobody's ever had wings coming out of their head!"

"The FTD Floral Man does!"

"What the fuck does the FTD Floral Man have to do with it? We're talking about God—none of this has anything to do with GOD!"

"Will you relax? I'm trying to make you laugh."

"I might be on my fucking death-bed here. Can't you be serious for five minutes? I wanna know what you believe in."

"What difference does it make? It's what *you* believe that counts."

"I don't know what I believe. I'm not sure—that's what scares me."

"Jack, come on, you're not gonna die."

"Why would the wings be on their *heads*? It's spooky! Why not on their backs?"

"Forget about the goddamned wings—it doesn't matter. What the hell's wrong with you?"

"But it doesn't make any sense! It's sick!"

"Okay, okay—the wings were on their back! They shot out of Eve's ass for all I care! What difference does it—"

"WILL YOU TWO SHUT THE FUCK UP!"

Jack and I both jumped. Then froze, in terror.

It was the guy in the next bed. He'd suddenly sat up and whipped the sheet from his face. It was a face straight out of hell, a toothless skull chattering atop a pale bag of bones, snow-white hair sticking up in mad little wing-like tufts, each shooting in a different direction, wild bushy eyebrows, the eyes bloodshot, bulging, full of angst and irritated fury.

Jack was clutching his chest, gasping. He was in shock, I think.

I opened my mouth but the dead guy cut me short:

"NO, DON'T SPEAK! I DON'T WANT TO HEAR ANOTHER WORD!"

"Hey, we were just talking—sorry."

"DON'T TALK! YOU'RE INSANE! YOU'RE BOTH INSANE! I CAN'T STAND ANOTHER MINUTE OF IT!"

Jack's vital signs began to flash. He fell back against his pillow, shut his eyes. He was breathing funny. The dead guy didn't seem to give a shit.

"Hey, old man, what's your problem? Don't be such an asshole—my friend has an addled heart, he's..."

"NURSE! NURSE!" the dead guy screamed.

And that's how Jack wound up on the critical list again.

AFTER THE GOLD RUSH

I took Lydia's check out of my boot, took it to the bank and cashed it. Thirty C-notes. Nice. I stuck them in my wallet, stuck my wallet in my backpocket. That bulge felt good. But I knew I wouldn't be feeling it for long.

I called Jenny and asked her to meet me at the jewelry store.

I had an engagement ring to buy and I needed a female's opinion. I didn't know a damned thing about diamonds—except that most women seemed to like big ones ...

"So, what's this all about?" Jenny asked.

I was pacing back and forth in front of RINGS AND THINGS, the only jewelry store in town.

"I need you to help me pick out a ring," I told her.

"A ring? What for?"

"I'm getting engaged."

"*Engaged*? Did you talk to Tia? Are you two back together again?"

"No, but I'm buying her a ring. I'm gonna get on a bus and go to Chicago and ask her to marry me."

"Lupus, you haven't talked to her for three months."

"Four—she won't take my calls. But I've written her every day."

"Has she written back?"

"Listen, Jen, I'm buying her a ring—do you wanna help me or not?"

"Lupus, you can't just show up with a ring and ask her to marry you! It's creepy. She'd think you were stalking her."

"I'm getting her a diamond. I don't know a thing about diamonds. I don't know what women like."

"Oooh, I do," Jenny said. "Follow me—I'll show you what we like."

I learned that what women like costs about three grand ... and then some.

***

Jenny and I were in the bar. We'd just finished cleaning the place, the lights were out, the jukebox was un- plugged, the open sign was off. We were wrapped around our drinks—vodka on the rocks—savoring the peace and quiet, the lack of sound, the silence. It had been an insanely shitty night and now all we wanted was oblivion. No consciousness, *no noise*, internal or ex- ternal.

"I can't believe you bought that ring," Jenny said.

"What? You helped me pick it out. I thought you liked it."

I was playing with a book of matches. I lit one, flipped it at her. She had a book of matches, too. She fired one back—and my hair went up in flames. She threw a bar-rag over my head.

"I do like it," she said. "I just can't believe you bought it. I mean ... well, you know what I mean."

"No—what do you mean?"

"You know damn well what I mean."

"Jen, I'm going to Chicago, and that's that."

"Suit yourself," she said.

"I will," I told her.

There was the smell of burnt flesh in the air. I looked in the bar-mirror. My hair was fried, the left side radically shorter than the right.

"Look what you've done to me!" I said.

She burst out laughing. She practically fell off her stool with it.

"Oh, God, I'm sorry, Lupus." She couldn't stop. "I'm sorry, I can't help it—it's funny!"

"I look fucking ridiculous!"

"I know," she laughed, "I'm sorry." She got up and began walking in circles, bent at the waist, holding her stomach, cackling.

I went behind the bar and fixed myself another drink. Sat there, drinking it.

"Lupus, I'm sorry ... I can fix it," she said.

"How?"

"My sister's a beautician. She used to practice on me. I picked up a few tricks."

"You know how to cut hair?"

"Sure ... sort of."

"What do you mean, *sort of*?"

"Your hair's rail-straight. It'll be easy, it's all one length."

"Not anymore."

"Lupus, I can do it. It'll be easy—trust me."

"What the hell? I can't walk around looking like this."

"Let me find some scissors."

"I think there's a pair under the bar," I told her.

She went back there, poured herself a vodka.

"You'd better pour me one, too," I said.

"I'll pour us three," she laughed.

Since I was sleeping in the office every night, Angel had given me the keys to the place, so I could let myself out in the morning without having to get her out of bed. I could come and go at my leisure now. The owners had ok'd it all. They'd even given me the green light to help myself to a few drinks now and then. But I'd been told not to go overboard with it—whatever that meant. It was like telling a goldfish not to spend too much time in the water bowl. I'd been good about it, though.

Jenny trotted our drinks over, along with a bottle of Crown Royal and a shaker full of Jagermeister.

"These scissors are pretty dull," she said.

"That's alright, let's do it."

"You sure?"

"Yeah, just don't butcher me."

"Don't worry. My sister's a beautician—I know what I'm doing."

"Maybe we should get your sister to do it."

"Don't be silly, it's 4 in the morning. Besides, she's a drunk, she'd fuck it up."

"Well, we can't have any of that," I said.

"No, we can't," Jenny laughed. She leaned over and gave me a little kiss on the cheek. It lasted only a fraction of a second, but it was a nice friendly kiss and it made me feel good inside. Jenny was alright. She was more than alright. If I hadn't been in love with Tia Correlia, I might have fallen head over heels for her.

We did a few shots of Jagermeister.

Then Jenny started chopping away ...

SYMBL.

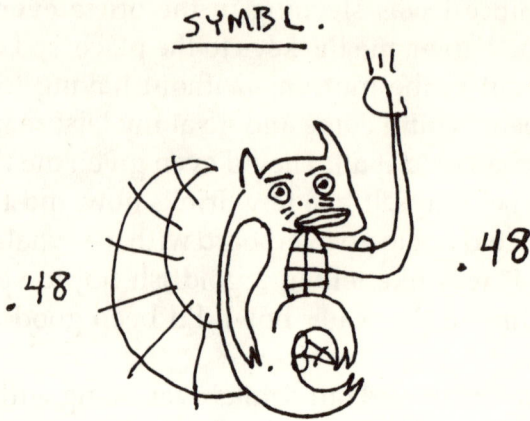

.48   .48

***

When I woke up it was daylight. Sun spilling through the front window, headache, nausea, end of the world, remorse.

I lifted my head off the table. Jenny was stretched out on the bar. Angel was standing over me, shaking her head. There were empty bottles sitting out, cigarette burns in the tablecloth, hair and vomit on the floor. The jukebox was blasting. AC/DC: "Hells Bells."

"Looks like you had quite a party in here last night," Angel said. She didn't sound too happy with me.

"It wasn't any party," I told her. "Jen and I had a few drinks. We got a little carried away, I guess ..."

"That's against the law, you know that."

"Yeah?"

"I'd fire you right now, Lupus—but I like you. Besides, there's only two weeks of summer left and I'm not about to hire anyone new at this point."

"Thanks, Angel."

"Don't thank me, Lupus. You timed your fuck-up well, that's all. Any other time, I'd fire your ass. You got lucky."

"Give me a fucking break. Jesus Christ ..."

"Wake Jenny up. Get that slut out of here before I fire her."

"Slut? What the fuck is that supposed to mean?"

"Just get her out of here before I change my mind and fire the both of you!"

"Listen, Angel—what the hell's your problem?"

"My problem? Look at you! You're nothing but a drunk! You and that whore over there—you're both nothing but drunks!"

"This whole town is nothing but drunks! Who the fuck are you? You don't know a goddamn thing about Jenny!"

"That's a laugh! I've worked with her for two years—I *know* that bitch! What the hell did she do to your hair, anyway? You look like an idiot. She told you her sister was a hairdresser, didn't she?"

"Fuck you, Angel." I got up, walked over to the bar and gave Jenny a shake. Angel was on my heels.

"That's right," she yelled, "get that bitch out of here before I fire her!"

Jenny let out a little moan, shifted her weight on the wood. Her eyes slowly opened, bloodshot and confused. I felt bad for her. I felt bad, period.

"Okay," I said, turning on Angel, "that's it! WE FUCKING QUIT! *FUCK* YOU!"

"GOOD!" Angel screamed. "GET THE FUCK OUT! AND TAKE YOUR SLUT WITH YOU!" She stormed off to the breakroom, slamming the door behind her.

Jenny sat up, rubbing her eyes with the backs of her hands.

"What's all the commotion?" she asked.

She looked at me, then looked again.

"Lupus, what did you do to your *hair*?" I checked the mirror behind the bar.

I had a bowl-cut.

***

So I spent my last two weeks in town shacked at Jenny's place. On the couch, of course. I had Tia Correlia to think about. I'd already fucked up once, I wasn't about to pull a repeat performance. Jenny liked to walk around the apartment in her panties and bra. She was unemployed now so she had no real reason to get dressed, I suppose. Still, it wasn't easy. Sometimes, she wouldn't even bother with the panties and bra. I walked around with a hard-on for two weeks ... It seemed to put a strain on the platonic nature of our relationship.

***

"Maybe I should be a secretary," Jenny said. She yawned and raised her arms over her head, stretching. Black panties, no bra, 22 years old. We were at the breakfast table, pouring coffee on our hangovers. I had to be at work in thirty minutes. Jenny was going through the Help Wanted ads. I was hiding my hard-on. I hid it well. I'd been hiding it for most of my adult life.

"Don't do it," I told her. "You'd be at the beck and call of some asshole all day. It'd be just as bad as waitressing."

"Want some more coffee?"

"Sure, thanks."

She walked over to the stove, brought the pot back, filled my cup.

"Well, I have to do *something*," she said.

"Keep looking. There's gotta be something better than that."

"That's as good as it gets around here. I've looked."

She sat down, sighed and ran her hands through her hair. She put her feet on the table, tipped back on the rear legs of her chair. "Does it bother you that I'm not wearing a top?"

"No, I don't mind." I was looking at her forehead, concentrating on it.

"You seem nervous."

"Why would I be nervous? I don't care what you wear."

"Do I have something on my forehead?"

"No." I shifted my gaze to her left ear, the ring dangling from it. She had a ring in her belly button, too. But to flee to that half of her body would have been counterproductive.

"Lupus, you're blushing."

I didn't say anything. I looked at the wall, the knick-knacks on the shelf behind her head. I felt like a fucking fool.

"The human body," she said, "is nothing to be embarrassed about."

"Who's embarrassed?"

"You know, if we were part of an African tribe, you wouldn't think anything of it."

"We're not in Africa, Jen. Things are different here."

"Well, they shouldn't be. It's silly. Nudity is natural, there's nothing dirty about the human body. I hate wearing clothes in my own apartment. Besides, it's hot in here."

She stood up, wriggled out of her panties, sat down again.

"I wish you wouldn't do that," I said.

"Jesus, Lupus—what's wrong with you? Haven't you ever been to a nude beach?"

"No. I'd walk around with an erection all day, it'd be ridiculous."

"God, that is so typical! You men—you see a naked body and all you can think of is sex!"

"Well, what am I supposed to think of—*Passover*?"

"Can't you just see a human body as a human body? Does everything have to be sex?"

"I can't help it, I'm sorry!" I could see she was a natural redhead.

"Pretend I'm your sister," she said.

She stood up, stretched her arms out and turned on her toes in a s-l-o-w, miraculous circle, giving me a long, hard look at her body. Full hips. Round ass. Firm breasts. A tight, maddening little package—all of it put together just right.

She sat down. "If you saw your sister walking around naked, you wouldn't wanna fuck her. You wouldn't even think about it."

"I don't know," I said. "I don't have a sister."

"Well, if you did!"

"If I did, I'd probably tell her to put some clothes on."

"Oh, forget it. You're hopeless."

She walked over to the refrigerator, grabbed an apple, dropped it, bent over to pick it up. She had a ring down *there*, too. It was torture. The girl had a body to die for, death death death, right there in the kitchen, death death death, wall to wall, ripe and ready for the taking.

"I have to go to work now," I told her.

"Okay," she said.

I didn't move. The clock ticked. The birds sang.

She stood there by the refrigerator, munching away at her apple. The early morning sun had turned her body into butter, into gold. Buttergold.

"Well?" she said.

"Well what?"

"Are you going or not?"

"Yeah. I'm late. I should probably go."

"Then go already. You don't wanna get fired, do you?"

I sat there.

"What's wrong with you?" she asked.

History's most complicated question. A friend in Atlanta had once told me that the truth would always win out. Fair enough, then.

"Jen, I'm afraid to stand up ... it's embarrassing."

"Oh, gawd, Lupus—you are so hung up."

***

It went on like that for the next two weeks. Jenny parading around the apartment in varying degrees of undress, vicious, beautiful, maddening, bending over oh-so-slowly for this, that and the other thing, combing the Help Wanted ads. Me feeling guilty for getting her fired in the first place, feeling guilty for not being able to see a human body as just a human body, innocent and uncomplicated, feeling guilty for wanting to fuck her uninhibited brains out every time her flesh passed my field of vision.

I remained faithful to Tia Correlia.

Jenny pranced and paraded. Threw her top off. Bent over for this, that and the other thing. Flashing that pretty little ring.

I slept on the couch and jacked off a lot.

Not working at the bar had curbed my alcohol intake,

but just a bit. No more free drinks. It put a strain on my wallet. I stopped going to bars altogether. Jenny and I drank in the apartment. It was cheaper that way. And, I must admit, far more entertaining.

I'd cork the bottle and watch her go.

The girl was turning me into a peep-freak.

Well, I'd lost the bar but I still had the grocery store. And a couple thousand dollars in the bank. I hadn't touched the nestegg. Without the tips rolling in, I couldn't add to it anymore. But I figured I had enough to set me up in Chicago for awhile once I got there.

Jenny didn't think I should go. She thought it was crazy.

"Lupus, why don't you forget about Chicago? You could stay here with me. You could paint."

"I gave up painting three months ago. Forget it, it's caused me nothing but trouble."

We were sitting in the livingroom. Bulblight. Bottle. Ashtray. Jenny had her pants on for a change. But her bra was on the floor.

"Your show was a success, Lupus. You sold almost everything. You can't quit now!"

"Sure I can. I'll tell you something, Jenny—I *have* sold almost everything. My whole goddamned life. Fuck it, I'm not going to do it anymore—I quit."

"What for? Tia? That girl doesn't want anything to do with you. Can't you see that?"

"To hell with Tia! I'm doing it for myself, I'm doing it to save whatever's left, if there is anything left."

"What are you talking about? You're just drunk, that's all. Things will look better in the morning, Lupus."

"Jenny, listen. I've been a fuck-up all my life. All I've ever done is let people down. A *thousand* tomorrow mornings won't change that. Drunk or sober, when I wake up, I'm still me."

"Lupus, don't say that. You haven't let anybody down."

"What the hell do you know about it?"

"You not painting is just plain stupid!"

I poured another drink. I didn't feel like talking about it anymore. All people ever wanted to do was talk. Day and night and in their sleep. Talk talk talk. I felt more comfortable staring at walls.

"Listen," Jenny said. "I'll have a job soon. Rent's cheap here, I can get it on my own. You wouldn't even have to work—you could just stay home and do your art. You're talented, why waste your time fucking around in a grocery store? All these shitty jobs you take—it's stupid!"

"Jenny, that would fly for about fifteen minutes. Then you'd get fed up and throw me out. That's what got me into trouble with Tia."

"Well, I'm not Tia, am I?"

"Jenny, it doesn't work. Believe me, you'd hate it. I'm not very good company when I'm painting."

"What's so fucking special about that girl, any-way?"

"What?"

"Why are you so hung up on her? What does that bitch have that I don't have?"

"You're drunk. Why don't you just go to bed?"

"I'll go to bed when I damn well please! This is *my* apartment. You're just a guest here."

"You're drunk. Everytime you drink, you lose it."

She leapt from her chair as if she'd just taken a bullet in the back, shrieked, picked up an ashtray and threw it against the wall. Threw her drink against the wall. Threw the bottle against the wall. Broken glass, rivers of liquor. Woman gone mad.

"*I'm* drunk?" she screamed. "*I'M* DRUNK?"

It was already happening. I wasn't even sleeping with her and it was already happening. The useless arguments, the drunken fights, the wild dramatics. Fireworks, explosion, idiocy. The inevitable friction between Man and Woman, the eternal clash and bang of the sexes. Adam and Eve drawing steel. War. All-out war. Always war.

I sat there. I sat there like a rock. Fuck it.

"Go to bed," I told her. "Get the fuck out of my face."

That seemed to put her over the edge. She ran into the kitchen, came back with a bottle of wine and hurled it at the wall—directly over my head. The glass and the grape came down, a rain of it. Cheap Chardonnay. But I was afraid she'd get her hands on the good stuff next, the Merlot, the Bushmill, the Tanqueray.

The girl had lost her mind. A line of decency had been crossed. War had been declared.

I jumped up, grabbed her wrist, spun her around. She screamed and raked her nails down my face. Blood.

"YOU CRAZY BITCH!"

I got her by the hair, pulled her to the floor, held her down as best I could. She thrashed and screamed—wild, strong, agile, insane. I didn't weigh much. I was a punk. I was going to get the shit kicked out of me by a frail, crystal-wearing redhead—a vegetarian. I tried to reason with her.

"COOL IT, BABY! DON'T MAKE ME BITCHSLAP YOU!"

She kneed me in the balls and wriggled away. I doubled up. White hot agonizing pain. Fire and explosion. Death in my groin.

"HA!" she spat. She stood over me, cursing, screaming. Kicking. And kicking. And kicking. Rib shots. The bitch was trying to murder me.

I rolled, caught her ankle, pulled her off her feet. She fell. There was a loud thump—her head hitting the floor. She put a foot in my face, trying to push me away. I bit it, hard. She kicked, got me in the nose. The blood began to flow.

I was losing! I was going to die! Fuck that.

I pulled her toward me, pulled and yanked and climbed those long naked legs until I had her ass in my face—I gripped her hips, rolled her over, got on top. Peach-colored panties, no bra, 22 years old. Our bodies were pressed together, hot and sticky. She spat in my face. I had a fullblown erection. Maybe I *was* a sick fuck.

She kicked and screamed. Thrashed and clawed.

My cock throbbed. My nose bled. I couldn't hold her there forever.

Something had to give.

I grabbed her by the hair, put her head to the floor and kissed her, hard, on the mouth. Lip to lip, tooth to tooth, nipple to nipple. A river of blood. My blood. Her blood. I kissed her. Held it.

All at once, her body went limp. The screaming stopped. She relaxed. I rolled off her. Panting, erect, in pain.

There was a moment of stillness, a moment of silence. We lay there on our backs, breathing in and out, winded, speechless. Then she sat up, slapped me across the face and ran to her room. She slammed the door behind her. Opened it. Slammed it shut again. Dramatic effect.

I lay on the floor, staring at the ceiling. There was a big ugly water stain up there. It looked like a mushroom cloud. Hiroshima. Nagasaki. It was obscene.

I'd have to talk to the landlord about that.

Jenny had a stereo in her room. She turned it on, turned the volume up. But I could still hear her throwing shit around, kicking things. I went to the kitchen, found a bottle of bourbon, walked back to the livingroom, brushed the glass off the couch, sat down, drank. My nose was still bleeding. I put my head between my knees, pinched my nostrils. I stared at the floor. My feet were bleeding. I counted my toes. They were still there, all 20 of them. I shut my right eye and the 20 digits became 10. Whenever I drank, my vision got gimped. I lay back, drank and listened to Jenny kick the shit out of her bedroom walls.

She had an old Ike and Tina Turner record. She was playing it. She was always playing it. In every song, Tina was singing about some prick who was fucking her over, beating her, cheating on her, stealing her money, destroying her soul, doing her wrong. The songs were obviously autobiographical—all about Ike, in other words. And Ike was the one who had written the fucking things. You had to marvel at that. You had to wonder about the dynamic there.

I didn't know a damned thing about Jenny. Not really. I didn't even know her last name. But any fool could have sensed the baggage she was dragging around, heavy, awkward shit, the kind that's hard to walk away from. Well, I had baggage of my own to deal with. Everybody did. Jenny had Jenny. I had me. There was no saving anyone. So I didn't know her last name— what difference did it make?

Jenny kicked the walls. The neighbors bitched.

I drank and listened to Ike and Tina create art from the wreckage of their relationship.

I'd gotten halfway down the bottle. I began to doze.

Then Jenny came storming into the room. She stood there with her hands on her hips. She wasn't wearing anything.

"WHO THE FUCK ARE YOU?" she screamed.

I didn't feel like fighting. The world was too noisy, even in times of peace. But her madness was interesting, I could understand it. She was caged, the way I was caged. She wasn't crazy. And it wasn't just the booze. She was reacting to something in the air, some dark, blanketing gas, something hidden and just out of reach, undefinable, maddening. She was trying to find the key, trying to claw her way out. I admired that. I was too tired to even rattle the bars. I'd been born tired.

"You're just going to sit there!" she said. "You're not going to do a fucking thing, are you?"

"I guess not," I told her.

"You're just the type," she said. "You're just the type to sit there. If I was to shove my pussy in your face, you probably wouldn't even stick your tongue out."

"Probably not," I said.

"FINE! I WOULDN'T STICK MY PUSSY IN YOUR FACE EVEN IF YOU PAID ME!" She ran to her room, slammed the door.

I sat there, lit a cigarette, looked at the wall.

It seemed to have gotten higher. Maybe it was just the booze.

Five minutes later, she was back again.

"Hey, look," she said. "I'm sorry. I don't know what got into me." She sat down, gave my hand a squeeze. "I'm sorry, Lupus."

"It's okay," I told her. "I'm sorry, too."

"I get crazy sometimes. I don't know why ..."

"Jen, it's okay. I shouldn't have bit you. Let's forget about it." She seemed completely sober. It was strange, the way she could do that. I'd seen it happen before. Maybe she *was* crazy. Maybe we were both crazy.

"How's your nose?" she asked.

"My nose is fine. It's been broke before. Is your toe okay?"

"You left some teeth marks. Nothing major."

"They say being bit by a human is worse than being bit by a dog ..."

"I'm not worried about it," she laughed. "You're a dog at heart, Lupus. All men are."

"Yeah, maybe."

"And now you're gonna trot back to Chicago with your tail wagging, trying to find your mistress. You're just a big dumb dog. I always knew that about you."

"I'm sorry, Jen. I can't help it."

"I know ..." She lay back and lit a Virginia Slim. "Hey, listen—are you hungry? I haven't eaten anything today. I'm dying."

"No, I don't get hungry much. I'll make you something, though."

"That would be nice," she said.

I walked to the kitchen, opened a can of tomato soup, put it in a pan, put a flame under it. I found a loaf of bread, some cheese, a stick of butter. I got it going, turned the flame low, let the bread brown and the cheese melt just right. At heart, I was a domesticated fool, a homebody. I might have been a flailing fuck-up, but I was going to make a good husband some day. Tia Correlia didn't know what she was missing. Goddamnit, why couldn't she be Jenny? Why couldn't Jenny be her?

I found a drink tray in the cupboard—filched

from the Sause Box, no doubt. I set the soup and sandwich on it, a glass of milk, a napkin, a spoon. I ran out
the backdoor and yanked a tulip from the neighbor's
garden. Yellow. With little shots of red.

I carried it all back to the livingroom. Jenny had
put some clothes on. Jeans and a t-shirt. She'd combed
her hair, fixed her lipstick. Jenny Somebody—she looked
real pretty.

I set the tray down in front of her, bowed.

"Oh, you even picked me a flower! Thank you,"
she said. "You're a sweetheart, Lupus. I always knew
that about you."

I lay on the floor and watched her eat. Women, I
thought, what miraculous works of art they are! What
lovely whirls of color! It was late, I was getting sleepy.
For the first time in five months I felt entirely at peace.

I let my eyes close. I asked her what her last name
was.

"What difference does it make?" she said.

When I woke up it was morning and Jenny was Jenny
and I was still me. And it was okay that way.

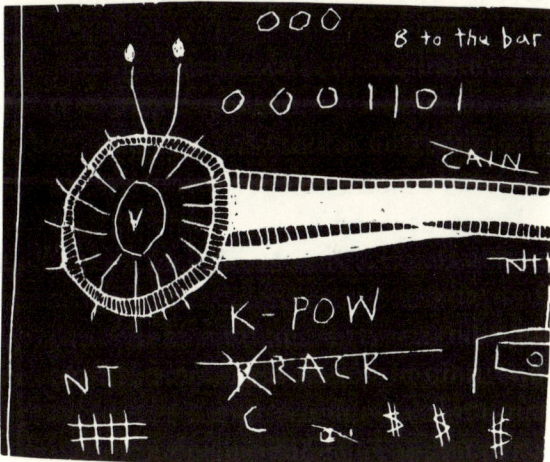

Mart (coil)
oil
PENICIL
← living cells
K ||||

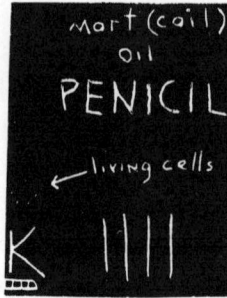

THE VALLEY OF HEARTS

I had to open the grocery store. I decided to go in a little early, get a jump on things. I unlocked the place, turned the lights on, punched the clock, got some coffee going.

It was my last day. Summer was over and so was the job. I wasn't going to miss it.

I poured myself a coffee, carried it to the front window. I stood there awhile, smoking, looking at Main Street. It was completely deserted. The tourists had all gone home. There were no cars, no people. A town of ghosts ... Silent ... Sleeping ...

Stillwater. They'd named it right.

The phone rang as I was watching the street. Loud, star-tling.

I spilled my coffee.

It was Linda Lee.

Jack was dead.

He'd died during the night, right around the time Jenny and I were knocking the shit out of each other. He'd died in that hospital in Ludington. He'd died in his sleep.

Jack Philly. Tough Guy.

Jack Philly. My friend.

I put the phone down. Sat there a few minutes. Looked around.

Then I stood, turned the lights off, put the Closed sign on the door, locked up, thought once, thought twice, put my fist through the window, and started walking.

The cemetery was only a mile away.

***

I never went to my father's funeral. I'd never even visited his grave. But I knew where the family plot was. I'd watched them bury my little brother there.

I walked through the gate, down a narrow, winding road, through a stand of trees, over a briar-patch and up a small hill. I knew where I was going. I knew exactly where I'd end up one day.

There they were. There they all were.

My old man. My little brother. Aunts and uncles. Grandparents. Cousins.

I felt bad that I hadn't brought any flowers. I searched around, found some dandelions. Gathered two bunches. One for my father. One for my little brother. They were buried side by side.

I laid the dandelions on the graves. Shots of yellow against the granite. They were only weeds. But they looked nice. Bright. They looked alive.

I stretched out, coffin-length, in the grass between the graves. I lay there. I lay there a long time.

Then I sat up.

Then I snuck away.

***

I closed out my savings account. The woman behind the counter pushed it toward me. Half cash, half traveler's checks. I thanked her. She had a tiny gold cross hanging from her neck. A valley of cleavage.

"Going on vacation?" she asked.

"I'm moving to Bali," I told her. "Missionary work. There's a small church being built even as we speak. I'm going to bring Christianity to the heathens, I'm going to get those people to put some clothes on. There are souls to save and money to be made—the market's wide open. If the show is a success in Bali, I may expand, move the operation east to Java. After Java, who knows? The sky's the limit, I guess. Maybe you would like to ..."

"Next!" she said.

***

There were no buses that passed through Stillwater. To come or go, you needed a car. I'd never learned to drive. I'd always been too drunk. I had no business with the DMV. The streets were safer that way.

I called the Greyhound station in Ludington. There was a bus leaving for Chicago at 10 p.m.

I'd packed my belongings in a suitcase the night before. It was stashed in the alley behind the bar, behind a mountain of bottles, by the dumpster. Everything I owned. I went and got it.

I didn't say goodbye. Not to Jenny. Not to Barley or Linda Lee. Not to my mother. Not to anyone. It would have been too messy. I didn't like a cluttered exit, I didn't like goodbyes.

I hitched a ride to the station with an old farmer. Pickup truck, overalls, Cat-Diesel hat. Johnny Cash on the radio. Merle Haggard on the radio. Hank Williams Jr. Windows down, no muffler. We didn't talk. Ludington was only fourteen miles away. And Johnny and Merle and Hank filled the gap just fine.

He let me out at the station. Waved and drove

away. I waved back. Those old farmers, they were alright.

I had six hours to kill. I bought my ticket and sat down on the bench out front. I closed my eyes. What I needed was a nap; a nap would help pass the time. But I was too nervous, too worked up. I took the engagement ring out of my pocket. I played around with it, rubbed it, polished it, fiddled with it and thought about the different ways to propose, what I would say to her, how I would say it. The more I thought about it, the more uptight I became. What if she turned me down, what if she refused? I didn't want to think about that. I couldn't.

Then I remembered the sackful of Xanax the fruitcake from the psych hospital had given me. I'd packed it, it was right there in my suitcase. I dug it out, took a handful and sat there on the bench. Staring straight ahead. Waiting for the bus. Waiting for the world to begin or end.

Something woke me. From within or without, something woke me. I sat up, fast. My mouth was dry and the crickets were singing. I was still in limbo.

And my bus was pulling away.

The world. My future.

Tia Correlia!

I jumped up, grabbed my suitcase and ran after it—all of it. Yelling, screaming, crying out; begging the driver to stop; begging the driver for one more chance; begging the driver to brake and let me on; begging the driver, just this once, not to leave me behind.

But the driver didn't stop. And the bus kept right on going. And I stood there in the highway, watching the tail-lights fade.

I stood there a long time.

No cars came along. Nothing came along.

I was standing on the yellow line. I was in the middle of fucking nowhere. Crickets and stars. A bus ticket in my hand.

That yellow line stretched forward, and back, for as far as the eye could see.

It was getting late.

I had a ring in my pocket.

Maybe I still had a woman to give it to.

I threw my suitcase into the ditch. And started walking.

ABOUT THE AUTHOR

Kurt Eisenlohr is a painter and bartender living in Portland, Oregon. His poetry and fiction has appeared in numerous journals and magazines including *Asylum, Verbal Abuse, River Styx, Another Chicago Magazine, Cokefishing, Way Station,* and *Stovepiper.* His chapbook, *Under Hand and Over Bone* was published by Alpha Beat Press in 1994. A new chapbook of his poems, is due out this year from Lummox Press. His art has been shown in many galleries and is featured on the Future Tense web site.

DINO   FRANK   SAMMY